Please enjoy

Loving Adonis

Sandi K. Whipple

Sandi K. Whipple

Copyright © 2014 Sandi K. Whipple
All rights reserved.

ISBN-13:978-1494939144
ISBN-10:1494939142

Printed by CreateSpace
eStore address (i.e. www.CreateSpace.com/TITLEID)
Printed by CreateSpace, An Amazon.com Company
CreateSpace, Charleston SC

No part of this work may be reproduced in any fashion without express, written consent from the copyright holder.

This is a work of fiction. All characters and events portrayed herein are fictitious and are not based on real any persons living or dead.

DEDICATION

A heartfelt thank you goes to my dear friend Margaret Clark-Price. She pushed me to complete this novel. Her faith in my abilities and her constructive opinions about *Loving Adonis* were not only helpful and more than appreciated, but they were truly priceless.

Intentionally
Left Blank

Sandi K. Whipple

PROLOGUE

"Dad's drunk again, buttons," thirteen-year-old Tom whispered to his eight year old sister, Angie, "so stay upstairs with me and keep quiet." They were huddled in the far corner of the room between a wall and a dresser. Angie squeezed her eyes shut and plugged her ears at the sound of her mother's cries. Tom struggled to remain brave, but more than one tear rolled down his boyish face and seeped into the lines of worry at the corners of his mouth. He was saturated with fear and loathing. He and Angie had been through too many violent weekends of screaming and flying dishes, a result of vicious outbursts from their drunken father, Leonard Henderson.

Very early on, running and hiding had become their only means of escape. Tom's anguish was unbearable knowing that his mother, Sylvia, couldn't do anything but withstand the terror and pain that rained down on her from the drunken animal his father became when he drank. Tom knew in his heart that one day the beatings would certainly end her life...if one could call her nightmare "a life."

He gently cradled his sister in his arms to quiet her sobs. Tom had suffered the pain of his father's cruel backhand and he feared for Angie. She was just too fragile and tiny to withstand any abuse. He had to protect her.

Through teary eyes, Angie looked up at Tom and whispered, "When I grow up, I'm going to leave here and never come back."

Sandi K. Whipple

Although he felt escape from their home in Silo, Montana, would not be soon enough, Tom squeezed Angie harder and replied, "Me too, 'Buttons', me too."

****

Sandi K. Whipple

CHAPTER ONE

Angie Gibbons was daydreaming as she walked toward the bank for her appointment, excited at the thought of her hard-earned independence just around the corner as a new business owner. Her shoulders back and her chin out, she contemplated how she was about to get a "piece of the pie" and make her own way.

Deep in thought and not heeding her steps, she was suddenly lost in the commotion of colliding bodies. Her purse fell to the ground and her body quickly followed after she bumped into the shoulder of another person sharing the sidewalk. A hot redness began to creep up her neck and onto her face. Her embarrassment and anger were fighting each other. She prayed for composure as well as words, but her mind and body were not cooperating.

Trying to straighten her now rumpled and dirty clothing, she looked up straight into a pair of piercing black eyes. "What the..!"

The words from the stranger were as piercing as his eyes. "If you'd been looking where you were going, you'd probably still be upright."

That was all it took for anger to beat out embarrassment. Grabbing her purse and rising from the dirty sidewalk, Angie hissed to this total stranger, "Look what you've done to my clothes, you big oaf. And I have an appointment!"

Now, taking notice of this stranger, Angie's mind began assembling the words to blast this man's impertinence when he simply smiled, turned, and disappeared into the heavy sidewalk traffic.

Sandi K. Whipple

With a deep breath, she willed her legs to move, now noticing her hose were torn and a small trickle of blood was creeping down her leg from a scrape on her knee. Too late to do anything about that now she decided. She was already going to be late.

****

Walking into the bank, she wondered if the chill she felt was due to the air-conditioning, or if her goose bumps were the reaction to the impertinent oaf of a man.

Red faced and looking downward, Angie was embarrassed by her appearance. She could almost feel people staring at her and whispering about her disheveled look. As she approached the desk, she saw the puzzled look on the bank officer's face.

"Angela, are you okay? You look like you've just been run over."

After seating herself in a chair, Angie took a long, slow, deep breath. "Carolynn, I was so excited about coming here. I was daydreaming and not paying attention to where I was going. I accidentally bumped into a man who was, by far, the rudest individual I've ever come in contact with. He obviously wasn't looking where he was going either. Look at me! He just knocked me down, smiled, and walked away. No regard to my filthy clothing, let alone an apology. He never even asked if I was okay!"

Carolynn told her, "Wow! At least you're not hurt. I mean physically anyway." Looking down at Angie's knee she grimaced and added, "Except for your knee. Want a Band-Aid?"

Sandi K. Whipple

Knowing it was time to put her pride aside, Angie chuckled and said, "No thanks. But a new pair of hose wouldn't hurt."

Carolynn was now chuckling with her. Then in a business tone she said, "I guess we're done with the headaches of paperwork Angela. Escrow and all the nasty old stuff for the loan are now officially finished. I'm happy for you, as you are now the proud owner of your own building, and soon to be flower business. Here's your keys. You got lucky you know. Bank owned foreclosure real estate doesn't normally close in just a few weeks." After a pause, she continued, "I guess that's pretty much it. Any questions?"

"Nope!" Angie could only smile.

The bank officer said, "Now that we're finished with all the business junk, and you know I'm not the Wicked Witch of the West, I thought it would be nice to chat a bit and get to know one another."

Angie relaxed, so relieved that the loan had been approved, all the waiting and wondering was over, and that the bank had chosen Carolynn for her to deal with.

"You'll soon find out in a small town like Nasons Grove, Illinois, everyone knows everyone, including their business, and I mean on every level," Carolynn told her.

Appreciating this woman's personality and friendliness, Angie smiled at her and said, "Could you please call me Angie? Most people do. At least those I consider friends."

"Only if you'll call me Carl."

Angie looked at her with wide eyes and a tilted head. "That's a strange nickname. Am I being nosey if I ask how that came about?"

Carl explained, "I got stuck with that tag in sixth grade. There was one boy who kept finding ways to tease me and make me cry. One day I finally had enough, and I beat the crap out of him. After that, he said I acted and fought like a boy, so he started calling me Carl. I guess that's pretty much when the name stuck."

****

On her drive home, Angie took in the sights as she recalled what Carl said about Nasons Grove being a small town. Funny how she never thought of it as small until she'd attended college in Evanston. But still, a town of eighteen thousand people wasn't as small as Silo, Montana. Besides, she loved this clean, beautiful town located on the banks of the Spoon River.

As she passed the many tree lined streets with well manicured yards and many Victorian homes, her thoughts were again drifting. After her brother deserted her by running away, and the death of her parents, all she had in her life were the uncompassionate case workers. They sure couldn't always be trusted to keep their promises. Angie had nowhere else to go. Or so the caseworker told her.

She remembered the day when she was only eleven years old, how the caseworker dropped her off at Aunt Ruth's doorstep, located on one of the tree lined streets.

Remembering how Aunt Ruth's love and kindness had quickly dissipated her fears, made her eyes begin to water. Not having children of her own, Aunt Ruth had loved and treated Angie as if she was her daughter, and taught her that not all facets of life were ugly. She even took on her aunt's last name.

Forcing her thoughts to the present, Angie began to formulate a way to tell Aunt Ruth she would be moving out in the morning. Her aunt knew Angie would be moving into the small apartment at the rear of her new flower shop, but not that she was leaving so soon.

Angie shook her head to clear her thoughts, and pulled into the driveway of her Aunt's old, two-story Victorian building.

After parking her car, she saw her aunt sitting on the front porch. Angie loved Aunt Ruth, with her short salt-and-pepper hair and somewhat dark complexion. She'd kept her figure, and still had the tiny frame of a much younger woman. Her bubbly personality and quick wit almost always kept Angie in check when things looked dismal.

Aunt Ruth hollered from the front porch, "Hi, sweetheart. Come sit with me and have some Chambord. I want to hear all about your day."

Angie sat in the cushioned chair at the patio table and kicked off her shoes. She poured a glass of the sweet black-raspberry-flavored liqueur and dropped in three ice cubes from the glass ice bucket.

With a grin on her face and dangling the keys in the air she said, "I got the keys."

Clapping her hands, Aunt Ruth told her, "Congratulations to you, you new business owner you! I guess you'll be moving out soon too." After a silent pause, she added, "Well, when you graduated from college, I knew it was only a matter of time before I'd lose you."

Angie saw the tear in the corner of Aunt Ruth's eye. And those two words *lose you* made it difficult to keep a jovial attitude. "Come on, Aunt Ruth, you're not losing me. I'll only be a few miles from the house, and besides, we'll be seeing each other a lot. You know I'm counting on you to help me with the shop, right?" Angie got up from the table. "Let me go change clothes, and can we both sit here drinking this Chambord until we have a heat on."

That was Aunt Ruth's favorite phrase for getting tipsy. Angie drank a little wine once in a while, and occasionally shared a glass of her Aunts favorite liqueur, but actually drank very little. She learned firsthand years ago, the negative effects alcohol could have on some people.

The next morning, Angie discovered packing was hardly a chore. Only two suitcases held what little clothing Angie found necessary to own. She smiled as she recalled the wise words from her mother: "There's no shame in having little, but there's a lot of shame in not taking care of what one has." God, how she would trade everything if she could have her mother back. She closed her suitcase, told herself that her goal now was to work hard, make her business profitable, and provide a comfortable life for herself. Angie's throat tightened and tears of joy began to form as she realized Aunt Ruth was her biggest ally, and would always be in her corner. How could she possibly not succeed with that kind of backup?

Sandi K. Whipple

****

After unlocking the door to her very own building, Angie walked through the office area into her unfurnished apartment in the rear. She silently thanked the previous owner for leaving the stove and refrigerator. That would save her a few dollars, but she needed some furniture. The bed would be new, but everything else she could find at second-hand stores. No telling when the shop would make a profit, so she needed to be thrifty at the outset.

Hearing a noise from the front shop, realizing she'd failed to relock the door, Angie stepped in to find Carl standing there.

Carl smiled and said "Hi! You told me you'd be here this morning, so, well, here's a fruit basket for your housewarming, or business warming, or whatever. Hell, how could I give flowers to a florist?" In a more serious tone, she continued, "Angie, please call me if you need anything, and, by the way, congratulations."

As she accepted the fruit basket, Angie was almost at a loss for words. She looked at Carl, and said, "Thank you", thinking it didn't really seem like enough. Waving her arms around she told Carl, "It doesn't look like much yet, does it? I am glad though that everything is gone. It gives me a clean slate to work with."

After Carl's goodbye and departure, Angie locked the shop door, and took the fruit basket into the apartment. She was touched by Carl's gift, and thought there may be the beginning of a good friendship.

She grabbed an apple from her gift basket and walked around the apartment. She thought about her first night in her new home, without furniture. Perhaps it was a mistake moving in so quickly when she had absolutely nothing. But the excitement of now having a business and a new home had made that decision for her. Oh well, one night on the floor without a bed or a cot wouldn't kill her.

Late the next morning, sunlight streamed through the windows, awakening Angie. She moved slowly in anticipation of a backache from sleeping on the floor. Once standing, moving her arms and legs and rolling her neck around, she was surprised to find she was pain-free. And it was a beautiful, yet unusually warm, spring day. It must be an omen of good things to come.

She just finished dressing when the banging on the shop door startled her. Closing the door to the apartment, she looked up and almost quit breathing at the sight of the gorgeous man standing at the door. After she opened and unlocked the door, he walked in..., and walked past her without even the hint of an invitation. She thought he looked like a mature, six foot tall, tanned brother of Adonis. When he turned to face her, she noticed the imposing dimple on his chin and a stunning face framed by thick, coal-black hair. His eyes glistened like lava jewels. The sleeves of his T-shirt were ripped off, exposing muscular arms that would make all body builders envious.

This man's gorgeous body wrapped in tight jeans was forcing her stomach to flip flop. Angie couldn't fathom where this incredible specimen of a creature had come from or why he looked so familiar. Suddenly it struck her! She'd never forget those piercing black eyes!

This was the man who'd knocked her over a few

days ago on her way to the bank. Oh God, what if he remembered her? Would he bring it up? Should she bring it up? What would she say?

Her temples throbbed with a racing pulse as she stared at him. Her stomach felt as though she'd been punched! Her knees were weak and she was struggling with the thought of what to do.

The man interrupted her thoughts as he read from the pink invoice on his clipboard and announced in a robotic tone of voice, "Walgren's Heating and Cooling Systems. I'm looking for Angela Gibbons." He stood there shifting his weight from foot to foot, as he waited for her to speak.

Angie felt sure that this stunning guy couldn't wait to get this job done and get out. "I'm Angela Gibbons," she responded, surprised that she actually had a voice. She decided that the incident a few days ago was best left entirely unmentioned.

"I'm here to deliver and install four flower coolers and an air-conditioner. Where do ya want 'em,?"

Forcing a professional demeanor, she said, "I want all four coolers on the far right wall. The air-conditioner will replace the old one located in the back apartment."

He walked around to survey the shop walls. He stopped in the middle of the room and crossing his arms he told her, "These coolers are too big to put all four on that wall. You'll only be able to get three over there."

Horror set in as her eyes opened wide enough to compete with the Grand Canyon. "But I measured the wall before I ordered them." Not only were they custom- ordered and expensive, but she needed all four of them. "I need the other wall for the racks and shelving for accessories, cards and stuff. I can't afford to buy smaller ones and eat the cost. Now what do I do?"

She knew she was rambling. Her hands began to shake and she was biting her lip. Excusing herself, she walked into the apartment and stared at an empty wall as she tried to regain her composure.

Footsteps behind her made her whirl. The Adonis man had followed her into the apartment and now she really couldn't breathe. What was he doing here? Before she could chase this thought any further, he said in a kind tone, "Don't worry—this is an easy fix...... If you just move that wall back a few feet, all four coolers will fit fine. I can do it for you, or wait until you have it done. We can set up another appointment if you want. Whatever you decide is fine with me."

Her composure now under control, Angie said, "I really need to get opened up here so if you could possibly do it all, I would certainly be indebted to you, Mr. . . . ?"

"Just call me Gary. I'll call the office and get two more guys out here and we'll have it all done in just a few days. Will that be okay?"

She felt a rise of panic. "How much more do I have to pay?"

"The wall won't be much, and the two extra men are included. If I can use your phone, I'll get on it right now Miss Gibbons."

Uncertain why she said it, she told him, "You can call me Angie."

****

Sandi K. Whipple

Angie felt her presence would be an intrusion while Gary Adonis and his men worked, so she went shopping. She bought furniture at a second hand store and was grateful when the kind owner, Mr. Hill, offered to deliver it free of charge.

She drove in a daze and meandered through the other stores in a hazy cloud of confusion. She couldn't get the Adonis cooler guy out of her head. She was baffled by this great looking man who puzzled and dazzled her, but why? Other men hadn't made her queasy or dizzy from just the sight of them!

She thought of her college boyfriend, Chad. He certainly had never made her feel this way. In fact, it had taken a long time to just become friends. Once they'd been dating for a while, he'd repeatedly told her she was the only girl for him. She remembered how they'd broken the balloons at the county fair, and made the tilt-a-whirl go so fast, they were both so dizzy they almost couldn't quit laughing. And how understanding he was at her fear of water. Well, not actually the water, just being so far out that it was no longer possible to see land. He loved holding hands, saying he wanted everyone to know they were together, a couple, more than just friends.

Her stomach lurched as she recalled the real truth of Chad when it was revealed during the second or third semester of her senior year, she couldn't remember now. It was that day in the library.

It was full of students studying for finals, so almost every table was full. She'd finally found a table with several other girls that had an empty seat.

Sandi K. Whipple

Though she tried, with such close seating, it was almost impossible to ignore some of the conversations taking place. It was when she heard the name Chad that her ears perked up. One girl named Susan was whispering through her tears that she just found out her boyfriend Chad was cheating on her, and that he'd told her she was the only girl for him. Those last few words had certainly set off the lights and bells for Angie.

After confronting Chad about Susan, his apology had included yet even another girl named Shelly! She remembered it had been painful as hell to find out she was actually one of three, who he'd said was the only girl for him.

The experience forced her to realize how naïve and trusting she'd been. She vowed that she'd never be taken advantage like that again.

****

When she returned to the shop with three large bags in her arms, she tried to juggle the load and open the door, with little success. She was about to try and set one bag down when the door opened from inside and again, she stood facing Gary Adonis.

"Thanks…"

Before she could finish, he took two of the bags out of her arms and headed for the apartment.

Following him, she was surprised when he placed them on the dinette table she purchased just a few hours ago. She hadn't expected the furniture she'd bought to be delivered so quickly. "Oh, I see Mr. Hill was already here. I was hoping I'd be back in time. By the way, thanks for carrying my bags, Gary Adon... oops."

She chided herself for thinking of him as Gary Adonis. How embarrassing it would be for her if he actually heard her call him that.

Gary looked around the small apartment. "So you're going to live here too, huh?"

"Uh huh."

He walked around, giving the room a hard look. He tapped on the back door and rattled the latch. He was surprised at how flimsy the set up was. "If I were you, I'd put a more secure door and lock on that back entrance." With that, he went back to work.

****

It had been a long and tiring four weeks for Angie. With the wall finished, the coolers installed, and all the vendors lined up for deliveries, Angie thought she would fall apart once she tackled the apartment. But it was now not only painted, furnished, and decorated well enough to be comfy, but she wasn't as tired as she'd expected to be. And, it was all hers. Well, hers and the banks.

Working for three years in the flower shop after graduating from college, to find out the owner was in foreclosure, had given Angie quite a jolt. Wondering what she wanted to do with herself was a question that had raced through her mind. She wondered where she would go. What kind of work would suit her?

Two weeks after learning of the foreclosure, Angie went through her finances and thought she might be able to swing it. She had a nice sum in her savings account. But foreclosures could be a nasty drawn out process. And of course it would depend on how much the bank would settle for. She thought well, that was all history now.

Walking into the shop, it was hard to believe it was only two days until the doors opened for business. She would just assemble a few shelves, and two racks, then deliveries tomorrow, and then open the door for business the next day.

Unlocking the shop door, Angie stepped out onto the sidewalk and looked up and down the street. As she watched the hustle bustle of people and traffic, she wondered why it was that the old owner couldn't make it. This was a great location. They'd sure had a lot of busy days when she was just an employee for those few years. It made her think maybe the prior owner just wasn't very good at handling money. But Angie was a math major, and very good at handling money. Turning to go back into the shop, she stopped to peruse the huge windows on each side of the entrance. Yep! Both windows were creatively painted saying, Angie's Flower Shop. She'd had second thoughts when the painter suggested she include the shop's number, but now was glad she had agreed.

She smiled as she walked into and looked around the yet unfilled shop. She found it hard to believe she was really here.

Suddenly, thinking back to the prior owner, Angie began to pace back and forth as her rambling thoughts moved faster than a locomotive. *What if this doesn't fly? What if I can't make the loan payments?* She needed to keep her inner strength and emotions in check. The jingle of the bell at the shop door jarred her.

"Aunt Ruth, what a surprise! What's in the huge shopping bag? Here, let me help you."

Aunt Ruth snapped the bag back and said, "Why? I'm not old and feeble. I'm only fifty-eight years young. I don't need any help, not yet anyway."

Chuckling at her own words, she moved into the apartment. "Oh, Angie, you must have been up until all hours every night since you've been here. This room is beautiful. I never knew so many different shades of blue could look so magnificent."

Aunt Ruth set the bag down on the dinette table and continued, "Now, then, I've brought something to celebrate your new home and business. Open the bag, dear."

As Angie reached in, she found three wrapped packages. Her excitement made it difficult to remove the bubble wrap. One package contained a large bottle of Chambord. The second included four small lead crystal glasses. In the last package was a beautiful glass ice bucket, just like Aunt Ruth's.

"Oh, they're wonderful. Thank you." Hugging her aunt, she added, "God, how I love you. The ice bucket is touching but, I'm not sure I have any ice."

"If you'll share, I could go get some..."

Both women jumped at the sound of the interrupting voice. They turned toward the shop, and stared at Gary Adonis, leaning against the doorframe of the apartment with his arms and feet crossed.

In his tight jeans, pale green polo shirt, and adorable cocky smile on his face, he looked gorgeous!

Angie realized she'd been so tickled to see Aunt

Ruth, she totally spaced locking the shop.

"I thought for sure you'd hear the jingle on the shop door." Smiling, Gary walked toward them. "I came by to drop off the bill for the job on the wall. Sorry if I'm intruding."

"Not at all," said Aunt Ruth, looking in the freezer for ice. "We're about to celebrate. Angie's shop opens day after tomorrow ... Oh, you were right, dear, no ice."

"I'll get some, and be right back." He disappeared as quietly as he arrived.

After a moment of silence, looking at Angie with a big smile and wide-open eyes, Aunt Ruth asked, "Who pray tell, was that?"

Angie grinned and told her, "Oh, that's Gary Adonis from Walgren's Heating and Cooling. He did the extra work on the wall and installed the coolers and air conditioner."

Aunt Ruth stated, "I must say, he has a very fitting last name. He *is* handsome, Angie."

"What did you say?"

Aunt Ruth was laughing and her head leaned to one side. "I'm talking about his last name, Adonis. Very fitting for such a handsome man."

Angie quickly informed her, "Oh, Aunt Ruth, I made that up. You know, like a joke because he's so good looking. I don't know his last name, and you can just forget what you're thinking. I see those wheels turning around and it's not going to happen."

Aunt Ruth told her, "Well, dear, you can't stay single forever, and he really is an Adonis."

"Aunt Ruth, you just forget you ever heard that

word and promise me you won't ever say it again. You'd embarrass me to death if he ever overheard it."

"Overheard what? Here's the ice," Gary said as he placed a bag on the table.

Oh God, I hope he didn't hear that, Angie thought.

"By the way," Gary asked, "what are we sharing?"

Aunt Ruth told him, "Chambord."

While looking straight at Angie, Gary made a strange face by crinkling his nose. "Never heard of it, let alone tasted it, but I'm game. Let's give it a try."

Aunt Ruth poured the dark purple liquid explaining it was a black raspberry flavored liqueur, and handing him a glass, she introduced herself. "I'm Ruth, Angie's Aunt."

"Nice to meet you. I'm Gary." He gazed around the finished apartment. "You've done a terrific job here. This place looks great. My compliments. No one would know there's an apartment back here. From the store front, the apartment door looks like a storeroom."

As the three shared their drinks and conversation, Angie and Gary took turns catching each other, as they were sneaking looks at one another.

After her third glass of Chambord, Aunt Ruth announced, "Well, I guess that's enough nerve juice."

Confused by the strange remark, Angie looked at her. "Nerve juice? What does that mean?"

Smiling like she just pulled a fast one over on her niece, Aunt Ruth said, "I have a date tonight. A first date, with a man named Frank, and I'm just a little nervous, that's all. Don't look so shocked, Angie."

"Aunt Ruth, I'm not shocked, I'm just surprised. In fifteen years, I've only seen you go on a date two or three times."

As Aunt Ruth reached for her purse she responded in a jokingly firm tone, "Then it's about time again, don't you think?" Smiling, she said, "Well, I'm off. I'll call you tomorrow, dear." Hiding her grin, Aunt Ruth gave a wave as she left. "Nice meeting you, Mr. Adonis."

Angie nearly fainted when Gary asked, "What'd she say?"

As she wiped at a spot on her skirt, knowing there was nothing there, she said, "I was still stuck on the fact that she had a date. I didn't hear what she said." She knew the moment the words were out of her mouth he'd probably see right through that lie.

Gary asked, "How about you? Care for some company?"

Angie could feel him staring at her. It felt as if he was slowly undressing her with his eyes. It was difficult not to watch those dark eyes as they traveled over her body. Her spine tingled, and she could feel her nipples getting hard. And how could anyone get goose bumps on their thighs?

Angie said, "Look, Gary, I've enjoyed our visit, and thanks for bringing the bill, which you could have mailed. You can just put it on the table and I'll mail a check. I have a lot to do tomorrow and I'll need to get an early start. So, if you don't mind. . ."

Gary crossed the room to where she stood. When he placed his hand on the wall above her, he leaned so close she could smell the sweetness of the Chambord on his breath. "My ego is now severely bruised, thank you. I haven't been thrown out of a woman's apartment in a long time."

It was getting even more difficult now to keep her composure. "I'm not throwing you out, not exactly. It's just that I have a lot of things to do tomorrow. The flowers and the accessories are arriving early. And I have to assemble the racks. And then I have to hang the shelves. . ." She was rambling. She was so damned nervous.

Moving back and away at the rejection, he said, "Okay. I get it. I'll go. I can help you tomorrow with your assembly project though. I'm actually pretty handy to have around."

Angie wondered if he was trying to find an excuse to spend some time with her. Looking up at him she asked, "Don't you have to work tomorrow?"

"I'm off tomorrow. What time should I be here?"

Angie smiled. "Why not just call me tomorrow, okay? The number is painted on the shop window."

"I guess I could do that." He looked at her for a moment, shook his head slightly, and walked from the apartment through the shop, and stopped at the front door. Turning back, he said, "I'll change the door and lock for you from the apartment to the outside so you can use the back entrance when the shop is closed. Good night, Angie."

With that, he was gone.

Locking the shop door behind Gary, Angie decided to take a bath and go to bed. Lying back in the tub, with her eyes closed, she realized she was upset that he hadn't kissed her. Would it have progressed to another level? Would his kiss have been soft and gentle or firm and aggressive? Thinking about his strong looking arms with those beautiful biceps, she thought firm and aggressive would be her choice. At least that's how she was feeling right now.

She was restless when she climbed into bed, as she knew tomorrow would be a busy day.

It took a long time for sleep to quiet her mind.

****

Early morning found her on her hands and knees looking for the screws she dropped while trying to assemble the shelves. The palm of her right hand was blistered and bleeding from pushing and turning the screwdriver. She had no idea the wood was so hard. Her own fault she thought. If she hadn't been watching her pennies so closely, she could have hired someone to do it.

When she heard the jingle from the shop door, her spine tingled. *He* was here! She turned, and seeing it wasn't him, her smile almost faded. She sat up and said, "Hi, Carl."

Carl looked around the shop. "Hey girl, I'm not trying to spy on you, I just came by to see how it's going." She bent down and gave Angie a hug. "I think I'm almost as nervous about tomorrow as you are. I thought I'd offer to help the first few days, because I know you'll be busy with everyone wanting to check out the new owner and all. Damn it…" She nearly tripped as she stepped over the unassembled litter on the floor.

"I'd better stay over here where it's safer." She leaned against a wall and said, "I could get a sitter, and when my big boy, Jim, gets home, he could watch the kids."

"I didn't know you had kids," Angie said with surprise. "And I assume Jim is your husband."

Carl shrugged and told her, "I guess the subject never came up."

Angie was almost sad at having to decline her offer. It was after all so kind of her. Arrangements had already been made for Aunt Ruth to help out, not only opening day, but on a part time basis. "Carl, it's a nice offer, but Aunt Ruth said she's bored to death so she'll help out the first few weeks. But thanks. If I get real busy, though, I might take you up on that offer."

Carl looked at the stack of wood shelving and unassembled racks. "Looks like I came at a bad time, huh? I'm uh, not too good at putting stuff together, so, how about lunch later?"

Angie told her as she waved her arms like wands over the rubble on the floor, "As you can see, I have so much to do today I can barely think straight. And deliveries will be here early this afternoon. So, I'll have to pass. But how about one day next week?"

Once again, Carl climbed around the accidents waiting to happen as she headed to the door. "Alrighty then, it's a deal, and, good luck tomorrow, Angie." Putting her fingers to her lips she said, "Kiss, kiss my friend."

"Thanks, Carl, bye."

Angie returned to her hands and knees. After looking around the floor for another ten minutes, annoyed, she still couldn't find all the screws. Her knees were starting to hurt from the hard floor and her back ached. "Damn it all to hell."

"That's not very ladylike, Miss Gibbons."

She jumped at the sound of his voice. She didn't care that he'd heard her, only that he was here. But why? She hardly knew him. What was it about this *Adonis* that she found so appealing? He looked smug, leaning against the door frame with his arms crossed, holding a six-pack, staring at her. And his cocky grin was causing an earthquake inside her.

Gary grinned and said, "I must say, the view from up here is amazing. What are you trying to put together down there?"

Angie sat straight up, her face now crimson red, giving away her embarrassment at his saucy, and what she considered teasing remark. She told him, "I dropped the screws for the shelves and I can't find them all."

With a smirk on his face, he stepped toward offering her his empty hand to help her up from the floor. "I'll make you a deal. If you'll put this beer in the fridge, I'll get my toolbox out of the truck and finish those shelves for you. Shouldn't take me too long. I have extra screws too. You might even open a beer for me. I'll admit, though, I'd rather stand here and watch you look for those screws. Like I said, the view from up here is great."

Ignoring his saucy remarks, Angie took his offering and she pulled herself up from the floor. She told him, "I'd appreciate the help, thank you." She was grateful, although she wasn't sure about letting anyone erode her new sense of independence. But she liked the idea of *his* help. Why, she didn't know. As she rose from the floor, she thought it was because of her blistered and bleeding palm. That had to be it. Certainly it had nothing to do with the fact that the man was incredibly good-looking, or that he had a body built for a sex marathon. As she entered the kitchen, she giggled, wondering where the hell that came from.

Returning with a tool box, Gary asked, "What's so funny? It can't be the beer bottle you keep rolling between the palms of your hands, can it?"

"No. My hand hurts and the cold bottle makes it feel better." She said, "Here," as she handed the beer to him.

When he took the bottle, Gary frowned as he held her hand palm up. He pulled it toward him for a better look. "What the hell did you do?"

Angie winced in pain as she looked up at him. "I didn't realize the wood shelving was so hard." Her mind was reeling with confusion and embarrassment. Yet she was touched by his concern.

"Gee Angie, I told you I'd be here today to do it." He let out a sigh and shook his head. "Why didn't you wait? Does it hurt?"

She pulled her hand back as if he'd burned it. "It's okay. It doesn't hurt much." The sensation of his touch coursed through her entire body like lightning. The result was causing weakness in her knees. She needed a diversion. She walked back into the shop, determined to hide her reaction.

She heard his slow steps.

Now he was directly in front of her. He looked down at her.

Her face was almost touching his as she looked

up.

He bent his head so their lips could touch.

Angie hesitated for only a moment. It had been so long since she'd been kissed, or even wanted anyone to kiss her. Right here, and right now, the butterflies in her stomach told her she wanted a kiss, and from him. She didn't push him away.

Gary realized she wasn't backing away. His thoughts were spinning. Her one moment of hesitation had set him on an exciting mission. It seemed an eternity before their lips finally met. Slowly, he probed further.

Angie froze when she realized her arms were around his neck and she was kissing him back. She quickly pulled herself away. "I'm sorry. I don't make it a habit to stand in front of a showcase window kissing a workman I hardly know."

He just stared at her with those burning black eyes and said, "Well, I guess the workman needs to get to work then, huh?" His flaring nostrils showed his anger.

He opened his toolbox, and for a few moments just sat staring at his tools. As he quickly started to assemble the shelves, he realized he was tossing and banging things around. When finished, refusing to look at her, he turned to the racks and stands, while Angie pulled merchandise from boxes and placed the items meticulously on the shelves.

Though still not looking at her, he broke the silence. "While you load those up, I'll go around back and put in the door. I picked one up on my way over this morning." With that, he stomped out.

Sandi K. Whipple

With the shelving and stands now assembled from the boxes that had been stacked in the corner for days, the excitement of everything coming together, began to jump around in Angie's brain. It really was going to happen.

Just as she finished the shelves and racks, the huge shipment of flowers arrived. She spent a lot of time placing them in the coolers. She tried arranging them by what she considered popularity. She knew she could develop a better working system as time went by.

Gary peeked in, several times when taking a break for a beer. He was amazed at how quickly and meticulously the tasks at hand were being completed.

Angie stepped back to examine her handiwork. She was finally ready to open the shop!

Gary interrupted her thoughts. Sarcastically he said, "The workman is finished now, Miss Gibbons. If there's nothing else, I'll be leaving."

His obvious sarcasm made her wince. Angie couldn't decide if she should react to it or not, so she simply said, "Thanks, Gary. If you'll just make out a bill, I'll write a check."

"I'll do that, Miss Gibbons," was his departing remark. With a wave of his hand that looked like a salute, he added, "See ya."

Fuming at his apparent dismissal of her, Angie made a survey to be sure everything was clean and ready for tomorrow. Satisfied, she locked up, turned off the lights, and retreated to the sanctuary of her apartment.

There were two keys on the dinette table. She assumed they were for the new back door. She walked over, tapped her knuckles on the surface, and discovered it was a steel door. Her sense of security was heightened by the reinforced protection. She felt as if she was now safe from the world outside.

She hadn't realized that setting up the shop had exhausted her. Angie opened the refrigerator, grabbed a beer, and sat down at the dinette table. She rolled the cool bottle between her palms, took a sip, and wondered what she was doing. She didn't even like beer.

She liked Gary though. She'd wanted him to kiss her. She wanted to kiss him. So why did she push him away when he did? And why in the hell did she have to act so damned superior and condescending by referring to him as the workman? She had nothing to be angry about. Didn't he do what she wanted? Maybe she was afraid of this man, this *Adonis*. Why would that be? Was it because he made her insides feel weird and it was difficult to think when he was around? What was with that, anyway? For some reason, her strength, independence, feeling of being secure and knowledgeable, all went flying out the window when this guy was either around or even in her thoughts.

She took a sip of beer and realized she'd been obsessing about Gary. She had to change her mood and decided a bath was what she needed. That night she slept dreamlessly.

****

The next day, Angie's Flower Shop opened for business. The foot traffic was beyond her expectations. People came and went, stood in line both to pay and place orders, and even to ask for advice. One customer even put in an order for six weeks later.

Angie glanced at Aunt Ruth and felt a pang of guilt that she was working so hard. "Why don't you go into the apartment and take break Aunt Ruth?"

Aunt Ruth just rolled her eyes and smiled. "I'm fine dear." She giggled when she added, "Go back to work, you're ignoring your customers."

Still, the day flew by, and Angie couldn't believe she was already closing. She gave Aunt Ruth a big hug. "You're a godsend. I wouldn't have made it through the day without you. Now that the door is locked and the closed sign is up, let's go sit, and have a drink."

Angie poured a glass full of Chambord with ice and placed it in front of Aunt Ruth. She opened the last beer in the refrigerator for herself. With the bottle above her head, she made a toast: "Compliments of Gary *Adonis*."

The remark made her aunt laugh. "I thought we weren't supposed to *ever* say that word again? And why would you say with his compliments?"

With a quick snicker, Angie said, "He was here yesterday and put the racks and shelves together for me. He brought a six pack and this is the last of it." She felt here was no point sharing or going into any other part of the day.

"Did he put in that new door, too?" Aunt Ruth asked.

"He did indeed. Then I treated him like a servant, he called me *Miss* Gibbons, saluted, and left saying, 'See ya.'" Careful Angie, she told herself. Unsure of Gary's intentions at this point, there was no need to offer any other information. Actually, at this point she was even a bit unsure about her own feelings towards him. After all, she hadn't known him for very long.

Disappointed that her niece didn't freely offer any further information regarding her and Gary's afternoon together, Aunt Ruth asked, "Was his help done professionally, I mean was he uh, I mean, do you think he had an ulterior motive ?" She just stood there looking at Angie and added, "Can I ask why, or what happened, to make you feel it was necessary to, what did you say, treat him like a servant"?

Until she was *sure* of her own feelings, Angie chose not to wonder about Gary's possible ulterior motives. She said, "I don't know. I was just tired from setting things up I guess, and I took it out on him."

Angie was grateful that Aunt Ruth seemed to accept the explanation and let it go.

They chatted and giggled for a while.

Calming down, Aunt Ruth said, "I am now physically disabled from the day's work."

Angie, still giggling at her aunt's feigned disability, said, "There are no roses in the refrigerators; the carnations were gone by four P.M., there are only a few bunches of miscellaneous flowers, and seven potted plants left."

Aunt Ruth said, "At one point, I counted forty-one people in the shop. Who would have guessed huh?"

Angie replied, "Thank goodness, I had had the foresight to arrange an early and large delivery for tomorrow."

Aunt Ruth asked if they needed to call a Brinks

truck to handle the day's sales, and that started them both giggling again.

Gasping for air, Aunt Ruth said, "I need to go home and die in peace. If I make it through the night, I'll be here at ten in the morning." Struggling to her feet, she let out a groan which caught Angie's attention.

"Aunt Ruth, are you okay? You're scaring me."

"I'm fine, dear. Just a little tired." At the door, before leaving, she turned to Angie and said quietly, "Angie, I am so proud of you, and I love you." Then in joking tone she said, "But if this keeps up, I'm going to have to seek other employment. You're a slave driver. And remember, dear, I have to leave early tomorrow. I have a date with Frank. See you in the morning, honey."

"Another date with Frank, huh?" Angie said. "Is this something you need or want to talk about?"

"No thank you, dear. Good night."

"I love you, Aunt Ruth. Good night."

After locking the door, Angie sat at the table and began to cry tears of joy and relief. Today was a bigger success than she dreamed possible. Her business was off to a great start.

She was too emotionally drained to eat or think. A hot bath and a good night's sleep would make her feel better.

CHAPTER TWO

While Aunt Ruth watched over the shop for a few hours a day, Angie spent countless hours visiting hotels, sending out fliers, and visited many restaurants donating free flowers for their dining tables. She was even placing advertisements in the local paper.

A few weeks later, Angie's business blossomed even more. Word spread that Angie's Flower Shop created innovative arrangements with unsurpassed quality. She'd acquired two hotels as clients, and their lobbies now boasted a new ambiance. Even a few walk-ins with questions left the shop with contracts for Angie to furnish, prepare, and deliver flowers for their weddings.

She would definitely need to hire some help, and soon. Aunt Ruth was wonderful, but she worked too many hours, far more than they agreed upon in the beginning, and she refused to accept a paycheck.

****

A few days later, Angie wrote up a few orders, invoiced a few clients, and hung the *Open* sign in the window.

Later in the morning when she was alone, Angie sat at her desk separating her already paid and yet unpaid bills so could get her filing done. She didn't remember paying it, and it wasn't in either stack, so where was the bill for the wall? She must have misplaced it. She hadn't received a bill for the steel door either. That's simple. Just call Walgrens and ask for them. The

Sandi K. Whipple

number was on the refrigerator invoice.

Might as well do it now, she thought, as she dialed the number.

"Good morning, Walgren's Heating and Cooling. May I help you?" a cheerful voice greeted Angie's phone call.

"Good morning. This is Angela Gibbons from Angie's Flower Shop. I seem to have misplaced the bill for the wall replacement in my shop. I haven't received a bill for the new back door either. If you'll furnish copies, I'll mail a check."

The cheerful voice that greeted Angie, hesitated for a moment and finally asked, "Are you sure, Miss Gibbons? We don't install walls or doors. Maybe you have us confused with another company."

Angie felt somewhat insulted, wondering if this individual thought she was crazy. "No, there's no confusion on this end. Your workman did all the work." And then some, she thought.

"I'm sorry about the confusion, Miss Gibbons. I'll check it out and get back to you as soon as possible," the representative apologized.

"Thank you."

Angie thought the phone conversation was strange. She sat there shaking her head, wondering how in the world a company could do such expensive work, and then screw up their billing. They're obviously not very organized over there.

Gary installed the coolers and air conditioner. Gary worked for Walgrens Heating and Cooling. On the very first day he agreed to the wall work, and even called his office. He brought the bill to her, didn't he? Yes, the day he shared Chambord with she and Aunt Ruth. Though, she couldn't recall a bill for the door. Oh well, she thought, it'll get straightened out. Get some work done Angie.

The rest of the morning was somewhat busy. She was alone. Aunt Ruth was running errands and had a hair appointment. Angie dealt with telephone orders, walk-ins, and orders from restaurants for their daily delivery of fresh table roses. Aunt Ruth came in every day while Angie dealt with all the deliveries.

Aunt Ruth hadn't been happy about it when Angie hired a gal named Patti, just for part time. Patti was a college student and needed part time work. She was young, just nineteen, had a bubbly personality, and had a flexible school schedule. As it turned out, she was not only a quick learner, but she reminded Angie of herself. And Patti could work afternoons for sure, and possibly a morning here and there.

****

She hadn't seen or heard from the *Adonis* since last week when he stopped by for Secretary Day flowers. She remembers how surprised she was to see him.

He'd walked in wearing a T-shirt with missing sleeves, a pair of 'oh' so tight blue jeans, and work boots. His clothing told her he was working. His dark eyes, mussed thick dark hair, broad shoulders, tanned muscular arms, and the firm cheeks under those tight jeans, had made her dizzy. The man had the body of a God. *Adonis* really should have been his last name.

He'd walked right up to the counter where she

stood and smiled at her. "Hi, Angie." I need some flowers for one of the gals in the office. It is Secretary's Day, isn't it?"

There they were again, those damned butterflies in her stomach.

"It is at that. And that's what we do here, sell flowers. What did you have in mind?"

He never took his eyes off of her. "I hadn't really thought about it. Your choice I guess. You're the pro after all."

She thought about apologizing for her attitude the last time they saw each other. The same time he'd kissed her. And yes, the same time he'd set her emotions into a spin.

Instead, she'd chosen not to engage him in idle conversation. Why didn't she apologize for the nasty 'workman' comment? She'd deliberately portrayed a business-like attitude as she picked out a beautiful bouquet of carnations, telling him they would be perfect for the gal in his office.

Once again, the jingle of the front door bell jarred her back to work.

CHAPTER THREE

"Good morning, Katie." Gary acknowledged his secretary. "What have you got for me today?"

"Good morning, Mr. Walgren. There are two jobs set for this morning, and three more for this afternoon. I've got Ted on both jobs this morning, and him and Tom on both jobs this afternoon. I'm worried about next week though. I think I might have overbooked, and it could be a tight squeeze, if not impossible, to get the work done as promised."

"Don't worry about it. Just don't book any more until I look over the ones you've already scheduled." Smiling at her, he added, "I'll figure a way to get it done. Maybe the office in Green Bend can spare a few guys; we'll see. Anything else?"

With tilted head and a puzzling look on her face, his secretary said, "Well, yes. A Miss Gibbons called from Angie's Flower Shop this morning. She said something about a bill for wall work and a door. She insisted that one of our guys did the work. I told her our company doesn't do that kind of work, but I'd research it and get back to her. I'm sure she just got her signals crossed somewhere, but I'm not sure how to tell her tactfully that she's mistaken."

Gary just shook his head. "I'll take care of it, Katie. If she calls again, just tell her I'm looking into it personally, okay?"

"Sure thing, Mr. Walgren."

Gary closed the door when he entered his office. He sat behind his over-sized mahogany desk wondering how he was going to handle the bill to Angie's Flower

Sandi K. Whipple

Shop.

His thoughts took him back to the shop the day he'd met her aunt. He wasn't in the habit of giving free labor, but, he sure remembered pushing the bill for the wall deeper into his pocket, thinking maybe he'd wait on giving it to her. He had no idea when he finally threw it away. And no, he thought to himself, it wasn't just a ploy to get her in the sack, was it?

As he gazed out the window, he remembered how Angie looked that day. The tips of her cute painted toenails cuddled in open sandals, her shapely satin-smooth legs, and the not-short-enough gray skirt. She had rounded, firm, large breasts, sky-blue eyes and shoulder-length light brown hair. He decided that day she sure was a beautiful, well-put together woman, and what he saw, he liked very much. He'd never met a woman like her. She could turn his insides to mush.

He remembered several years back when he'd met Gloria. She was quite the looker, but she hadn't turned his insides to mush, ever. Their relationship was a close one, but never any bells or whistles. Gloria was tall, a bleached blonde with grey eyes, and generally quite passive. She was a buyer for a department store and had traveled a lot. When he'd discovered she was seeing other men on her out-of-town trips, he was, well, devastated wasn't the right word. But he was sure as hell crushed. He'd thought they were on the road to becoming pretty serious about each other. Wasn't fidelity supposed to be the most important part of a relationship? Obviously not for her. And for him, well, sharing just wasn't in his nature.

But, what was it about Angie? Her eyes became

daggers when she got angry, and he couldn't resist the thought of stealing a kiss in the hope it would calm her. And her stubborn independence —it was something to be admired. When he'd kissed her that day in the shop, she'd kissed him back. Why hadn't he tried again? Sure, he was mad because she'd treated him like a workman. After all, he was trying to be more than just her workman, wasn't he? His last attempt to get next to her had failed miserably as well.

He'd walked into her shop to buy flowers for Katie on Secretary's Day, and she'd been strictly business, not giving him even a little opening. He tried several times to make conversation, and all she gave him in return were short, curt, answers. He never took his eyes off her as she moved around the shop. Her refusal to be social, and be only business like wasn't just a disappointment, but another blow to his ego. He could have moved head on and forced the issue by asking her to dinner or something. But rejection fear struck him, so he didn't.

He knew he needed to get closer to her. *Wanted* didn't seem to apply here. When had it become a *need*? She had a strange magic that had him imagining her reaching out and pulling him toward her. He laughed out loud. That was sure as hell corny. Enough daydreaming.

Because he and Tom worked like a crew of four, he decided he would work on two of the jobs with Tom. He would bring over one of the guys from his office in Green Bend to work with Ted on the others.

Gary viewed Tom as a great guy, a fast learner, a hard worker, and loyal. He'd been with him for eight years and even helped set up the Green Bend office a few years back. He remembered when Tom came looking for work. He revealed he'd moved around for a couple of years but hadn't kept any steady jobs. It was time to settle down and stay put as he had a family to support. He promised to work hard and had certainly proven himself. He learned the business faster than most. And when he took the state licensing exams and passed on the first attempt, Gary knew he was management material.

He called Tom's cell to get his opinion on the jobs.

Tom agreed that Gary's choices were good but said, "We can't keep pulling the Greenbend guys over to Nasons Grove, Gary. It's starting to get a bit busier there too."

Gary asked him, "What are you going to do about new water lines for the boiler job?"

Tom told him, "I checked all the piping and lines yesterday. I think we can save and re-use close to half of the stuff, which could save us a ton of money."

"Say Tom, do you think you can do without me for an hour? Or maybe even two?"

"Sure", Tom told him. "If you're gonna make it all day though, tell me now, so I can shuffle a few bodies."

Gary laughed and said, "No. I promise bud. A few hours at the most. There's just something I want to do first. But in case…"

"Ya-Ya, I got it! I'll see you when I see you then. Bye, Gary."

Gary smiled. Yea, Tom was more a friend than

an employee.

Ready now to leave, Gary opened his office door, stepped out and said, "Katie, I'll be gone the rest of the day. I'll keep my pager on but call Tom first for any problems. If you can't reach him or he can't fix whatever it is, then go ahead and page me," he said as he left the office.

"Sure thing, Mr. Walgren."

****

Gary drove like a man on a mission. He felt even a detour couldn't keep him from accomplishing his goal of seeing Angie and maybe scoring a date with her.

Arriving at Angie's shop, the anticipation of seeing her made him a bit giddy. Climbing out of his truck he tried formulating what he would say to her. After all, he couldn't just barge in the door and say "Will you have dinner with me?"

When he entered the shop, he was surprised to see there was someone besides Angie or Aunt Ruth behind the counter.

"Hi, is Miss Gibbons around?" Gary asked the stranger at the counter.

"No, sir, she's out for the afternoon. May I help you with something?"

"Actually, no. This is kind of a business call. When do you expect her?"

"She went to Green Bend today and said she wouldn't be back until just before the shop closes. Her aunt will be in later though. Maybe she can help you?"

"No thanks. I'll stop by another time. You're

new here, aren't you?"

"Yes, this is my second week on the job. I'm Patti."

"Well, it's nice to meet you, Patti. I'll be seeing you. Bye."

As he left the shop and climbed into his pick-up, his mind was reeling. He thought this is great. She has extra help, so business must be pretty good. With extra help, he could drag her off to lunch somewhere.

He laughed as the image of a caveman came to mind. He'd like nothing more right now than to drag her away somewhere and see if her kisses were really what he had been spending his nights dreaming about. Would she respond to his touch? Would she moan or cry out when he exposed those beautiful breasts of hers and massaged them? Or when he ran his tongue around their rosy tips? And how would she react when he trailed soft kisses from her neck all the way down her spine, then to that beautiful round firm bottom of hers?

He remembered the day he'd seen her in the shop on all fours. He'd wanted to touch and caress that beautiful behind.

Damn it. Good thing he was daydreaming in his truck. His arousal was more than obvious. This either had to stop or he had to do something about it.

****

While browsing other flower shops and comparing the competition in Green Bend, Angie found a few small antique clocks for her shop and headed back to Nasons Grove.

Sandi K. Whipple

As she drove out of Green Bend, she noticed a building that appeared to stand out from the others on the street. It was newer. A professional, well-designed sign on the building read: *Walgren's Heating and Cooling Systems*. Angie had no idea her *Adonis* worked for such a large company.

The thought hit her that she used *that word* again. Aunt Ruth would think it comical, knowing how adamant Angie was about not using it. Every time she thought of Gary, that word just popped into her head. She couldn't help it.

Wouldn't any woman who'd been kissed by him feel that way? He was, after all, quite a hunk, and sexy as hell, with the softest, most gentle hands for a man of manual labor. She remembered when he kissed her in the shop. If he kissed her again, would he let her stop his advances again? Why was he so easily stopped anyway? She'd been on the pill since she was a senior in high school, so if that something more happened... she needed to stop thinking these thoughts right now.

She was aroused simply by thinking about him. If a mere thought did that to her, then actually making love with him might be her demise.

Demise? What did that mean? With him, would it be a good thing or a bad thing? She had to figure out a way to find out. Realizing she was already parked in front of the shop and was still daydreaming about her Adonis, she sighed as she left her car.

"Hi ,Patti, any messages?"

"Nope," she replied. "I had three drop-in orders and I wasn't even nervous putting them together. The customers seemed pretty pleased so I guess I did okay."

Sandi K. Whipple

Sifting through some more papers, she added, "Oh, by the way, your aunt came by, checked through the mail, and said there was nothing pressing. She offered to help but I told her I had it under control."

Patti stopped to catch her breath, and then continued: "She said she'd call you later, then she headed off to have lunch with a guy named Frank. How was your trip to Green Bend? It's not a bad drive, huh?"

Angie thought it was almost comical the way Patti prattled.

"And, oh yeah," Patti added, "Some hunk came by to see you. No message though. He said it was just business. I sure could have done business with him. Monkey business, that is."

"Patti, really."

Patti roared with laughter. "Well, gee, Angie, the guy looks like an Adonis!"

When *that word* hit Angie's ears, she felt a shocking sensation in the pit of her stomach and with widened eyes, she asked, "Why would you use that word, Patti?"

"What word?"

"That, that, — descriptive word."

Giggling, Patti asked, "How come you're having a problem even saying it, Angie? It's not as if it's a dirty word or something. Try it, Adonis, A-don-is. See, it's really an easy word to say."

With a wave of her hand, Angie said, "All right, already. I was just shocked you would think that way at your age, that's all."

"Angie, I'm not blind! I may only be nineteen years old but I've read about the Greek Adonis! And besides, I know a sexy-looking guy when I see one."

"I only meant to question your choice of words, Patti. If I've offended you, I'm sorry."

"I'm not the least bit offended. But me thinks you know exactly who I'm talking about and me thinks, by your reaction, you think he's sexy, too." Leaning on the counter with her chin in her hands, Patti started to giggle when she said, "Want to talk about it?"

"I'm fine and it's nothing. So no, I don't want to talk about it."

"Okay. I have a class tonight so I need to skedaddle. I only have three day-classes next week so if you need me to work more hours, I'm available." She gave Angie a hug and was gone.

Hiring Patti had been a great move. She was a bright young girl. She was artistic, learned quickly, was devoted to the shop, and considered her job to be fun. She always had a smile and the customers adored her, as did Aunt Ruth. Angie recalled how hiring Patti had upset her aunt, due to her young age. That feeling had quickly dissipated once Aunt Ruth met her.

The grumbling of her stomach told Angie it was late and nearing the end of the day. The antique clocks also confirmed it was time to close the shop. She changed her focus and started her closing routine. She locked the front door, hung up the closed sign, and headed for her apartment in the back. After straightening a few things, she climbed in the shower.

Gary approached the fifteen-foot walkway between the buildings that led to Angie's back door. When he knocked hard on the new steel door, he was smiling. It seemed an eternity before Angie answered.

When Angie heard the pounding noise on the door, she quickly wrapped a towel around her head, and another around her body, then ran to answer it.

When she opened the door, she was gasping for air. The moment she realized it wasn't her aunt, she screeched, "Agh!"

Gary's face lit up like a Christmas tree. Standing there looking at the voluptuous body wrapped in towels, he asked with a mischievous grin, "Do you always answer your door half-naked?"

"I am not half-naked, and I thought it was my aunt. What are you doing here anyway?" she responded, embarrassed at her attire.

"I thought I might talk you into having dinner with me," he said, and slipped past her into the apartment. He turned to look at her with serious black eyes but his smile gave away his animal intentions. As calmly as possible, he said, "A provocative outfit like that could be pretty dangerous."

Angie instinctively put her hands up to the body towel as if trying to glue it to herself and replied, "As you so eloquently put it, I'm hardly dressed for dinner but, thanks anyway. Maybe another time."

"You look great as far as I'm concerned. And I doubt any male over the age of fourteen would disagree. But, I don't mind waiting if you'd like to change."

Why did he have to look at her with that cocky grin that made his eyes appear half-closed?

Although her heart hammered inside her chest, she told him, "I've had a long day, Gary. I was on the road for more than half the day. I just finished dusting and mopping the shop." She was nervous and knew she was rambling. "I have a lot to do tomorrow, and besides, I wasn't expecting you. . ."

Walking slowly toward her with his head slightly tilted and a sheepish grin on his face, Gary said, "Do you know, whenever you get nervous, you jabber on without really saying much and almost every time we see each other you do that? Do I make you nervous, Angie?"

Fidgeting with tendrils that had escaped the towel wrapped around her head, she told him, "No, of course not. It's just that I'm tired and I planned to just kick back and relax tonight. That's all."

"I could help you do that if you'd like. I'm a pro at helping people relax."

As he moved even closer to her, she looked around for an escape route. She slipped around him and headed for her bedroom. As a means to stop him in his tracks, she said, "On second thought, I *am* hungry. Dinner sounds good. Have a seat while I get dressed. I won't be long." She turned and almost ran into the adjoining room.

Gary walked around the apartment wondering if he'd find any pictures of men. He didn't see any. He thought maybe that was a good sign and perhaps an opening for him.

Angie interrupted his thoughts. "Okay, I'm ready. I hope I didn't take so long you've lost your appetite."

In a split second, Gary took note of the cream-colored dress with spaghetti straps, pulled-back hair, and clear-painted toes wrapped in dressy sandals.

He told her, "Nope. I'm even hungrier than I was

before." Laughing, he added, "Though at this very moment I'm not sure I'm referring to my hunger for food."

Angie shook her head and said, "Oh stop it", as she feigned a punch to his shoulder.

They drove to the restaurant and chit-chatted about their day. Seated in a quiet corner of the restaurant, Angie ordered a glass of wine with a shrimp salad. When Gary ordered a large draft beer, Alfredo pasta with sausage and broccoli, and lots of French bread and butter, Angie started laughing. "Are you really going to eat all of that?" She felt relaxed for the first time since they'd met.

"You bet. I read somewhere that everyone should eat three square meals a day. I always have breakfast but I usually skip lunch, so by dinnertime, I eat enough to equal two meals. That comes to three meals a day, right?"

Gary leaned back in his chair, smiled as he looked at Angie, and said, "I know this is going to sound like a cliché, but you're beautiful when you laugh, Angie. You should do it more often."

As Angie unfolded her napkin as a means to hide her discomfort from the compliment, with a mischievous grin Gary added, "Though I'm not sure yet if I like you better in an upright position or lying on the sidewalk."

At that moment, Angie was sipping her wine. The saucy remark caught her off guard and she spit wine all over the table.

Now, not sure if she should once again be angry or embarrassed, she smiled at him and quietly said, "I didn't think you'd realized it was me. I knew when you showed up at the shop that first day it was you I'd collided with." Angie was smiling at him when she said, "I was pretty mad when it happened. I guess I should apologize for the *oaf* remark, huh?"

"Naw! I think we were both kind of daydreaming and not paying attention." With outright laughter, he told her, "I was going to help you up but I thought better of it when you hollered at me."

As she stared at the wine splatter on the table, and thinking back to the collision of bodies, Angie decided it was time to drop the subject completely. "Tell me about yourself, your family, and how you ended up doing the work you do."

"I grew up in Highland Park, Illinois, just outside of Chicago. I hated the city once I grew up."

Curious, Angie asked, "Why?"

Gary told her, "Because there were so many people, I mean people everywhere. I couldn't stand the constant hustle and bustle. And I hated traffic all the time when I was going from one job to another. Ever see rush hour around the Chicago area? It sucks!"

"What kind of work were you doing?"

Gary told her, looking down at the tablecloth, "I worked for my dad in his heating and refrigeration business, and then he died."

Angie looked at him and said, "I'm sorry Gary." After giving him a moment, she asked, "So what about the rest of your family?"

Gary brought his eyes back up to hers. "There were three of us, my mom, my younger sister, and myself. We voted to sell the business and move here. My mother started another company here, and organized it like Highland Park. I did most of the grunt work. Once it became profitable, Mom sold out. So here I am, 33 years old, and still doing the grunt work, but I really love it. How about you?"

Now that Gary had suddenly put the spotlight on her, Angie said, "I graduated from college a few years ago and went to work at the flower shop. I absolutely loved being creative and matching different flowers and different colors. And seeing the smiles on the faces of people who purchased my creations, well, like I said, I loved it. When I found out my boss was in foreclosure, and that I'd soon be out of work, I thought I could build it up and make a decent living, so, I bought it from the bank."

Gary asked, "What about your parents? Any brothers or sisters?"

Angie reacted inwardly to his question thinking, *I hate talking about the past*.... Biting her bottom lip, she formed a response and said, "My parents died; that's why I came to live with my aunt. My brother left home when he was fourteen and I was nine. I haven't seen or heard from him since." Angie paused and lowered her head. "This isn't a favorite subject of mine, Gary. Could we talk about something else?"

The waiter's arrival saved Angie from the cloud of sadness that seemed to envelope her. When she saw the huge amount of food placed in front of Gary, she was delightfully sidetracked.

With a jovial tone in her voice, she asked, "Are you seriously going to eat all that? And the bread? You won't be able to move if you do."

"Oh, don't worry about me, I'll be fine. Maybe

later I can demonstrate just how I can move."

After dinner, they strolled through the town streets for a while. They talked about happy and funny things that they'd done in their lives.

Angie described climbing the stairs while attending Northwestern, and looking up to see Sean Connery, and how she proceeded to fall 'up' the stairs landing directly at his feet. When she told him, to her embarrassment, the University paper even wrote about it, they both broke into laughter.

Gary asked if Sean Connery helped her up, and Angie nearly choked when she told him "of course not, silly."

Gary told her how he drove his Dad's car through the garage when he was learning how to drive a stick shift, and closing his eyes as he awaited death because he knew his Dad was going to kill him. When Angie remarked, "that obviously didn't happen, I mean you're here", Gary jokingly punched her shoulder. Not until they reached the car did either one realize that they walked and talked with Gary's arm around her shoulder.

As they climbed into the car, Angie thought how it just felt so normal and comfortable, and wondered why that was.

At Angie's apartment, when she opened the door, Gary walked in right behind her. "You got any beer?"

Smiling up at him, she said, "Actually, yes I do." She reached into the refrigerator and when she turned to hand the beer to him, he was just inches away, towering over her and sporting that cocky grin she adored.

Taking the beer, he said, "I thought you didn't drink beer?"

Sandi K. Whipple

  Before she could respond, Gary set the beer down. He moved forward and backed her up against the counter, their bodies almost touching. He placed his hands on both sides of her so she was unable to retreat. Smiling down at her, he whispered, "Did you buy the beer with me in mind?"
  She could only look up at him. She was unable to speak. She wondered if he would kiss her.
  He pushed her hair to one side and kissed her gently on the neck. His kisses continued down to her shoulder as he slipped the spaghetti strap of her dress off her shoulder and continued his kisses toward her covered breast.
  She bent her head back and he moved to her other shoulder continuing with his kisses while pulling down the other strap.
  Angie whispered, "Gary, this isn't the right time for this. And, I have a very busy day tomorrow. I'm sure you have to work too, and . . ."
  The rest of her words were stifled when he said, "This isn't the time to start rambling, Angie. You don't need to be nervous. I wouldn't try to put you in a position that you didn't want to be in." He slowly pulled the straps of her dress back where they needed to be. Kissing the tip of her nose he told her, "I'll call you Angie." When he reached the door, he said "Lock this", and quietly closed the door.

****

  Gary called the shop the very next day, asking Angie to get together the following Sunday.

Sandi K. Whipple

When Sunday came, they decided to take a long walk in the park. They found a vendor selling kites to children. Gary bought them each one.

After putting his together, he began teasing Angie. "Aren't you done yet? Come on 'pokey', do I have to do yours too?"

Finally finished putting hers together, Angie said, "Okay hotshot. Let's have a little contest here and see whose will be the highest in thirty minutes." Then she took off and her kite started rising. When she looked back, Gary had just started trying to get his in the air.

When Angie won, Gary accused her of cheating, and threatened to tell all the children who had quit playing, so they could watch the crazy adults.

The following Sunday they drove to the airport and went gliding. Angie was frightened at first. Gary had to calm her. He told her, "Look hon, I'm licensed and the glider is very safe, really it is. Trust me Angie." As it turned out, Angie had the time of her life, until after landing that is. Gary informed her they had to walk back. When she realized he was teasing, she lunged for him and hollered, "The time will come to get even."

For weeks the two were together every Sunday.

They went bowling, and Gary had so many gutter balls, Angie decided that it wasn't his game, and they should stop. When Gary pulled out his wallet at the counter to pay, the young kid told him they only had to pay for one, since one of them didn't hit any pins. Gary told him, "Look here young man. There were two of us on the alley, two of us throwing a ball, and I'm paying for two!" The kid said, "Whatever you say mister." When Gary turned around, Angie was gone. He found her leaning on the exit door laughing, with tears streaming down her face. He started laughing too and told her, "Cut it out, will ya?

The day they went to an Art Gallery, Gary caught her yawning on three different occasions. He finally asked her, "Are you enjoying this?" When she told him she was, he laughed at her and said, "Come on you little liar. Whose idea was this anyway?" Neither of them took responsibility for it.

One weekend they decided to walk through the flea market. Angie bought so many knick knacks and small antiques, Gary had to make three trips to put them in the car. Angie finally complained and told him "I can't find anything else that I can't live without." Gary took her shoulders, turned her in the direction of the car, and told her, "Good, because if you buy anything else, you'll have to ride home on the roof." They held hands all the way to the car.

One Sunday they went to the zoo and spent the day making animal faces and noises at each other at every cage. Gary told Angie, "Your noises aren't even close kiddo." She fired back with, "Oh yea, well your faces are really pretty sad too."

After leaving the Zoo, they had dinner at a little café on the old highway. During dinner they laughed while comparing how awful the faces and noises were that they'd made at the zoo. And they wondered how many people, who observed their antics, thought they were both crazy.

When they reached Angie's apartment, she invited Gary in for a beer, which had become a habit on each of their Sunday outings.

Sandi K. Whipple

    When Angie closed the refrigerator and handed Gary his beer, he set it on the counter. Wrapping his arms around her, his mouth met hers with a kiss that was aggressive, yet gentle. Exploring her soft, warm mouth, his tongue searched for hers. The feel of her arms reaching around his neck and her deep sigh found him groaning with desire, and her tongue was now frantically searching for his.

    Unzipping her dress with one hand, he massaged a breast with the other. Pulling her arms from around his neck, he placed them at her sides as he continued tasting her warm giving mouth. He slowly pulled down on her dress. When it fell to the floor, he brought his hands up to her breasts, surprised to find them bare. With his mouth still locked firmly to hers, he massaged her breasts, flicking his thumbs over her already peaked and hard nipples.

    Angie's heart raced and the pressure inside her body began to build. She pressed her hips against his.

    He lifted and carried her to the bedroom. His lips were locked to hers as he placed her on the bed. He reached down to remove her lacy underwear and flicked his tongue first across one breast, then the other,

    Angie stared up at him as he removed his own clothing and removed a condom from his pocket, opening and placing it on the side table. Her eyes moved slowly down from his handsome face to his broad shoulders, to the hard muscles of his arms, to his hairy chest, and finally to his more-than-obvious aroused manhood. She thought he was not only beautiful but, his body was absolutely perfect, which put the real Adonis to shame.

Sandi K. Whipple

He blanketed her body with his and rained more kisses on her face and neck, spending a glorious amount of time in pleasing her.

When his kisses reached her first breast, he used his entire mouth, sucking in as much as would fit, then flicked his tongue over the taut, hard nipple.

Angie arched her back in response to Gary's wonderful foreplay. She began to push her breast toward him as if begging for more. Her breathing became heavy and she gasped for air. Angie's moans, along with her obvious enjoyment, pushed him almost beyond his own limitations. When she felt the heat of his manhood and flesh pressing against her thighs, she lifted herself to him and whispered, "Please, Gary. . ."

He couldn't hold off much longer. With lightening speed, he reached for the condom, surprising himself how quickly it was in place.

When he entered her, she wrapped her legs around his waist as her body matched his fevered desire. He filled her insides over and over again. She moaned and made soft noises that sent him into a frenzy of passion, and he thrust deeper into her.

When her body stiffened and became motionless, his explosion came.

It took a long time for the rocking motions and convulsions to subside.

Later, he lay contentedly with her in his arms. Her slow steady breathing told him she'd finally succumbed to needed sleep. He gazed at her peaceful face, nestled in the crook of his shoulder.

It was that moment that Gary realized he'd be unable to share this incredible woman.

His eyelids began to close. His final thought was he never before wanted anyone in his life as badly as Miss Angela Gibbons.

When he awoke, the other side of the bed was empty. He quickly hit the bathroom, threw some water on his face, dabbed his mouth with toothpaste, and pulled on his jeans.

The scent of coffee led to Angie's homey kitchen.

Humming, Angie stood at the counter wearing panties and a T-shirt.

Walking up from behind, Gary wrapped his arms around her and placed each hand over a breast. Nuzzling her neck, he mumbled, "Good morning. It's too early to be up."

Angie tilted her head sideways and offered free access to her neck. "Good morning yourself," she whispered. "Want some coffee and breakfast?"

"If breakfast comes with dessert, sure. I can start with dessert, then move on to breakfast."

She giggled and placed her hands over his to assist in the breast massage. Her scent aroused him and he turned hard as steel. He roughly turned her to face him, lifted and placed her on the counter. He pulled her T-shirt over her arms and threw it to the floor. He took both her hands in one of his, raised them above her head, and pinned them against the cupboard. Aggressively stepping between her legs, Gary separated her thighs. He leaned back and gazed at her. He bent and took a breast into his mouth, while grabbing and massaging the other.

Angie gasped at the touch of his warm mouth and

morning-rough beard. One nipple was aroused and tortured by the continual circling and sucking of his mouth and tongue and the other by his thumb and fingers. She felt her chest would explode. She squirmed and tried to pull her hands free for want of touching him, but he was too strong. The more she struggled, the tighter he held her. The more he sucked her breast, the harder he became. Just when she was sure she could take no more, he released her and lifted her off the countertop.

With one hand holding her by the waist, he removed her panties with the other.

Suddenly time stood still.

They just stared at each other.

It was Angie who broke the silence. "Gary, you're making me feel things I've never felt before," she whispered.

Lifting her up and setting her back on the counter he told her, "I want you, to want me, as badly as I want you, Angie."

Bending, he kissed his way from her breasts to her stomach, all the while looking up into her eyes. Moving to his knees, he placed her legs over his shoulders. He reached behind her, grabbed her buttocks, and pulled her to him.

Angie gasped and almost stopped breathing when his warm lips assaulted her. Her level of arousal was nearing its peak as his warm mouth and tongue dictated the pathway.

Gary lifted her from the counter and headed for her bedroom. He quickly removed his jeans and placed his body over hers. He propped himself on his elbows so he could gaze into eyes. Angie focused and stared at her *Adonis*.

Gary's soul and being were moved as he looked into the depths of her eyes and saw intense satisfaction. Her face appeared to be aflame with a beaming smile.

That was the signal his body needed to take her again. With his desire now a fierce hunger, he entered her with a single deep thrust and remained there without moving.

Angie moved into him and raised her hips, signaling her desire for more.

Her incredible needs were new to him and his skin tingled at her touch.

He considered himself an experienced lover, but his rising emotions made him feel as though this were his first passionate encounter. This was not just sex.

As Angie struggled to lift her body into his, Gary held her firmly. Moving his hips backward, just short of leaving her, he plunged inside her over and over again, trying to delay his flood a little longer.

Without control, the pace became faster. Angie matched him stroke for stroke until they cried out, and became frozen in the moment.

Beads of perspiration on Gary's forehead began to dissipate.

Angie's breathing slowly subsided.

With no notice of time or place, they dozed off for a short time.

The sound of a siren from a nearby ambulance awakened Gary. He was up and dressed by the time Angie opened her eyes and looked at him.

With a soft voice Gary told her, "I'm sorry

Angie. I should have used a condom. I only had the one. I haven't been with anyone in a long time but I had no right to…"

"Stop, Gary. I haven't been with anyone for a long time either. Besides, I'm on the pill if that's what you're concerned about. We were both too worked up to be concerned about something that seems not to have been a major concern."

Gary sat on the side of the bed next to her, and kissed her gently on the forehead. "I've got to get to work, Angie." Standing up, he straightened his clothing. "I'm on two time-consuming jobs this week, and I'll be tied up until nine or ten every night. I'll try to call you, but if I don't, I'll call you by the weekend, okay?"

With a sleepy voice, Angie said, "No problem. I'll be busy myself this week." Staring at the ceiling, she added, "I've been working on a project for a long time."

Gary slowly approached the bed and asked, "What project would that be hon?"

She'd told him about her brother that night in the restaurant, so she reminded him by telling him, "I haven't seen my brother since we were kids and he ran away. Aunt Ruth is a little upset about it, but I've hired a Private Investigator to see if he can find him, because I don't think he can find me. I have to at least try. And I'm meeting with the private investigator this week."

Now standing, Gary asked, "Where'd you find this private investigator? I hope not from the Yellow Pages."

Angie giggled in an attempt to lighten her own mood. "Of course not, silly. My friend Carl found him."

Sandi K. Whipple

With a puzzled expression on his face, Gary looked at her, and without a word, walked to the door.

"I would have helped you find a PI if you'd asked me Angie. But you let me know how the lead from your friend Carl goes, okay? See ya," was his abrupt parting remark.

Angie thought she heard a bit of rancor in his voice. She sat on the bed completely dumbfounded and wondered, *What the hell was that about?* She mulled over the incident for about ten minutes and, deciding it was nothing more than a temperamental man, she dismissed it. She jumped off her bed, picked up her clothing, took a quick shower and opened the shop.

CHAPTER FOUR

"Want to tell me what's eating at you this week?" Tom asked Gary as he handed a spool of wiring to him. "You've been a bear to work with. You speak only when spoken to, and then it's a one-or two-word sarcastic answer."

"That's not true," Gary answered dejectedly.

"Oh, yes it is." Tom continued with a raised voice. "Yesterday you had Katie in tears for no reason at all. All she did was give you a message from a woman who just wanted to pay a bill. And why the hell did you throw away Katie's flowers from her boyfriend? They weren't in your way. You even snapped at Lucy over in Green Bend. She called me at home and threatened to quit, saying you were obviously unhappy with her work. It took me almost an hour to calm her down. So out with it, Gary, what's your damned problem?"

Gary lowered his chin, nearly touching his chest. "Gee, Tom, I didn't know I was that bad. Have I really been a bear?"

Tom just looked at him with raised eyebrows.

Gary began to bare his soul. "I've been seeing this woman on the other side of town, and for me anyway, it's getting pretty serious. She said something about another man and I, well, I acted like an ass, and the whole thing's driving me nuts."

With a chuckle, Tom said, "Aha! Hence the mysterious unpaid bills for wall removal and door installation that someone did. I knew it. Katie said the woman told her the worker who installed the coolers did the extra work that hasn't been billed. Well, old buddy, you're the one who installed her coolers, so I guess you did the extra work. She must be a looker for you to be giving away free labor, not to mention supplies. What I don't understand is why she'd call asking for a bill unless…Gary, does she know you own the company? Or is she under the impression you just work here?"

Trying to look engaged in his wiring work, Gary told him, "Well, we've never actually discussed it. I told her about my father and the move here and how my mother sold the business. Guess I never mentioned she sold it to me. But, you might be right. She got mad at me once and referred to me as the *workman.* She might think I just work here."

"She called you the workman, and she's still breathing?" Tom said with humor.

Color rising in his face, Gary responded, "I was still trying to impress her, so I kept my cool."

Tom laughed so hard he had to set down his tools for fear of losing his balance. He finally grabbed his stomach and sat on the floor. "Looks like the old confirmed bachelor here finally got bit. But, for a woman to tear you up like this, she's got to be something really special. What happened during this mentioning of another man to set you off?"

Sensing his friend's sympathetic ear, Gary explained, "She told me how excited and grateful she was that her friend Carl had done her a favor. Hell, Tom, I could have done it for her but she didn't ask me. Instead, she asked this guy Carl. When she told me, I snapped at her and walked out. All I could think about was Gloria and how she had cheated on me for two years and how stupid I was not to see it. Now, I'd like to think

Sandi K. Whipple

I might have been mistaken, but I'm not sure how to go back. I'm so damned confused. I was on the verge of telling her how much I cared for her. Now that I know about this other guy, I'm thinking maybe I was wrong about her."

Tom patted Gary on the shoulder. "Jealousy can play tricks on the mind, old buddy. You gotta admit, you wouldn't be this worked up if you weren't jealous. But, isn't it possible that this Carl is just a friend? Remember, this isn't Gloria"

With a heavy sigh and a wave of his hand, Gary seemed to tire of the conversation. "I'd sure as hell like to think so. Let's drop it and finish up here."

****

When Angie recalled Gary's departure a week ago, and his flippant "see ya," the mental images of their encounter sent flames shooting through her stomach like volcanic lava. The constant rumbling affected her mood and she couldn't find anything in her day to make her smile.

Why the hell had he left so abruptly? Did he have a girl at home or, perhaps, a date? That would be Chad all over again! She found herself more than infatuated with Gary and the thought of sharing him made her nauseous.

Adding to her already distraught mood, one of Angie's clients had yet to decide on the number and colors of her wedding flowers. Another client, Claudia Williams, wanted her wedding arrangements to be a myriad of colors and her indecision caused such stress that Angie was ready to refuse the job. Claudia's mother finally stepped in and attempted to calm her daughter's frenzied chatter. She gently explained that her choice might hinge a little on the gaudy side and convinced her to leave the decision-making to the expert. Hoping to end further debate, the mother turned to Angie, "After all, it is your specialty and you did come highly recommended."

Leading them toward the shop door, Angie continued, "I think you're probably in need of a hot cup of tea and a croissant and I know just the place." She gave directions to the mother and daughter as she gently eased them out the door.

Once the shop had quieted, Angie filled out the necessary paperwork. She felt comfortable with the choices and arrangements she envisioned. She found Patti in the front of the shop and explained she was leaving for lunch.

She headed to the restaurant to meet the private investigator, who'd driven from Chicago as he told her it was on his way to another appointment anyway. He'd explained to her his preference of meeting face to face with a new client, and besides, it was only a few hours away.

She thought about her brother, whom she missed terribly. It depressed her each time she thought of him, wondering where he was and what he was doing. Why hadn't he said goodbye or told her where he was going? Why hadn't he come back to get her? Maybe he had but found her gone. He didn't know about Aunt Ruth, so how could he know she was in Illinois?

Sandi K. Whipple

When she entered the neighborhood restaurant, she explained to the hostess she was meeting someone. Hearing her words, a gentleman sitting nearby raised his hand.

Angie walked to the table and before she could say a word, he stood to introduce himself to her. "You must be Angela Gibbons. I'm Alan Krenshaw." Angie shook his hand and sat across the table from him.

His fifty years belied his tall and lean, well-built frame. He appeared patient as he listened to her story, interrupting only for clarification. She was relieved to note that his professional demeanor didn't allow him to notice her few tears as she spoke of some painful moments. He merely took notes and asked questions.

Once Angie finished her heart wrenching story, Alan gently he explained, "You need to understand, Miss Gibbons, there's a possibility I may not find your brother. You need to be prepared for that if it turns out to be the case."

After wiping away the last of her tears, Angie said, "I understand, Mr. Krenshaw. I just appreciate your trying for me."

"I'll be calling you on occasion and I'm sure you'll want to call me." He handed her his card saying, "Here's my cell number. I also think we might as well be on a first name basis, if that's okay with you."

"Not a problem, Alan, and thank you again."

They finished their lunch with a bit of chit-chat, and when they parted at the door, Angie felt a bit more relaxed and eager to get back to work.

****

Sandi K. Whipple

Angie and Patti worked steadily for the next few days making arrangements, filling orders, and restocking. The days flew by and Angie was lost in her work. The end of the week finally arrived.

As Angie was locking up the shop on Saturday, Patti started out the door and said, "I've earned a long weekend bath! If I go down the drain, call 911!" She giggled at her own joke and waved goodnight to Angie.

It was now eight o'clock, and Angie hadn't moved from the sofa for three hours. She finally got up, turned on a lamp, and opened the refrigerator. She sighed. There was nothing to eat.

A hard knock on the door startled her. She couldn't imagine who would be visiting at this hour. When she opened the door, she was surprised to see Gary, especially since he hadn't called for over a week.

"What a surprise, Gary! Come in." When he entered, she closed the door, turned, and looked at him.

When he reached out for her she threw her arms around his neck. They just stood silently, holding each other for what seemed a long time.

Gary whispered, "God, I've missed you. I've been miserable."

"I've missed you too. And mine was no bed of roses either," Angie responded with a grin.

The pun made them both chuckle as Gary took her hand and led her to the sofa. He sat in the corner and pulled Angie onto his lap. With another sigh, he sat still and just looked at her — really looked at her.

With a puzzled expression, Angie asked, "What are you looking at?"

"You. You're beautiful. I need to apologize for storming out of here like I did the other morning. I had a lot on my mind and I acted like an ass. Am I forgiven?"

Just grateful that he was here, she would have forgiven him. Smiling, she told him, "If you'll take me somewhere and feed me, then yes, you're forgiven."

"It's a deal. Where you want to go?"

"Italian okay with you?"

"Hey, hon, I'm a pasta man or did you forget?"

Di Nido Bistro, the chosen eatery for the night, was dark and cozy and quite romantic. Their hunger pangs pushed them to order without hesitation.

When their selections arrived, Gary devoured every bite of his antipasto, spaghetti, and veal parmigian.

"You'll get fat if you don't watch out," Angie kidded.

Wiping his mouth he said, "That could never happen as long as I work it off."

With a giggle and lifted eyebrows she asked, "Is there a special or favorite exercise you prefer?"

"Of course there is. I might even be persuaded to show it to you later," he said with a smile.

Their hunger satisfied, Gary asked for and paid the bill. They agreed to forgo a walk and went directly to Angie's apartment.

In the kitchen, Gary grabbed two beers, went to the living room, joining Angie on the sofa. He asked about her meeting with the private investigator.

She tried to repeat everything she could remember that the PI said, stressing that her brother might never be found.

Gary tried to comfort her and urged her to think positive because the odds were certainly in her favor. Especially if the private investigator was worth his salt.

The phone startled them. Angie picked it up as Gary watched her every move.

"Oh, hi, Carl. A picnic? Tomorrow? What time? Sure. Sounds like fun. Can I bring anything? Are you sure? Okay then, two o'clock it is. Bye."

Angie sensed a mood swing by the expression on Gary's face. "You're awfully quiet over there. Something wrong?"

"Actually, yes, there is." Hoping to hide his negative reactions to Angie's obvious delight at speaking with Carl, Gary stood, walked slowly toward her, and backed her against the wall. Gazing into her eyes he told her, "I'm starting to feel fat. I think I need to work off tonight's dinner. I did promise to show you my favorite exercise, didn't I?"

Stammering and turning a bit red in the cheeks, Angie coyly responded, "Well yes, I do believe you did."

Grabbing her hand and pulling her toward the bedroom, he said, "Well, no time like the present, I always say."

"When have you ever said that? You don't always say that. I've never heard you say that before."

As his mouth covered hers, he chuckled and said, "Oh, shut up."

****

The next morning, streaming sunlight from the window awoke Angie. She sat upright, stretched, and realized she was alone. Was that bacon and coffee she smelled? She hastily threw the covers back, ran to the bathroom, splashed her face, and brushed her teeth. Looking at her image in the mirror made her smile. Her lips were as swollen as her nipples were sore from last night's lovemaking marathon. But boy, did she feel great! She tied her robe around her waist as she followed the breakfast aroma.

"Ah, sustenance," she said, entering the kitchen.

There was Gary, in jeans and bare feet!

"Morning, sleepyhead. Want some coffee?"

"Indeed I do. Where'd the bacon come from? There wasn't any last time I looked. And what time is it, anyway?"

"It's almost eleven o'clock. After your snoring woke me up, I threw on my jeans and went to the store to buy some groceries. How can you expect to have a sleepover and not be able to feed your guest? Makes for a shoddy hostess, don't you think?"

"Hey! I don't snore. Do I? Oh, you got a paper, too. Can I help with something? Maybe squeeze the oranges for juice, or run to the hen house and grab a few fresh eggs?" She continued with her giggling chatter. "Or maybe cut a slash in a maple tree in search of syrup?"

He set the skillet to the side of the burner. When he reached for her, she dodged him and was laughing when he caught her, lifted her up, and held her in the air.

"You're pretty feisty this morning, aren't you? What brought that on?" Gary asked with a grin.

When he finally set her down, she spoke in a soft tone that he almost didn't hear.

Sandi K. Whipple

Angie looked at the floor as she said, "I missed you and was sad when I woke up and you weren't there. At first, I thought you'd walked out and left me again."

His look was so pale and serious she was afraid he might balk at the knowledge of her amount of caring. Thinking it might lighten his apparent mood swing, she quickly added, "But then I smelled bacon and got excited at the thought of food. Priorities, you know."

Over breakfast, she mentioned she'd never slept so late in her life, and noted it must have been really late when they finally fell asleep.

Swallowing his coffee, Gary looked at her with a somewhat serious expression. "It was four thirty when I was lying next to you watching you sleep."

She reached across the table and squeezed his hand. Angie murmured, "You were watching me sleep?"

He smiled and nodded. Enough was said. Together they cleared the table, washed and dried the dishes, and cleaned the kitchen.

They agreed that Angie would shower first. When she stepped from the bathroom, the bed was made and the previous night's clothing was neatly folded and lying on the covers.

Gary smiled as he looked at the towel on her head and the one wrapped around her. With a tilted head and a mischievous grin he said, "I think I've mentioned this before, but I feel compelled to repeat it. That's a very dangerous and provocative outfit you're wearing."

She made a little pirouette and told him it was the latest fashion. When he reached for her, she side-stepped his grasp and told him it was his turn in the shower.

Pretending to pout, he said, "Okay, I can take a hint."

With a new-found perspective on the growing relationship, Gary's refreshing shower seemed to put lightness in his attitude. Pulling his shirt over his head, he realized his hair was still damp but decided to forego any more toweling.

When he stepped from the bathroom, his wonderment as to Angie's whereabouts was answered by the sounds of her moving around in another room. In search of her, he went to the living room. She wasn't there, but he saw that the door to the shop was open. He walked through the doorway and saw her holding a bouquet of flowers.

When Angie heard his steps she picked up a plant and a bouquet from the counter, turned to face him, and asked, "Which one?"

Not really sure what she was talking about, Gary wrinkled his nose and asked, "Which one what?"

"Which one do I take to Carl's picnic as a gift? The flowers or the plant?"

With a sudden shift in his mood, he realized he couldn't contain his jealousy about Carl. He was struggling to keep his composure. "Either one is nice, I guess."

He slowly approached Angie, leaned over, kissed her on the cheek, and turned to leave. He hollered over his shoulder as he walked through the apartment and out the back door, "Have fun at the picnic, see ya."

Sandi K. Whipple

"Hey, where you going?" she hollered back. "I wanted to ask you to go with me to the picnic." When she heard the door close, she realized he hadn't heard her invitation.

****

That afternoon, as Angie steered her car toward Carl's house, she felt an inner struggle with her own frame of mind. She realized she was becoming rather sullen and somewhat depressed about Gary's, once again, sudden departure.

When she arrived, Carl had Angie join her in the back yard as they both sat in a lounge chair. Angie told Carl that she'd been looking forward to meeting her children. She went on to say how disappointed she was that they weren't home.

"Jim just took them to a birthday party," Carl told her. "He'll pick them up tonight. Besides, maybe it's lucky for you that you won't meet them. Lord knows they're spoiled and I'm not sure if my mother or my brother is to blame. But then, my Jim spoils them too. Oh hell, Angie, so do I."

They were laughing when Jim arrived home. He walked up to Carl and gave her a kiss on the cheek.

Looking up at her husband, Carl held his hand and said, "Hi, honey." Realizing that Angie hadn't yet met her husband, she told her, "This is my Jim. Jim, this is my friend, Angie."

Following a bit of polite introductory conversation, Jim said, "If I'm gonna be a good host, I need to stoke the barbeque. You two have a good time." With that, Jim walked to the other side of the backyard.

Carl turned to look at Angie. "Okay, Angie, tell me. What's carving away at your mood today? You're not yourself. It's high time you tell Madam Carl everything."

"Oh, Madam Carl is it?" Laughing she added, "I think I like that title."

Hesitating, and wondering if she could bring herself to really tell her, she said, "Carl, I'm kind of involved with this guy."

Carl couldn't contain her knee-jerk comment and interrupted Angie by saying, "There's no such thing as *kind of involved,* Angie. Either you are or you aren't. So, are you? Involved, I mean."

"Yea, I guess I am. But sometimes I just don't understand him. Like today for instance; we were having a beautiful morning. We had breakfast and did the dishes together and everything was fine. Then when I asked him which he thought were better to bring to your picnic, flowers or a plant. Then he just snapped! He told me to have a good time, and as he left he hollered 'see ya'. I mean damn Carl, his mood change just came out of nowhere. It happened a few weeks ago too. I'm not sure how to deal with his mood swings, and now, I'm wondering if I should even try."

With a grin on her face, wide open eyes, and a tilted head, and a light tone in her voice, Carl said, "You had breakfast together? You mean as in 'Good morning' together?"

"Carl, will you please be serious about this? And yes, I mean as in 'Good morning' together."

"Why, you sinner, you." Carl turned her head toward the patio and yelled, "Jim, honey, would you bring us two sinners a beer?"

She looked at Angie and laughed. "Then, my dear friend, I want to hear it all. And I mean every last detail, especially the racy stuff."

The two friends spent the rest of the afternoon laughing and talking about Angie's shop and Carl's job. Carrying their conversation toward the grilling pit where Jim was busy preparing burgers and chicken, there was a bit of men-bashing included. Surprisingly, Jim was amused, although he feigned insult.

With appetites sated and conversation exhausted, Angie thanked her hosts and gave each one a hug goodnight. Driving with her car windows down to let in the evening breeze, Angie arrived home at nine thirty.

She reminisced about the afternoon's laughter, the wonderful meal, the fresh air, and her new friendships. It had been a fun day and that was the reason, she surmised, that she found herself so exhausted and eager to don her pajamas.

When she finally climbed into bed, her thoughts were of Gary's lovemaking the night before. How could he just flip out like he did? Had she said something to upset him? Did he have plans somewhere else and had just then remembered? A tear rolled down her cheek just before she fell asleep.

Sandi K. Whipple

CHAPTER FIVE

Patti arrived late, and Angie had to open the shop. As a result, Patti kept Angie from starting on her list of many errands.

With a terse tone in her voice, she told Patti, "I'm driving over to Green Bend today to look for more antiques. They sell so fast I can't keep up. When the accessory boxes arrive, would you arrange the shelves and put them up? I'd appreciate it. And don't forget to tear down the boxes or the garbage man won't take them."

With a defensive attitude, Patti replied, "Angie, I've been doing all those things for quite a while now. I know what to do. I haven't screwed up yet."

Realizing she'd been curt, Angie said in an apologetic voice, "I'm sorry Patti. I have a few things on my mind right now and I don't mean to take it out on you." Heading for the door and shaking her head at her own stupidity she added, "I'll see you later this afternoon."

Patti sensed that Angie was struggling with something and decided not to pry. She gave her a smile and told her to drive safely.

Angie drove as though she were in a fog. She hit the five antique shops in Green Bend and had a back seat full of wonderful finds. Though some were a bit pricey, she felt the profit margin would still be phenomenal.

On her way out of Green Bend, she passed Walgren's Heating and Cooling Systems. It reminded her to once again request that damned invoice.

Sandi K. Whipple

With wandering thoughts, she found herself wondering about Gary. She hadn't seen or spoken to him since he walked out of her apartment with his last 'See ya" episode. And that was two weeks ago. She missed him and doubly missed his strong arms around her. She missed the wonderful and exotic way his lovemaking made her feel. She hoped he missed her too. Since he hadn't called, he probably didn't. Should she call him? Maybe it was time she ended the entire thing. She didn't want to fall in love with someone whose moods seemed to flip-flop so frequently. Wow, she thought, did the word love really enter her mind? She remembered reading once that love could make one both naïve and stupid. Is that what she was becoming?

For a very long time, Angie hadn't thought about falling in love, at least not since she and Gary started seeing each other. When he was good, he was so good in every way. He'd share his thoughts and his feelings – not to mention that terrific masculine body of his. But when he wasn't good, he was confusing and frustrating. Missing him was painful. Maybe she had fallen in love.

Before she knew it, she was parked in front of her shop. Strange, she thought. The closed sign hung on the door and almost all the lights were off. She didn't unload the car. Instead, she ran to the door and jiggled the handle. It was unlocked. She walked in and heard someone crying.

Dear God, it was Patti, sitting in the back. She ran to her. "Honey, what's the matter? Are you okay? What happened? Why is the shop closed?"

"Oh, Angie, it was awful, and I was so scared. I had no way to reach you..."

"Patti, tell me, what is it, what happened?"

"It was awful, Angie..."

She grabbed Patti's arms and shook her violently while practically screaming at her, "Damn it, Patti, tell me right now, what was awful."

"It's Ruth."

Angie's hands flew to her face and she almost quit breathing. "Oh, God, no. What happened? Where is she?"

Through her tears Patti tried to explain. "She came by, and then went to the bank like she always does, and said she had nothing to do today, so she helped empty the boxes. We were just talking and she keeled over. I called 911. They took her to St. Andrew's. I'm sorry, Angie."

Already heading for the door Angie told her, "It's not your fault, Patti. Lock up. I've got to go to her."

****

Not once looking at the speedometer, Angie couldn't even remember stopping at red lights or stop signs. Her head was spinning and her heart was beating almost as fast as the waterfall from her eyes. Alone in the car, she kept saying aloud, over and over again, "Dear God, please..."

Parking in a handicapped spot when she arrived at the hospital, she told herself *screw it*, I'll pay the fine! From the parking lot, Angie ran to the emergency room.

In a raised voice that she couldn't prevent, she told the woman at the sign in desk, "I'm here to see Ruth Sorenson."

After looking up the name, the woman behind the desk asked, "Are you a relative?"

"Yes, I'm her niece, Angela Gibbons." Visibly shaking, Angie continued, "Where is she?"

"I'll page the doctor and he'll be right out, Miss Gibbons, then he'll explain everything to you.

"Explain what? Damn it! I want to see my aunt."

She had no idea tears were still rolling down her face until a doctor appeared and handed her a tissue.

"I'm Doctor Greenburg and your aunt is fine, for now, anyway. I'll take you to her in a minute. I'd like to talk to you first. Let's sit down for a moment, shall we?" He walked with a hand on her elbow and led her to the waiting area. "Your aunt suffered a mild heart attack and needs to stay with us for a few days."

Angie's hand flew to her mouth.

"As I said, it was mild. My opinion is she'll recover just fine. She's still pretty young so I'm certain she'll recover with no complications. When she goes home, I'll send a special diet and a list of do's and don'ts. As long as she follows those instructions, she'll probably outlive both of us," he told her with assurance in his voice.

Angie lowered her hand and a sense of relief flooded her as Dr. Greenburg continued, "Normally, in cases like this, I wouldn't allow visitors on the first day. But, she's screaming and demanding we contact you. I think you're the only one who can calm her down. Follow me, I'll take you to her," he said as he got up from his chair. "Your aunt is one tough cookie," he added with a chuckle and led her to the room.

"Ruth, I believe you know this young lady? I've told her she can only stay for a few minutes, so if you give me any more trouble, I'll send her packing, got it?"

Ruth just grumbled and said, "Yes, yes, yes, I've got it."

Angie ran to her aunt's bedside and once again burst into tears and hugged her aunt so tightly she almost couldn't breathe herself. After nearly two minutes she finally let go.

"Oh, honey, please don't cry. I'll be all right," Aunt Ruth said as she attempted to give assurance to Angie.

She continued as Angie pulled up a chair, sat down, and looked at her, "Oh, honey, really, I'm going to be fine. I guess I'll just have to make a few changes in the way I live, huh? Nothing major though. So tell me, did you score any really good finds today in Green Bend?"

As she wiped her face and blew her nose, Angie said, "Aunt Ruth, when I found the shop closed, I knew something was wrong. I found Patti crying and blaming herself. It took me almost five minutes to get her to tell me what happened."

Excitedly, Aunt Ruth asked, "Why is the shop closed? Not because of this? I mean, not because of me?"

"Calm down, Aunt Ruth. One day won't hurt. And I'll need to talk with Dr. Greenburg before I let you have anything more to do with the shop. I'll need to hear from him what your limitations are, and that it's okay for you to work. So, you'll be here for a few days, what do you want me to bring you?"

Sandi K. Whipple

"Just Frank."

Angie raised her eyebrows. "What did you say?"

"Just a few magazines, dear," Aunt Ruth said with a giggle, "and maybe a crossword puzzle book. Don't forget a pen. And maybe you could sneak me in a tiny bit of Chambord?"

Angie had to smile at that. "Okay, you got it." Then shaking her head, as if to say *not gonna happen*, she added "except for the Chambord."

Angie hugged her Aunt and was thrilled to hear her giggling when she left. When the elevator doors opened, a man stepped out and bumped right into her. Angie looked up to apologize. "Pardon me, sir. Oh, Mr. Hill, how nice to see you again. By the way, I never got to thank you for delivering my furniture."

"You're more than welcome, Miss Gibbons." As he turned to walk away he added, "By the way, congratulations on the success of your flower shop."

The drive home from the hospital gave Angie time enough to catch her breath and calm the anxiety over Aunt Ruth.

She found the shop locked and Patti gone. Entering her apartment from the back, she kicked off her shoes and decided she could empty the car later. She lay curled up on her bed, holding a pillow to her stomach, and began to cry. The only real person in her life since she was eleven years old had been, and was, Aunt Ruth. Dear Lord, she almost lost her today. She was very nearly gone as quickly as her mother, all those years ago. Was it her fault? Was she working her too hard? She tried to slow her down by hiring Patti but Aunt Ruth was so stubborn. She cried hard and wasn't sure if her ears were ringing or if it was the phone. She couldn't care less at that moment.

A short while later after crying herself to sleep, something woke her. There was no mistaking the sound of fists banging on the steel door. She tried to ignore the sounds, but whoever was pounding wasn't going away. With tears once again beginning to stream down her face, she whipped the door open and screamed, "What is it?"

Without a word of forewarning, Gary reached for her and wrapped his arms around her. "Sweetheart, I'm so sorry. I came by when Patti was leaving and she told me about your aunt. I tried to call you but there was no answer. Are you okay? What can I do? Just tell me, honey, and it's a done deal. Here, baby, let me close the door."

Trying to dry her tears, Angie was stunned at his presence. "Oh, Gary, it was awful. I almost lost her. And where was I? Gallivanting around Green Bend. It's my fault. I've worked her too hard."

Gary felt compelled to comfort her and ease her feelings of guilt. "Are you trying to tell me you've worked your aunt into the hospital?"

"Yes."

Picking her up, he carried her to the bedroom and placed her atop the pillows. He held her to his chest until her sobbing began to subside.

"Angie, listen to me. You were in Green Bend on business, not gallivanting. Ruth is a vibrant, active woman. She's a living being. You can't control her any more than someone can control you, or me. She could have had the heart attack anywhere. It just so happened she was in your shop. I'm sure she'll be fine, sweetheart."

Listening to his caring words and feeling a little more comforted, Angie whispered, "Please stay with me tonight; I don't want to be alone."

That statement gave Gary's heart a boost, knowing that Angie wanted him to stay. It made him feel that she found his presence comforting. "I'll be right here, honey. I'm not going anywhere."

An hour later she fell asleep, and her peaceful slumber caused his eyes to close as well.

A few hours later, Gary woke to the sound of water running in the bathroom. The apartment was dark. He rose out of bed and tapped on the door. "Angie, are you okay?"

She opened the door and lifted her head. He reached out to her and pulled away the wet washcloth she held over her eyes. When he saw her eyes so red and swollen, he fought the urge to shed his own tears for her apparent pain. He put his arms around her and held her.

"Gary,... "
"What is it, honey?"
"I'm hungry."
"Well then, I guess we'd better feed you."

He walked her to the sofa and made her sit. He headed to the kitchen, opened and then closed the refrigerator, turned to her and laughed. "Why is it you never have any food in this place?"

"There's food in the cupboard."

Opening the cabinet door, he chuckled. "Wow, what a find. A can of chili, and a box of macaroni and cheese. There isn't any milk for macaroni and cheese so I guess it's gonna be chili. Got any crackers?"

A little embarrassed by the lack of sustenance in her kitchen, Angie sheepishly told him, "I just ran out, but they're on the grocery list."

"It's only nine o'clock. Why don't I go and get us some take-out?"

"Can I have some Popeye's chicken?"

"Popeye's chicken it is. I'll be back in a few minutes." He kissed her cheek and headed out.

When Gary returned, he found Angie curled up on the sofa and sound asleep. He put the chicken in the refrigerator, carried her to bed, removed his work boots, and climbed in next to her.

He was up before the sun. Angie still slept. He tiptoed into the shop, looked around the desk, and found Patti's phone number. He called and introduced himself as a friend of Angie's. After briefly explaining last night's events, Patti agreed to open the shop and work the entire day. She would miss a class, but it was okay with her. Besides, there wasn't much she wouldn't do for Angie.

He wanted to be there when Angie woke but he needed clean clothes and a shave. He closed the door and headed home to grab a few things.

Returning to Angie's quiet apartment, he sat on the sofa and read the paper with the TV volume on low. Halfway through the business section, he looked up and saw her walk out from the bedroom with a sleepy expression on her face.

"What time is it?"

Sandi K. Whipple

As he observed her disheveled look he said, "It's almost noon. You slept long and hard, Angie, something you needed."

Angie's hands flew to her face and she screamed, "Oh my God. The shop!"

Immediately rising from the sofa, Gary raced to her and put his arms around her. "It's okay, Angie. I called Patti. She was happy to open and close for you. She said to tell you to just rest and she'll talk to you tomorrow." Looking at her he added, "Your eyes sure look better."

Angie nearly went limp with relief. "Thanks for taking care of things for me. Is there anything to eat? Didn't you go get chicken last night?"

If she's hungry, Gary thought, she's feeling better. "I did, but I'll make breakfast if you want. I bought groceries this morning."

"Chicken is fine, thanks." Then she questioned, "Aren't you supposed to work today?"

"I called in sick," he told her as he headed to her kitchen.

"So you're going to lose a day's wages because of me?"

"You're worth it — and more."

He put chicken and mashed potatoes on a plate and micro waved them. Then he placed some coleslaw in a small bowl.

They were sitting at the table when the phone rang.

Angie got up, crossed the room and answered it. "Oh, hi. Yes, I'm okay. I'm going to go see her in a little while. Patti's running the shop today but I'll get back to normal tomorrow. Thanks for your concern. Me too. Bye, Carl."

Gary felt a sudden pain starting to rise in his chest. Carl again! Although he was starting to seethe with jealousy, Gary controlled his temper and acted as calmly as possible. "Carl must be a really good friend."

"Probably the best I've ever had," Angie told him.

Gary was watching her closely. "I'm your friend too, Angie. You know that don't you?"

"Of course I do. But Carl's friendship is different."

Reaching a near boiling point, but still feigning a calm attitude, he wondered just how different.

Gary rose from his chair. "I see. Well, you're up and about now, so I'll be on my way." He grabbed his stuff from the bedroom, walked to the steel door, turned to look at her, and with a sarcastic and flippant salute, he said, "See ya."

Wow, there he goes again, Angie thought. Another mood swing for no reason and then he walked out on her. Boy was she getting sick of that 'see ya' line.

Hurriedly, Angie dressed and tidied up the apartment. She needed to get busy and forget the so-called rift she just witnessed with Gary.

She went to the shop, thanked Patti, and asked her to continue to work when Aunt Ruth came home. Patti readily agreed. Angie threw on a pair of sunglasses and drove to the hospital. For now, everything else could wait.

****

Sandi K. Whipple

A week later, Aunt Ruth was thrilled to return home. Angie offered to move in for a while but she emphatically refused the offer, explaining the shop was Angie's priority. She told Angie she could check in on her regularly. Besides, Frank had agreed to help take care of her, and she was actually quite flattered and excited about the idea of being pampered by him.

Angie interrupted her thoughts. "You know, I'd really like to meet Frank. If he's going to be spending so much time over here, I'd at least like to know who he is."

Aunt Ruth tried her best to act as if she was perturbed by her niece's nosiness, knowing it was purely just love and concern. "You don't trust my judgment, dear? I'm not a teenager you know, and I do have some life experiences. Just because I never remarried after my George died, over twenty years ago—and he certainly was the light of my life —doesn't mean that I'm a naive woman."

"I'm sorry, Aunt Ruth. I didn't mean anything by that. It's just that I'm worried about you. A heart attack is a big deal."

"I know, honey, and I promise to follow everything on that foolish list of do's and don'ts. I'll even promise to eat the terrible food on the diet sheet, or at least some of it." Aunt Ruth grinned at her forthcoming confession, "I added Chambord, so now the list looks a little better."

They were giggling and chatting amiably when the doorbell rang. Aunt Ruth started to get up but Angie waved her back down.

Sandi K. Whipple

"I'll get it," Angie gently scolded and then, upon opening the door, said, "Well, hello, Mr. Hill. What a surprise to see you here. Can I help you with something?"

"I'd like to see Ruth Sorenson."

Puzzled by his request, Angie said, "Of course. Please, come in."

Angie showed him into the living room and before she could say a word, Aunt Ruth lit up like the sun and hollered, "Frank! Thank you for coming."

Angie stood dumbfounded as Mr. Hill crossed the room and gave her aunt a big hug and a kiss.

"Angie dear, this is Frank Hill. Frank, this is my niece, Angie."

Angie had to smile. "We've already met. I bought my furniture from Mr. Hill's second hand store. I had no idea that he was your Frank. I mean the Frank. I mean, oh hell, I don't know myself what I mean"

Aunt Ruth was beaming! "Ah yes, the second-hand shop—Frank's hobby since he retired. I've even helped out there, haven't I, Frank?"

He was smiling and still holding Ruth's hand. "You have indeed. After this latest episode though, I think those days are gone." Turning to Ruth's niece he said, "By the way, Angie, please, call me Frank."

Angie could see from just looking at the two that Aunt Ruth was in good hands.

****

A month later, Angie and Frank were sitting in Aunt Ruth's living room. Dr. Greenburg had given Ruth a nearly clean bill of health, and she was happy as a lark. After a concerning conversation, Frank assured Angie he would continue to monitor and watch Ruth like a hawk. Aunt Ruth acted offended by his statement, but Angie knew it was all for show. She was tickled pink to have Frank taking care of her aunt.

When she left, Angie knew her aunt couldn't be in better hands.

The next morning, alone at the shop, Angie reflected on her memories that didn't include a show of affection between her parents. She never saw them kiss, hug, hold hands, or do any of the little things that seemed natural to Frank and her aunt. Those little gestures obviously made them both very happy. Maybe that was the reason her parents were so unhappy. They never did anything to make each other content. Not that she could remember. But there must have been a time when things were better. After all, how did she and her brother get here?

The jingle of the shop door interrupted her mental ramblings.

"Hello Mr. Di Nido," Angie said with a smile. "How are you?"

"Hello, Angie. I'm fine, thank you."

Angie was a little surprised at seeing him. "Your daily flower delivery is still three hours away. What can I do for you?"

"I'm here to order some roses for my wife. Our anniversary is this weekend. I'd like to have them delivered to the restaurant Saturday night while we're having dinner. Think you can arrange that?"

Sandi K. Whipple

Mr. Di Nido was Angie's favorite customer and client. "Of course I can. What color roses would you like? Did you want long-stemmed or perhaps potted miniatures?"

"Oh, I'm lost there," he told her. "What do you recommend? You're the expert."

Happy to help and offer her expertise, Angie said, "For this occasion, I'd certainly recommend long-stemmed, and in a large crystal vase."

"Long-stemmed it is then. And I'd like red. Can you deliver them Saturday night about seven thirty?"

"Not a problem."

As he reached for his wallet, Mr. Di Nido said, "I need to pay cash for these. My wife does the paperwork for the restaurant and pays all the bills. I don't want her to feel these are from the restaurant. I want her to know they're from me."

Angie leaned back against the counter and smiled. "Your wife is a lucky woman, Mr. Di Nido. I'll take care of it. We can settle up next week. I'd like to look around for a vase first. I'll try not to spend too much."

"Don't worry about the cost, Angie, and believe me, I'm the lucky one, not my wife."

Walking him to the door, she said, "I'll see you Saturday night then, and thank you, Mr. Di Nido."

She wrote up his order and jotted a note to find a very special vase. As she moved about the shop, a slight draft caught her attention. She noticed the door wasn't completely closed. Hmmm, she thought, that's been happening quite often. She scribbled another note to get it fixed.

CHAPTER SIX

As soon as Gary entered the office, Katie accosted him.

"Mr. Walgren, Miss Gibbons called again about those missing bills. I told her we're still researching the matter but she's starting to get pretty testy about it."

"I'll take care of it. Thanks for letting me know."

"It's my job to let you know, Mr. Walgren. And if you don't mind my saying, you've been very quiet and distant lately. Have I done something wrong or offended you?"

Shocked by her statement, Gary stopped in his tracks. Turning and looking directly at her he said, "No, Katie. If I've given you that impression, I'm sorry. Truth is, if I lost you and your expertise around here, this office would be in trouble." Gary realized he really never let Katie know how much he appreciated her and all her hard work that showed him she was devoted to the company. "I think you're irreplaceable. I've had a lot of things on my mind lately, that's all. Personal things that I need to work out," he smiled. "Are we okay now?"

Katie seemed content with Gary's explanation. "We are, Mr. Walgren. I'm here to stay. I guess you're stuck with me."

"Good. I need you around here to keep me on my toes. Do you have next week's schedule?"

"Actually, I have three weeks of schedules. We've been so busy that Lucy and I are on the phone with each other every day trying to figure out how to shuffle bodies around to get it all done."

"Really? How come no one told me?"

Sandi K. Whipple

"Tom's been dealing with most of it and working until nine or ten every night and even some weekends. He told Lucy and me not to bother you."

Gary was somewhat touched by his employees care for him. "I'm flattered that you're all looking out for me. So what do you think needs to be done about all this shuffling? I mean your opinion, not Tom's or Lucy's or anyone else's, just yours."

Katie felt it wasn't her place to suggest anything. But, she thought, he did after all ask her for her opinion. "I think as busy as we're getting, we should hire two, maybe three more men. I'd start with two. I wouldn't jump right into three."

Gary smiled at her, thinking to himself that she was a lot sharper than he ever gave her credit for. "It's a done deal then. Run an ad in the paper and set up some interviews. You screen them first."

"Okay. I'll get right on it." Then his whole statement hit her. "But, you trust me to do the initial screening?"

Gary chose this moment to show his appreciation. "Of course I am. You know as much about the work and procedures as any of us. And, as the company administration supervisor, I would think that's part of your job."

As she sat in total shock, Katie asked, "Excuse me Mr. Walgren, but when did I get that title?"

With a broad grin he told her, "Now, and it comes with a raise."

He walked into his office, closed the door, and laughed out loud because of the look on Katie's face. He should have given her a raise and promotion a long time ago. The girl was worth her weight in gold and she was as efficient as his mother had been - maybe even more so. When he buzzed the intercom and she answered in her typical professional and pleasant tone, he said, "Katie, could you locate Tom and get him on the phone for me?"

"Right away."

Moments later Katie buzzed him back. "I have Tom on line two for you."

She was definitely efficient.

"Hey, boss, what's up? I'm in the middle of tearing out a damned 1902 boiler and I'm pretty busy."

"Hi, Tom. I just wanted to let you know, I'm going to hire two new guys, maybe three. Seems we need to relieve a little pressure on you. You'll have to train the new guys, though, so maybe I'm just shifting the pressure, huh? And how come you didn't tell me how hectic things were getting? I don't expect the company foreman to work until nine or ten every night either, let alone on weekends. It stops right now. Got it?"

Taken aback, Tom was hesitant before he replied, "Did you say *company foreman*? When did I get that title?"

Gary tried not to sound jovial. "Today. And it comes with a raise. Do you need me out there today? I could shuffle things around and come help if you do."

"Thanks for the promotion, Gary. I really appreciate it." Still somewhat shocked, Tom continued, "I think I've got things under control out here, but if you'd take care of three estimate requests Lucy has over in the Green Bend area, it would sure help me out."

Sandi K. Whipple

"Done. Talk to you later." Gary said as he placed his phone back into the cradle.

What a fool he'd been. Pining over a woman and ignoring his business. Well, things were going to get back on track at Walgren's Heating and Cooling, but what about Gary Walgren's personal life? He thought about the many times he'd allowed his temper to get the best of him. But hell, that was when he was younger.

Years ago, he thought he'd matured and learned to keep his temper in check and to quit taking things so seriously. But Angie opened up a whole new bucket of emotions he never knew existed. He hadn't seen or talked to her in weeks. Hell, she was driving him crazy. Sex with other women had never been what it was with Angie. She was so completely different. It wasn't just sex with her. Other women had great bodies, but Angie's was beautiful and seductive and warm and giving and - shit! Now he was rambling just like her. He really was losing it.

He got off his *'keester'* and headed to Green Bend to take care of those three estimates. Thereafter, he headed to his sister's house for dinner.

****

"Hey, stranger, you're late," his brother-in-law greeted him at the door.

Gary patted him on his shoulder. "I know, sorry about that. I had an ugly day. How goes things around here?"

They walked toward the patio and his brother-in-law replied, "Great! Your sister is in the kitchen with your mother getting the hamburgers ready for the grill. Want a beer?"

Gary let out a great sigh of impatience. "Why do we always have to have hamburgers? Just once I'd like to have a steak."

His brother-in-law started to laugh. "Talk to my wife, Miss Thrifty. She says steaks are a luxury because they're too expensive. She acts like we're broke all the time. It pisses me off once in a while too."

Smiling at the reality, Gary told his brother-in-law, "Glad it's you and not me, 'cause I love steak."

"Well, tonight you'd better love hamburgers if you know what's good for you. I know there's only your mom and your sister but, somehow I think we're still out-numbered."

They were laughing when the women came out to the patio. Gary hugged his mom and kissed his sister's cheek.

With an arm around his sister, Gary asked, "Where's the kids?"

His brother-in-law, stoking the coals, turned and said, "I didn't know until just recently there's a place called summer camp that actually boards the little monsters. I'm researching to see if there's any all-year camps available."

With a shocked look on her face and a roll of her eyes, Gary's sister laughed aloud and added, "Yeah right! That came out of the mouth of the same grown adult man who almost cried the first night they were gone. He even asked if I'd checked the references of every single person who works at that camp."

They all had a good laugh as they began to gather around the patio table.

During dinner, Gary explained how busy his company was lately and that he'd decided to hire three more men. He told them about Katie's and Tom's promotions and how he just suddenly gave them a title and a raise. It tickled Gary to see the expressions of shock on each of their faces. His brother-in-law thought it was a smooth move and his sister said it was awesome. His mother expressed her pride and admiration for her son who seemingly was following in the footsteps of her late husband.

Later, following dessert and hot coffee, Gary kissed his mom good night as she climbed into his brother-in-law's car for her ride home. She turned to Gary, told him she was proud of his accomplishments, and made him promise to call her. Gary was left with a warm feeling in his chest as he stood on the street and watched the car disappear around a corner.

Ambling back into his sister's home, he found her in the kitchen finishing up the remaining coffee cups. It was good to finally find time to be alone with her. "I need to talk to you about something, Sis, and I need your advice. When I'm finished, tell me what you think I should do, okay?"

She nodded with a raised eyebrow and pointed to the kitchen table where they both took a seat.

"Well, it's like this" Gary began. "I've met this woman. She's smart, strong-willed, independent, beautiful, sexy, compassionate, warm, giving, caring, and I'm hung up on her. But, it's been a roller coaster ride because of me. A couple of times, I've behaved like an ass. I know I was pretty upset when I found about Gloria, but I never thought I was actually a jealous guy. But damn it, Sis, I've never felt like this before. I'm miserable when I'm not with her and when I am with her, I don't want to share her. I've turned into a real ass. Got any ideas?"

Trying hard not to laugh, his sister nonchalantly put a hand over her mouth to cover her grin with just a finger on her bottom lip. "For starters, does she wear a lot of green clothes? I think she might be too young for you. From your description, minus the sexy part, of course, she sounds like a girl scout."

With heightened voice, Gary said, "Cut it out, will you? I'm dying on the vine here."

With a sorrowful tone, his sister quietly responded, "Sorry, just kidding. But I admit I'm a little stumped here. I don't think I've ever seen you like this. Certainly not because of a woman, not even Gloria. I don't know what to tell you, Gary. All relationships are different with good and bad issues. Hell, even though I love my husband, he can also be an ass."

With a slight pause, she suddenly realized a reason behind his behavior. Without considering her words, she blurted out, "Hey, do you love this gal?"

"I don't know. I only know I think about her every waking moment and when I'm asleep, I dream about her. The only thing that makes me feel better is putting my arms around her and seeing her smile."

His sister gently touched his arm. "Damn. I wish I could do something for you. You've got it bad. It kills me to see you like this."

Sandi K. Whipple

Gary looked at his watch and realized it was late. "I've got to go, Sis. Tell the other 'sometimes ass,' I said goodnight. By the way, next time we do this, I'm bringing steaks."

His sister's head snapped to attention. "But, Gary, they're so expensive."

He smiled because he knew she was serious. God, she was a tightwad.

Driving toward home, the falling shadows of night made Gary somewhat melancholy. He knew he'd be busier than normal this week but, come hell or high water, he was going to see Angie on Saturday.

CHAPTER SEVEN

Angie earmarked a couple of hours each week to be with Aunt Ruth. During one of her weekly visits, she greeted her on the front porch. "Well, Aunt Ruth, it seems I'm no longer needed here," Angie said, trying to pout. "Frank is a better cook and housekeeper than I am, and obviously a better organizer. I mean, he runs a business, takes care of his own place, takes care of this house, cooks your meals, and runs your errands. I sure tip my hat to him."

Making herself a little more comfortable on the porch chair, Aunt Ruth responded, "Actually, dear, he's not quite as organized as you think. He really doesn't do much running back and forth. When he's not at his second-hand store, he comes here to stay."

With a scowl on her forehead, Angie put her hands on her hips. "What exactly does that mean?"

With joviality and a lilt in her voice, Aunt Ruth responded, "Which part, dear?"

In almost a growl, Angie glared at her. "Aunt Ruth?"

"Now don't get all in a huff, dear. Frank is staying here. I asked him to. The running back and forth was just getting to be too much."

Angie didn't fail to see the grin on her aunt's face. There was more than friendship involved here.

"Well," Angie said in a soft tone, "I love Frank for taking such good care of you."

Giggling, Aunt Ruth told her, "Me too. By the way, your friend Alan stopped by yesterday. He wanted to ask me a few questions about your mother. Her background and stuff like that. I mean, she was my sister. He said he thought he might be able to fit a few more pieces into the puzzle. When he left, he said to tell you he'd be in touch."

This was encouraging news to Angie and she felt a bit lighthearted. "Good. He's diligently working on it." She cringed when she looked at her watch. "I need to get back to the shop. Patti has to leave early today and my new delivery man wants a rundown on his duties even though he doesn't start till Monday." She gave her aunt a big hug and said, "Bye. I love you."

****

When Angie entered the shop, Patti said with concern in her voice, "Angie, the door is getting worse. I have to close it myself almost every time." She continued, "Alan called and left a number. It's on the desk. Are you sure it's okay if I cut out early?"

"Of course it is. The delivery driver starts Monday so that should free up a lot of time for all of us." Angie rattled on and suddenly realized that Patti had nearly frozen in her steps.

"I see that panicked look on your face. Don't worry about your hours. There'll be plenty if you want them. With all the future bookings, having picked up another hotel along with two more restaurants, you can trust your job is secure. Now, go away."

Patti let out a deep sigh of relief. "Thanks, Angie."

Although it was close to closing time and with Patti out the door, Angie turned her mind back to business. She prepared two dozen long-stemmed roses in an absolutely beautiful crystal vase she'd picked up especially for tonight's occasion. The hand-written card from Mr. Di Nido was placed amidst the roses and the completed arrangement was put in the cooler. She locked the door and hung the closed sign.

Back in her apartment after a long relaxing bath, Angie fixed her hair and makeup and chose a simple but elegant cocktail dress. The beautiful sapphire necklace and earrings Aunt Ruth had given her completed the look. One last glimpse in the mirror told her she looked like a million dollars.

With a few minutes to spare, she thought she'd check the shop door. Maybe the closure thingy just needed to be adjusted. She dragged a chair, kicked off her pumps, propped the door open with the chair, and climbed up.

She was on tip toes when she heard a familiar voice, "Um, 'whatcha doin' up there?"

Without turning and looking at Gary, Angie continued to stand on her toes and fiddle with the thingy. "I'm trying to find out what's wrong with this closure thingy."

Fascinated and enthralled by the beautiful creature on tiptoes, Gary placed a hand on Angie's waist to prevent a fall. He chided her gently and said, "And dressed appropriately for the job, I see. I'm actually pretty good at fixing thingies, if you'd like me to look at it."

Angie only looked down and smiled at him. "Hi, you."

He lifted her off the chair, turned her face toward his, and just continued to hold her waist. "Hi, yourself."

Gary let go of her and stepped up on the chair. "Yep, the closure thingy is shot. They're not expensive and pretty easy to install. I can do it for you, if you want."

Stepping down beside her, he gave her an intent look. "Angie, you look great. No, that word isn't good enough. You're beautiful." He could feel himself beginning to seethe with jealousy when he asked, "Got a hot date?"

Angie could feel the color rising in her cheeks. "No. You know Mr. Di Nido, who owns the Italian restaurant we've been to in town?"

He nodded and nearly held his breath as he waited to hear why she was so dressed up.

"Well, it's his anniversary, and he ordered some special roses for his wife. He asked me to deliver them tonight at seven thirty. It's a special occasion for a good client, so I thought I'd dress up to deliver them."

Smiling broadly at him, she added, "And thanks for the compliment. I guess that means I look okay."

Taking a step backward, Gary crossed his arms and lowered his voice as a means of grabbing her attention. "I may not be dressed for the occasion, especially with you dressed like that, but, if you have no pressing engagement, Miss Gibbons, I'd consider it an honor if you would allow me to accompany you and buy you dinner."

With a bit of excitement rising, Angie was fearful her voice might shake. She cleared her throat to gain her composure. "I think I'd like that."

Sandi K. Whipple

Her racing pulse had to be slowed and sensibility restored. Angie attempted to quell her excitement by taking some extra time to find her keys and bag. With a flip of her hair over a shoulder and an artificial sigh of sophistication, she turned toward Gary. "Okay, I'm ready."

With amusement in his eyes, Gary said, "Ah, excuse me, Angie, but aren't you supposed to take the flowers with you?"

With reddening of cheeks, she pretended to cough. "Uh, huh." Bending her head a bit to hide her embarrassment, she carefully retrieved the anniversary arrangement from the nearby cooler. She couldn't believe she almost forgot them. What was she thinking? She'd been totally engrossed in his surprise visit.

She was wondering if he was over his mood swing. This last episode had taken a while. What was it? Five or six weeks? Maybe seven? Whatever it had been, it seemed like an eternity.

During the short drive to the restaurant, their light chatter gave Angie enough time to get over her embarrassment about nearly forgetting the flowers.

Upon entering the restaurant, Gary's arms laden with the exquisite vase and roses, they approached the table where the Di Nidos were seated. A silence filled the entire restaurant. After setting the surprise gift on the table, Gary made a short bow and said, "A special delivery, ma'am. I believe you are Mrs. Di Nido?"

"Yes, I am," Mrs. Di Nido said, with a surprised look on her face.

Smiling broadly and gently touching Angie's elbow, Gary guided her to his side.

Sandi K. Whipple

Angie nearly choked while holding back tears at the thought of the happy couple. She said, "We'd like to wish you a wonderful and happy anniversary."

The restaurant guests broke into applause. Mrs. Di Nido cried as she gingerly opened the dainty envelope and read the enclosed card.

"Thank you so much," she said to her husband and kissed his cheek.

Gary quietly stepped back, grasped Angie's hand, guided her to the maître d' station and requested a table for two. He continued to hold her hand as he walked her to her seat and held the chair for her. He sat across from her and picked up her hand.

Earlier, Angie began to choke up and was now dabbing at a few tears as she gazed toward the Di Nidos' table. "Did you see how touched and happy Mrs. Di Nido was? I'm so happy for them. What a special love they must share."

For a brief moment of distraction, the waiter took their drink order and quickly backed away.

Gary reached across the table and took her hands in his. "Why does that kind of love surprise you, Angie? I know not all couples share a love like that, but most do. My sister and brother-in-law would die without each other, and my mother was devastated when my father died."

Still feeling a bit melancholy, Angie responded, "I understand. I've just never witnessed it. My parents were horrible to each other, physically and emotionally. I guess seeing the Di Nidos like that made me feel a little envious."

"Are you lonely, Angie?"

Sandi K. Whipple

Quietly, almost too much so, she replied, "Sometimes, maybe."

The waiter's arrival saved Angie from further explanation. With their drinks delivered, red wine for Angie and a beer for Gary, the dinner entrées were ordered, again, the waiter backed away with a slight bow.

Looking directly into Angie's eyes, Gary said in a hushed voice, "I can't explain how much I've missed you. I couldn't quit thinking about you even in my sleep. It isn't easy for me to sit here apologizing to you, knowing I was such an ass again, but I am sorry. Did you miss me just a little?"

"No, Gary. I missed you a lot. I'm trying really hard to understand why you get so moody, and then just walk out and leave without any explanation."

Gary was trying to explain without admitting to his jealousy. "I guess I just get something stuck in my craw, let it fester, then freak because I don't know how to handle it. If you tell me this apology is redundant, you'll probably see a grown man cry in public. I really am sorry."

Angie placed a hand on his arm. Before any more conversation could take place, dinner was served.

Angie was amazed to see the small portion on his plate. "Where's the rest of your dinner? That's not all you're having, is it? You usually eat that much as an appetizer."

Gary's laughter could be heard tables away. Angie found herself laughing alongside him.

Sandi K. Whipple

"I haven't been eating much lately. I was afraid of getting fat. I haven't exactly been able to engage in my favorite exercise."

Angie nearly choked. Her shocked reaction caused Gary to chuckle. The waiter nearby moved toward the table and asked if she was okay. This merely added more humor to Gary's laughter.

When Angie was able to breathe properly again and steer the conversation elsewhere, an ice bucket and a bottle of champagne were delivered to their table.

The waiter told them, "Compliments of Mr. Di Nido. Shall I open and pour, sir?"

Gary smiled and said, "Yes, please, and express our gratitude if you would."

"Of course, sir." After the champagne was poured, the waiter disappeared.

This was an absolute first for Angie. There'd never been a time in her life when she'd had more than a beer, or a glass or two of wine, let alone champagne.

She drank the bubbly as if it were cola! Gary assumed she was really enjoying it, so he ordered another bottle.

When they left the restaurant, it was no surprise when Angie suffered a giggling attack all the way back to her apartment. Once inside, Angie began to really stumble over her words. "Bet you don't want a beer, do ya! We had enough booze to raise the river a whole inch."

She was feeling strange, and why was it difficult to walk? When she bumped into the wall and almost tripped over her own feet, Gary reached out to break her fall.

It was difficult to hold back his laughter. "Have you ever had champagne?"

Not realizing her words were rather elementary, she waved her hands in the air. "Sure! You betcha! Lotsa times. And if you'd stand still for a minute, I'd kiss you."

Covering his amusement with a serious tone, he told her, "Boy, are you going to hate yourself tomorrow, my love."

"I don't hate me. I don't hate you. Hell, I don't hate anybody! And am I really?"

"Are you really what, sweetheart?"

"Am I really your love?"

He gently picked Angie up and carried her to the bedroom.

"Sweetheart, you're pretty toasted right now. There's a real good possibility you won't feel very good in the morning, or even remember much about tonight."

"Toasted?" Giggling she added, "I'm not wheat bread, you know, my name is, uh, oh yeah, Angie. See, I'm okay. I'm Angie and you're Gary *Adonis*."

"You really are rambling, honey. Let me help you get undressed."

"You get undressed and I'll get undressed. Let's all get undressed, how's that?"

Unzipping her dress, Gary took great care in laying it on the top of the dresser. As drunk as she was, making love to her was out of the question. Removing the rest of her clothing would be pure torture. As she swayed, he found it difficult to hold her upright. He unhooked her bra and placed it with her dress. When he turned back, she'd fallen backward onto the bed in a fit of giggles. As difficult as it was, he finally removed her pantyhose and panties, which joined the other garments on the dresser. He lifted her off the bed so he could pull back the covers. When he tried to lie her back down, she wrapped her arms around his neck.

"Make love to me, Gary."

Wanting to, but knowing how drunk she was, Gary sadly said, "Not tonight, honey. You're too drunk and you won't even remember it tomorrow."

A hurt look crossed her face. She grabbed his hand, placed it over her breast, and moved his palm in a massaging pattern. Groaning, he told her, "Angie, we can't do this tonight."

"Okay, fine. Then let's do it, and tomorrow we can say we didn't."

She wasn't giggling any more. Gary noticed a stern expression come over her face. "Don't you dare leave me again."

He set her down so he could undress, and she sat upright on the edge of the bed watching every move he made without saying a word.

When he started toward her, she put her hands out and wrapped them around his firm backside. Very slowly she massaged his buttocks, all the while staring into his eyes. He didn't move a muscle, except, of course, the manly one, which was now grown to capacity.

In one smooth motion, she dipped her head, taking him into her mouth. She heard him gasp from the shock. It was pure lust. She pulled him into her, forcing him deeper into her mouth.

Sandi K. Whipple

When she started slowly moving her head forward, then backward, Gary found it difficult to breathe at a steady pace. When her tongue started working around him, he knew he would go to heaven in a very short time. Her warm mouth and soft lips caressed him and her tongue teased him nearly to a point of no return.

Angie's movements became increasingly pleasurable for him. Knowing he would burst any second, Gary pulled away from her, picked her up, and lay over her on the bed. As he settled over her he whispered, "Oh yes, Angie. Yes, you are my love."

In a seductive and gruff voice, she said, "Move off me."

Shocked by her demand, Gary lifted his head and looked at Angie. "What?"

She repeated herself, "I said move off me."

He did as she asked. Quick as an alley cat, she placed her thighs over him and pressed the heat of her center on to him. The feel of hot flesh rubbed against him. Every nerve ending in his body began to awaken.

Leaning over his face, she kissed him hard on the mouth. She lifted herself and placed her hand over his manhood. As she guided him inside her, sitting fully down on him, she began to groan. She suddenly threw her head back, closed her eyes and whispered, "Want all of you inside me." Moving up and down, she increased her pace.

He reached up and grabbed both of her breasts, unable to be gentle. He couldn't stop watching her. God, she was beautiful. Gary thought she appeared to be experiencing pure bliss one moment, and pain the next.

Sandi K. Whipple

Her hot body and frenzied movements seemed to be driving her to another level of emotion. Watching her facial expressions and hearing her moans, Gary thought she'd retreated to another space and time.

Angie found Gary's hands and covered them with her own. Together they massaged her breasts in unison with his thumbs forcing her nipples to double their size. Her pace was rapid and he couldn't hold off any longer.

She cried out his name and trembled as her spasm tightened her muscles around him. At the same time, his hot convulsion erupted deep inside her.

Moments later, totally spent, she fell on top of his chest. When he was able to breathe normally, he repeated, "Yes, Angie, honey, you are definitely, without a doubt, my love. Angie, Angie, honey, are you awake?"

She was out cold. He rolled her on to her back. Was she exhausted from their lovemaking or had she just passed out? He figured it was the latter. Would she remember this tomorrow? Would she remember what a tigress she'd been? Would she have any idea how she ignited him and turned his emotions upside down and inside out all at the same time? He knew he wanted this hot, seductive tigress with her beautiful body far beyond tonight or tomorrow. She'd wrapped herself around his heart and soul. He was in love with her. Would she let him love her? And what about Carl?

Reaching out, he pulled her body into his like a cocoon. He wrapped his arms around her cautiously so as not to hurt her. When she let out a soft sigh and cuddled even closer, his heart warmed at the reality of their perfect fit.

The next morning, while Angie slept, Gary shopped for groceries, stopped at Wal-Mart to buy the closing mechanism, fixed the shop door, read the paper, and was watching an old black-and-white war movie.

It was past noon when Angie stepped from the bedroom clad in a silken robe that clung to her firm breasts and beautiful rear.

Standing with her nipples protruding from the barely closed robe, she had no idea how beautiful she was or how aroused he was seeing her dressed like that.

"I hate you, Gary," she greeted him.

"Really? Why is that?" he asked with a smile.

"Because you obviously beat me up last night and left me to die. I fooled you though, huh? I might make it. If you offer me anything other than coffee, after I get sick, I'll call everyone I know till I find someone to lend me a gun. Then trust me when I say *you'll be sorry*."

It was difficult to keep from laughing. He could tell she was suffering just by looking at her.

As he rose from the sofa, he tried to control his amusement. "Have a seat and I'll pour you some coffee."

Angie cringed when she said, "Forget the cream. It might curdle when it hits my stomach."

He couldn't hold back any more and started to laugh. She smiled.

"Angie, have you ever had a hangover?"

"No, and I've never had champagne. And for the life of me, if I have much longer to live, I'll never understand how anyone can actually rise from their bed feeling like this, and have the proverbial hair of the dog." Trying to send him daggers with her eyes, she said, "And if you don't quit laughing at me, I promise you, I will not die alone."

When the phone rang, Angie just made a face and looked at the floor. "Please answer that for me and tell whoever it is that the funeral is on Tuesday."

Still laughing, Gary picked up the phone hoping it would be Carl. See how he'd like hearing a man answer her phone.

"Oh, hello, Ruth. No, she's right here. I'm just helping her out today. Hang on."

The cord wasn't long enough so he held the phone toward her. Angie smiled when she stood up. "I need to study the concept of portable phones. It may take me a few minutes to get there so please hold on to it."

Taking the phone she said, "Hi, Aunt Ruth. How are you, how's Frank? I'm fine. Absolutely not. Besides, I promised Patti more hours. Well, if Frank refused to let you go back to work for him, what in the world makes you think I'd let you back in the shop? Oh. And Frank's cooking? You bet. I'll be there with bells on — if I'm not dead by then. Nothing, it was a joke. I love you, too. See you Wednesday, bye."

Gary had difficulty curtailing his laughter as she nearly crawled back to the chair.

"Why don't you go fix something, or do something, or, hell, anything. Just quit laughing at me. Go fix that closer thingy on the shop door. I'll promise you anything if you'll quit laughing."

"I fixed it while you were passed out."

"Can't you see I'm in pain here and might die? Show a little sympathy will you? And I was asleep, not passed out. I think."

Gary subtly changed the subject. "How much do you remember about last night?"

"I remember a lot, why?"

With a slight nervous tinge to his words, he replied, "Give me an example."

"I remember the first glass of champagne and how it tickled my nose. I think I remember coming home. Yes, I do. I know, because you wouldn't stand still so I could kiss you."

"Anything else?"

"Just that you beat me up and left me to die." Showing a bit of difficulty at the task of rising from her chair, Angie added, "I think I'll go take a shower for an hour or two. Maybe I'll feel better. If you hear breaking glass, it'll be me falling through the shower door. If it happens, please call 911."

Still trying not to laugh he asked her, "Want to take a drive if you survive the shower?"

As she headed for the shower she answered, "Sure, that would be great."

Standing under the rush of water was therapeutic. She would live after all.

Bringing up their conversation in her mind, she knew there was no way she'd admit she remembered making love to him. Nor would she admit to knowing the level of his arousal. She recalled her need to be erotic and make him feel as desirable as she felt each time they made love. She wasn't sure why that was important to her, but it was.

Sandi K. Whipple

    Flip-flopping her thoughts she recalled his latest 'see ya' episode. Angie knew if there were another similar incident, there would be hell to pay.
    The shower water was beginning to get cold so she'd have to analyze that idea another time. She needed to get dried, dressed, and focus on bringing herself back to life.
    They drove down by the river, strolled hand in hand in the park, sat on a bench and talked, laughed and devoured too much ice cream. They took turns pushing each other on a swing. After having hot dogs for lunch, they were flat on their backs on the ground, joking while finding different shapes in the clouds, and pretending to cry as the wind tore the shapes away. The entire day was picture perfect as it ended while they sat with arms around each other watching the sunset.

    .

CHAPTER EIGHT

The next morning the sun shone brightly and the birds sounded a bit happy as Gary arrived at his office with an extra spring in his step.

"Good morning, Mr. Walgren," Katie greeted him. Was he really whistling? Wait till Lucy heard about this. No way would she believe it, especially because of his on and off brusque manners during the last few weeks.

"Good morning, Katie."

"I've pre-screened seven applicants so far and told them I'd call if you want to interview them. If you'll tell me when you want to do that, I'll schedule them right away."

"Which day this week is going to be the slowest?"

"We don't have a slow day for almost a month. Maybe you could squeeze in one interview in the morning and another in the late afternoon every day."

"Good idea. Coordinate them with the work schedule, then let me see it so I can work on timing."

"Did you say work on your own timing?"

He just smiled. "I did," as he closed his office door. He opened it and added, "Don't disturb me until further notice."

Once he was alone and in privacy, he dialed the flower shop.

"Angie's Flower Shop, may I help you?"

"You can help me in more ways than one. Want to know how?"

Giggling, Angie said, "Better to talk dirty on the phone than just get another breather, I guess. Go ahead, tell me, and please, do be descriptive."

"Mornin', babe. I just wanted to thank you for a great weekend."

"You're more than welcome. Believe me when I say, the pleasure was all mine."

He laughed. "That's sure as hell debatable. Listen, hon, I've just been informed that my schedule this week leaves me only enough time to shower and sleep. If I'm lucky, I'll be able to squeeze in a meal or two. I won't be able to meet you for lunch this week after all. I feel like crap about it and I'm sorry."

Suddenly fearful of another one of his disappearances, she nearly whispered her reply. "I see. You're not leaving me or walking out on me again, are you?"

"Not on your life. How about dinner this Friday?" The sound of the bell on Angie's shop door stopped Gary from saying more.

"It's a date. I have a customer so I better run. See you Friday —and I hope you're getting paid overtime."

After hanging up, he was disgusted with himself for ever putting her in a position to feel the need to ask him if he was leaving again. Getting up from the desk, knowing he needed to get to work, he promised himself to make it up to her.

On his way out of the office, he told Katie he was headed for the job site in Green Bend. "Let Tom know I'm on my way."

"I've scheduled your first interview at four thirty today. I'll call your cell to remind you." She handed him the week's schedule, including the seven interviews.

With a flippant "Alrighty, then," Gary was out the door.

Katie sensed something was in the wind. She called Lucy right away. Maybe she knew what it was.

****

By Thursday afternoon, Gary was ready to interview the seventh applicant. He'd narrowed it down to two and they were a done deal. If number seven looked promising, he'd go ahead and hire him, too.

He helped Tom on three jobs, working until seven and eight o'clock each night. He allowed the late hours so they could remain on schedule.

When he visited the Green Bend office, Lucy asked if the schedule she had shuffled around met with his approval.

Gary smiled knowing what he was about to say and do. "What are you asking me for? It's your office. You're the Green Bend office manager. With the exception of Tom and me, the crew takes orders from you anyway. For that matter, most of the time, so do Tom and I," he joked.

Lucy nearly choked. "Office manager? When did that happen?"

As he headed for the door, knowing Lucy couldn't see the grin on his face, Gary simply stated, "Just now and it comes with a raise."

Sandi K. Whipple

With a desire to jump up and down, Lucy controlled herself and tried to stay calm. She hollered to his back, "Thank you, Mr. Walgren." Once he was out the door, she hurriedly grabbed the phone.

"Katie, you're right. Something's definitely in the wind."

****

A few days later, Gary hooked up with Tom and told him, "Ok, we have three new guys. We'll have one for each office and a floater to go back and forth. Our schedules are clear Monday morning. We'll meet with them and fill them in."

"Thanks, Gary. I was starting to spread myself pretty thin."

"Don't do it again, Tom. I sure don't want you exhausting yourself or stressing out. Hell, if I lost you, the damned company would be in trouble. You and me, we've built this business into a thriving company with a potential for even more growth. Our reputation is good, and our business is great. It's time to slow down and for you to get reacquainted with your wife, and for me to..."

Tom interrupted him. "Am I allowed to ask how it goes with the woman who was killing you?"

Gary laughed. "She's still killing me, but her methods have changed."

"So things are good then?"

"So far, for the moment anyway. I'm taking her to dinner Friday. Lately, we've been making old man Di Nido rich."

CHAPTER NINE

Aunt Ruth was in the living room pouting while Angie and Frank cleaned up and washed the dishes. Frank had been adamant about not letting Ruth help.

"Frank, that was the best spaghetti I've ever eaten," Angie said. "Mr. Di Nido would be envious."

"Thanks."

"How is she, really, Frank? I can see she's in good hands and I love you for the way you take care of her, but, I'm still worried, especially since she asked me if she could come back to the shop a few days a week. Of course, I told her no."

"I knew you wouldn't let her," Frank said. "She already asked me to let her work a few days at the store. I've hired a retired guy like me who's bored and looking for things to do. Now I can spend more time with Ruth. Dr. Greenburg said she's doing great and he wants her to get out and about a little. Light shopping, short walks, the hairdresser, you know, stuff like that. He'd rather she didn't drive for a few more months though."

"Angie," Aunt Ruth called out.

"Coming." Angie hurriedly put away the towel she'd been using.

"Go ahead, I'll join you in a few minutes," Frank said.

Angie sat across from her aunt and smiled at her. God, how she loved this tough, old, witty woman. "Yes, what is it?"

"Tell me about the shop, dear. How's Patti doing and does it look like the new delivery fellow will work out?"

Sandi K. Whipple

"Aunt Ruth, you're a gossip monger! Patti's taking a few more classes at night so she can work more hours. And Chuck is working out just great. He even made a few dollars in tips yesterday."

"Want to tell me what Gary *Adonis* was really doing at your apartment on Sunday?"

Entering the room and hearing Ruth's question, Frank almost choked.

Aunt Ruth looked at him lovingly and asked, "Frank, dear, are you okay?"

"I don't think I want to know what that means, Ruth," he laughed as he went up the stairs. "I'll leave you two alone for a while."

When Angie heard Frank's footsteps on the upper floor, she said in a deep low almost whispering voice, "Aunt Ruth how could you? He was only there to pick me up. We had plans to take a drive that's all. It was no big deal. And don't you look at me like that; I'm telling the truth. And would you please not use that word Adonis, especially in front of people? One of these days you'll say it in front of him and we'll all be embarrassed."

"No, dear, you'll be embarrassed. And you're not telling me the truth, Angela. I know you, remember? Something's going on. I can tell by the look on your face. I'll find out eventually, you know. After all, this is a small town. Nothing here is sacred, not for long anyway."

They talked and giggled like young girls for almost an hour until Frank returned.

Sandi K. Whipple

"I have to work tomorrow," Angie told them as she got up. After a hug for each one, she drove home to her empty apartment.

****

Late afternoon on Friday, just before closing time, Alan called.

"My aunt told me you went by to see her."

"I actually got a few good leads from her," Alan told her. "She has one terrific memory. With her help, I traced your brother to a small town in North Dakota, where your father was from. Then he moved to Wisconsin. He left there several years ago." Alan inhaled and continued, "It wasn't too difficult tracing his steps to that point but it's getting a little tougher now. I'll keep on it, Angie. Just be patient. These things take time."

She heard the jingle of the shop door and looked up to see Gary smiling at her. She smiled back and waved at him to come in.

Turning her attention back to the conversation with Alan, she said into the phone, "I know. It's just that it's been so long. I hope you know how hard it is for me to not get excited. Thanks, Alan. Bye."

Replacing the receiver, Angie greeted Gary with, "Hi you. You look as if your hectic week hasn't even fazed you. Miss me?"

Once again Gary had to fight himself to control his seething jealousy. Who the hell was Alan? It wasn't bad enough there was Carl? It took great effort to keep a calm voice. "I just came by to tell you I can't make dinner tonight. I didn't want to cancel over the phone."

Angie took a deep breath, and then let it out slowly, showing her obvious disappointment. "I see. Is something wrong?"

With a forced smile, he replied, "I guess I'm just beat. It was a busy week for me. I want to go home and crash. I hope you're not mad."

"Of course I'm not mad. But I think, rather than kill his employees with all those hours, your boss would have enough brains to hire extra help. It'd be cheaper than paying overtime, too. You do get paid overtime, don't you?"

"I get paid enough, Angie, but thanks for the concern."

"Well, go home and kick back. I'll call Carl and see if we can go catch a movie or something."

"That's great. Call Carl. Go see a good movie. See ya." With that he stormed out.

At least this time he gave her a reason, but something wasn't right.

She phoned Carl and they agreed to hang out for the evening.

****

Meeting for dinner, Angie said with sadness in her voice, "Thanks for keeping me company. Though I'm not sure dinner here was one of my better ideas." Di Nido Bistro was, after all, hers and Gary's hangout.

Lifting her glass of water, Carl said, "Listen, pet, I told my husband my dear friend was depressed and something was wrong. He told me to go try to cheer you up. He'd never admit it to his macho friends, but he loves playing 'Mr. Mom.' Let's get a drink, then you can tell me what's tearing you up. You look like hell."

Angie smiled. "I encountered a teeny problem the last time I drank, but, you go ahead. I'll just have sparkling water with lime."

While the waiter delivered their drinks, Carl looked at her. "It's this guy you've been seeing, isn't it? All is not hunky-dory in Denmark, huh?"

Angie looked a bit downcast. "Oh Carl, he did it again — kind of, anyway. He came by because we had date for dinner. He gave me a lame excuse and stormed out with that damned 'See ya.' God, I hate that. He said he was tired from working hard all week and wanted to go home and crash. But he was clean-shaven and dressed nicely. If he were tuckered out from a hectic week and just got off, one would think he'd still be in his work clothes," she said as her mind trailed off.

"And?" Carl said in an attempt to interrupt Angie's wandering mind.

"I just think he was lying to me. I know I have no claim on him, but I thought we were developing something special. Now I'm not sure. I think he might have had a date with someone else. The very thought of him seeing another woman makes me ill."

Sensing Angie's unease, Carl asked, "What's really bothering you?"

"I don't know," Angie said with flailing hands. "When we're together, he's wonderful. He's got a hearty down-to-earth laugh. When he smiles, his eyes go half-closed; he's handsome, compassionate, loving, warm, and did I say he's very good- looking? I'm miserable when we're not together, Carl. I don't know how to handle this," she said as she took a sip of water. "I'm sorry to bother you with my problem."

"Don't ever be sorry about sharing anything with me, Angie. I'm your friend, and that's what friends do. They make sure they're there for each other. Tell me something. You say you know you have no claim on this guy, yet the thought of him with another woman makes you ill. Are you in love with him?"

"I swore years ago I'd never let *real* love be a part of my life. I saw first-hand what it does to some people. But the way he makes me feel when we're together, even if it's just holding hands, well, I don't know, maybe I am."

Carl was leaning forward in order to catch every word, and now, with a bit of skepticism in her demeanor, she said, "You're a great gal, Angie. If you want this guy, go after him. Shake him up a little. See how things really are. See where you stand. At least, once you know, you'll figure out how to deal with it. Personally, I'd like to kick his damned teeth in. It sounds to me like he's just slime. Want me to put a contract out on him?"

Angie pretended to give her a shocked look.

Carl decided to change the subject. "Enough depression. Let's eat, I'm starving. What's good here? And thank God you picked me up because you've just been assigned the designated driver." Carl summoned the waiter, asking, "May I please have another drink?"

"Thanks for being here, Carl," Angie said with a sigh. "I agree, let's change the subject. By the way, the PI, found a trail on my brother. He traced him through two states and then hit a brick wall. But hell, that's something, right?"

Over coffee and dessert, Carl had a brainstorm. "Hey, why don't I fix you up? I happen to know a great guy. You're both single, independent, hard- headed, and both miserable. You guys have a lot in common. A match made in heaven. Interested?"

"Thanks, but no thanks."

"I promise you, he's cute.

"Nah."

They stayed until closing time, laughing and doing what they did best: men bashing.

Sandi K. Whipple

CHAPTER TEN

Driving away from Angie's, Gary attempted to keep his cool. He'd fought to control his temper when he heard Angie's conversation with a guy named Alan.

How could she do that? And right in front of him. What was it she said to him? "It's been so long?" "It's hard not to get excited"? It wasn't even Carl; it was a different guy. Who the hell was Alan? He felt like she'd kicked him in the gut. He couldn't pretend he hadn't heard. In fact, her conversation had blatantly forced him to quietly swallow their phone dialogue and he wasn't that good at acting. Evidently there wasn't just one other man in her life, but two.

He needed to tread carefully. After all, he had no claim on her or any right to be jealous. They weren't married, engaged, or even living together so he had no right to be upset about another man, did he?

He had no justification to tell her she couldn't see Carl or Alan, whoever the hell they were. Damn it. He just wanted to be with her and not have to share her.

He needed to be alone to ponder the situation along with his roller-coaster emotions. He knew he didn't want to control her life and tell her whom she could or could not see. And then there was the issue about his owning the company. When she found out he was the owner, he knew it would make her furious. He couldn't imagine her anger if she thought she'd been used or deceived. Even Tom thought the lack of billing her, and failure to acknowledge company ownership was just a ploy to get her in the sack. Well, maybe it was, at first. But damn it, that was a long time ago. His feelings had gone way beyond that now.

Fighting his thoughts of anger and passion, Gary found himself sitting in his car in his driveway, and having no memory of the roads he'd just traveled. Thinking how ridiculous he must appear, he went inside and headed to the refrigerator. With a couple of beers and tears, he finally fell into a very troubled sleep.

****

The weekend was no better for Gary. When the sun came up on Monday morning, he put his feet on the floor and thought about the day's workload.

After he arrived at the office, the first person he ran into was Tom. Before the day could be approached, Gary cornered him to share his heartache and confusion.

After thinking it through, he decided to share everything with Tom. "Before, it was just this guy Carl, but now there's Alan too. And she's not even discreet about it. She called Alan by his name while looking right at me with a smile. She even told him how much she appreciated him by saying 'it had been so long.' When I lied and canceled dinner, she had the nerve to tell me she was going to call Carl to see about going to a movie. I'm not sure, but I think I'm really screwed here."

Taking a moment or two to catch his breath, Gary continued, "And she keeps bugging Katie about those damned bills. If I tell her the truth about that now, I know all hell will break loose. You know she'll think I did the work just to get her in the sack." After stopping long enough to take a deep breath, Gary added, "I know I don't have a right to tell her or even ask her not to see other men, but the thought of her next to another guy makes my blood boil. To top it off, I've been working on a personal business deal that could sour and cost me big time if I don't start paying attention and get back on track here. I feel like I'm drowning."

Tom was concerned for his friend. "You've got it bad. Have you thought of telling her that? You know, the thought of her with another guy makes your blood boil? Have you considered asking her about Alan? Maybe he's just a friend like she said Carl is. Women can have platonic male friends, you know. The bill issue— well, I wish I could help you on that. I haven't the slightest idea how you're going to get out of that one."

Katie buzzed, telling them the three new guys arrived.

"Well, I guess we'd better get back to work. Thanks for listening, Tom."

Once the interviews and hiring were over, there were now nineteen people whose welfare was in the hands of Walgren's Heating and Cooling.

If the business deal he'd been working on over the last several months were going to fly, Gary would sure as hell have to do some body shuffling.

He buzzed Katie on the intercom. "Would you call my attorney and tell him I'm on my way? I'll leave my beeper and cell on in case you need me. You got anything pressing for me before I go?"

"No. Just another message from Miss Gibbons wanting her bills. Want me to keep putting her off?"

Sandi K. Whipple

As he opened his office door he told her, "It isn't fair to ask you to keep doing that without an explanation, but as a favor to me, I wish you would. If you'd rather not, I'll understand."

"It's nothing I can't handle, Mr. Walgren. I've handled tougher people than Miss Gibbons and still come out smelling like a rose."

"Oh yeah, who?"

"Why you, Mr. Walgren," she replied with a giggle.

He laughed and said as he left the office, "Katie, you're priceless."

****

Gary drove to his attorney's office and arrived about 15 minutes early. He was immediately shown into the office. After a cursory greeting, his attorney, Ralph, opened the conversation. "You understand, don't you, Gary, that by buying out all three locations of Pederson's Plumbing and Heating, you'll become a very rich man? I'm concerned about you though. I don't know what's going on with you lately and I know I'm just your attorney, but, you look like hell and this buy-out is gonna spread you pretty thin for the first few months. I think maybe running back and forth to five different cities while still doing a lot of the grunt work yourself, will put you in an early grave."

"I've just had a few personal problems, Ralph. I'll work them out. And about spreading myself thin, I wanted to talk to you about that. I've decided to turn Walgren's into a partnership. I'll be *giving* half of the business to my new partner. He's more than earned it." Making a stab at some light humor, Gary continued, "After that, there'll be two guys headed for an early grave."

"I think I know exactly what you're thinking and of whom. Not a bad decision, Gary, and a great tax relief for both of you."

"Good, I'm glad you agree. How long will it take to close this then?"

"Well, I'll need to draw up the partnership agreement first and then the buy-out will be from the partnership, not you. It should only take a few weeks if the Corporations Commission in Springfield isn't backed up."

Gary stood and shook hands with his attorney and friend. They'd known each other over ten years and Gary trusted the man completely.

"Thanks, Ralph. Let me know when the papers are ready to sign," he said and headed off to his luncheon appointment.

Upon arrival at the restaurant, Gary found his table and waiting party. As he sat down, he said, "I'm glad you could meet me, Heather. I hope you kept your promise about not telling Tom."

"Not to worry. I've been dying to check out this new place anyway. The French name, *La Virage*, just sounds romantic. So, what's all this hush-hush, Gary, and how can it have anything to do with me or Tom?"

"For starters," Gary replied, "I owe you an apology for working your husband so hard lately."

"It's ..."

Gary put his palm up and said, "No, let me finish, Heather. What I'm about to tell you has to be kept confidential, for the time being anyway. I'll let you know when that changes. In fact, I may impose on you to help set up the celebration when the time comes."

"What celebration?" Leaning forward on her elbows, Heather added, "This already sounds intriguing."

Gary explained his plan and said, "That's it, I guess. So if you'll help me out here, and keep this all under your hat, I'd sure appreciate it."

"I don't know what to say, Gary. 'Thank you' doesn't seem to be enough. Tom will be speechless. He really is devoted to you. I swear, I won't breathe a word of this."

She walked around the table and gave him a hug, kissed his cheek, and left. Not knowing he was being observed, Gary looked down at the check, put a few bills on the table and walked out.

CHAPTER ELEVEN

It was late morning when Angie arrived at the shop. Shocked at seeing her aunt, she asked, "Aunt Ruth, what are you doing here?" Angie was flustered when she saw her aunt behind the counter. It was understood that after her heart attack she was no longer to work here. Assuming there was bad news coming, she asked, "Where's Patti? Is she okay?"

"Calm down, dear. She just needed to run to the bank before you got robbed. I came by to see you so I told her I'd hold down the fort till she got back. You know it's not very smart to leave that much money lying around. The bank is only two blocks away. And where have you been? It's not like you not to let Patti know where you are during business hours. She was worried and, frankly, so was I."

"I'm sorry," Angie said with a slight frown. "I had an appointment at La Virage this morning, the new French restaurant over by the waterfront. Have you heard of it? Anyway, Mr. Solis, the owner, wanted to set up arrangements for a daily delivery. He saw my flowers at Di Nido Bistro and said he was impressed. So, I have a new account. If this keeps up, I'll have to move out of my apartment so I can stretch the shop all the way to the back of the building."

With a slight change in her voice, Angie continued, "Anyway, what's up? Why the surprise visit?"

Aunt Ruth leaned on the countertop with her elbows. "Frank's talking business. I think he's discussing the sale of his store. We were supposed to go to lunch, but he'll be tied up for several hours. Since I'm without a luncheon date, I thought you might like to take me."

"I'd love to," Angie said as she turned at the sound of the brass bells jingling on the front door. "It's pretty much lunch time now, and here comes Patti, so now we can go now if you want to."

With quick instructions to Patti as to where they could be reached, Angie guided Aunt Ruth out the door and into the car.

Following a ten-minute drive, Angie parked in the lot of the La Virage. She said, "I've never been here to eat so I thought we might try it out. If I'm going to be doing business with the owner, I suppose I should frequent the place on occasion."

Upon being seated, Aunt Ruth said, "This place is beautiful. If the food is half as good as the place looks, I'll be in heaven."

They spent most of their lunchtime talking about Frank. Aunt Ruth seemed to be walking on air. She was happier every time Angie saw her. Too bad it wasn't contagious.

As they were enjoying dessert, Aunt Ruth asked, "Angie, isn't that your *Gary Adonis* over there, on the left?"

Angie looked up and froze. It certainly was him. She stared, unable to take her eyes off the woman seated across from him. She was tall, slender with blonde hair, and very beautiful. Angie stared dumbfounded as she watched them in deep discussion with their heads almost touching. So there *was* another woman in his life. Angie felt sick. It was suddenly difficult for her to breathe. There'd been someone else all along. She knew he'd lied to her that Friday when he canceled their dinner date and that woman was probably the reason. Her heart almost stopped when they hugged and kissed.

Aunt Ruth's shaky voice brought Angie back to the moment. Touching her arm, Aunt Ruth said, "Angie, are you all right, dear? You look strange. You're scaring me. What is it? What's wrong? Shall I call Frank?"

Angie made an attempt to maintain her demeanor without causing concern for her aunt. She lied by saying, "I'm sorry, Aunt Ruth. That last bite of dessert got stuck halfway down. For a minute there, I couldn't catch my breath. I'm okay now. Are we almost ready to go? Do you want me to take you home or shall I drop you at Frank's store?"

"Home will be fine, dear. I don't want to interrupt him." She was still concerned for her niece. "Darling, are you sure you're okay?"

"Yes, of course," Angie said smiling. She didn't want her aunt knowing how badly shaken she'd been while witnessing the loving couple. There was no doubt from the scene that they were just that—a loving couple.

****

A few days later while going over her books, Angie decided business was better than ever and getting busier each day. Between the weddings, hotels, restaurants, walk-in traffic, and phone orders, she sometimes felt frazzled. Now, two funeral parlors in town were requesting her services.

Sandi K. Whipple

Her consistent advertising, many visits to hotels, restaurants, churches, wedding shops, and even funeral parlors had been exhausting. Obviously though, looking at the books, all that hard work and effort was paying off. To realize she'd come this far since opening just seven months ago, well, that was just mind boggling.

She began to think she really might have to give up her apartment and use the entire building for the shop. That would mean at least six new flower coolers and of course, more shelves and stands. One consolation was that she might not have to get a loan for the expansion since business had been so good.

She had just closed the shop and finished taking a few measurements. She jotted them down and set them aside for further review at a later time.

Now in the comfort of her apartment, she was leaning back on the couch, just staring at the ceiling. Here she was, alone on a Saturday night, with her mind starting to wonder in many different directions. The possible shop expansion, moving, and of course, Gary, were all rolling around in her head.

She felt as though her whole world had imploded a few days ago at the La Virage. Seeing Gary with that beautiful blonde, well, it made her believe that he obviously didn't feel about her the way she felt about him. If he did, he wouldn't see other women and think enough of them to kiss them in public.

He'd become the only man in her life and she had no desire to date anyone else. He had to have known that, didn't he?

She thought a hot bath would soak away her distraught mood. When that didn't work, she wrapped herself in a down comforter, curled up on her bed, and cried herself to sleep.

The ringing of the phone woke Angie early the next morning. With a brief hello and some polite chitchat, Alan gave her an update on a lead in Martinsville, Illinois. It seemed a merchant knew a Tom Henderson and he said that Tom had moved into town, married, had a baby and shortly thereafter left town with his family. He continued on with his progress report by telling her of his intention to drive to Martinsville and talk to the merchant in person. He seemed excited with what he considered his best lead yet. "Keep the faith," he said, before hanging up.

This was good news and gave a little bit of cheerfulness to Angie's morning. She called Aunt Ruth to invite her and Frank to Sunday brunch but they already had plans. She called Carl to see if she was up to a little shopping and lunch, but she and her husband had plans as well. Patti and her boyfriend weren't home.

Everyone had someone, except her. She decided she had to entertain herself, so she went out for a newspaper, picked up some Popeye's Chicken, and spent the day searching the newspaper for a potential new residence. She felt certain the business would be pushing her out of her apartment sooner than she'd anticipated.

****

Monday morning was hectic. Patti couldn't come into the shop until two o'clock and the delivery van broke down. It took Angie and Chuck almost an hour to load the flowers into her car. The phone constantly rang and the La Virage wanted a double delivery for a banquet that day.

    By the time Patti arrived, Angie was frazzled to the max but at least things were starting to slow down. She asked Patti to finish out the day, went into her apartment, and closed the door. She took two aspirin for her headache, turned on the television, curled up on her sofa and promptly fell asleep. Hours later, a loud pounding sound startled her.

    She quickly turned on a lamp and, walking toward the sound, realized it was someone banging on the door. When she opened the door, she was shocked to see Gary holding a huge bouquet of flowers and a bottle of champagne.

    With a forlorn expression on his face, Gary gingerly stepped toward the opening of the door. "Patti was already locking up the shop so I had to buy these from your competition."

    When he received no response from Angie who was standing still and staring at him, Gary went on, "I couldn't stay away from you any longer, Angie. I know you've heard it from me before, but I really do promise to try real hard not to be such an ass, and I'm sorry."

    Seeing the sincerity written on his face, Angie threw her arms around him and began to cry. Gently lifting her off her feet, Gary stepped inside, turned, and kicked the door shut. He set the flowers and champagne on the table. Now that his hands were free, he wrapped his arms around her.

    "Don't cry, sweetheart. I feel bad enough for being an ass. I know the distance between us was my fault. I'm going to work real hard to control my moods. Please say you forgive me."

Angie was unable to speak and Gary felt he could say nothing more. All they were able to do was hold one another.

A few moments passed and Angie was able to find her voice. "I've been so miserable. Let's not even talk about it, let's just start over. Please?"

Standing back he said, "You're asking me when I'm the one who should be asking you?"

She put his face in her hands and kissed his eyes, nose, mouth, cheeks and back to his eyes, all the time whispering, "Gary, oh Gary . . ."

Her body began to tremble with need of his closeness. Pulling his shirt from the waist of his trousers, she slipped her hands under his shirt to feel his flesh. She looked up at him as she unbuttoned his trousers and when she pulled the zipper down, his black eyes turned an exciting *coal*, filled with desire. She sorely missed seeing that look.

By the time they reached the bedroom, there was a trail of clothing. Gary threw her onto the bed, climbed over her, and kissed every square inch of her beautiful body. He started from her eyes and didn't stop until he reached her toes. Working his way back up, he placed one hand on her stomach, separated her thighs with the other, and when he reached into her with his tongue, he pulled her to him at the same time.

When her breathing grew heavy and her moaning became loud with her begging sounds, she lifted herself wanting more of what was taking her to another world.

Crying out his name when she finally arrived, he chose not to stop or release her until she was silent and motionless. As she lay there, not yet in a full state of consciousness, he moved over her and filled her in one quick thrust.

He watched her face as he stroked faster and faster. He could see as well as feel that she was regaining her equilibrium as she responded to his every movement. When she wrapped her legs around his waist, he felt the impending visit to that other world would be together. And so it was!

Lying next to her, Gary watched her for a long time. She was cuddled up to him, sound asleep. He pondered her many assets and looked at her naked body. He thought he might actually love this woman. He was aware that he'd once again become aroused. He massaged a breast and her nipple stood to attention. When he started thumbing the other, she squirmed and tried to move away. He pinched them harder and she turned onto her stomach. Straddling her, he placed both hands around her waist and pulled her up on her knees. "No way, Angie. You can't get away from me that easily."

He entered her from behind, rubbing her back while holding her firmly against him. It wasn't long before she was pushing herself into him with each stroke. They moaned loudly as they reached their climax together, and then became motionless. He held her to him until he could no longer feel her contractions squeezing his manhood.

Letting her go, she collapsed onto her stomach. He placed an arm over her and knew she was already asleep. Smugly, he thought, take that, Carl. And you too, Alan, whoever the hell you guys are. He made up his mind. He would wine, dine, and exhaust her in bed and make sure there was nothing left for Carl or Alan. When those guys finally realized he was in the picture, they might just give up. Yep. That's the plan.

When Angie opened her eyes, it took her a minute to realize she was alone in her bed. Had she dreamed of lovemaking? Or had she and Gary made mad, passionate, every-which-way-but-loose kind of love last night? When she heard the sound of water in the shower, she realized it wasn't a dream.

She put two pillows behind her head, sat up, and pulled the sheet to her waist. She leaned her head back and rested her eyes. Her nipples were swollen, hard as cement and sore as hell, but they felt wonderful and she felt great. Giggling, she wondered if that made sense.

She stroked her lips with her fingers and tongue to feel how swollen they were. She felt a presence, opened her eyes, and saw Gary watching her every move. She gazed at his naked and beautiful body as he became aroused.

He had a strange smile on his face. "Damn you, Angie, don't do that."

She quickly put her hands in her lap. "Don't do what? My lips are swollen and sore. I was just rubbing them." Smiling up at him, she added, "I feel like a million bucks though."

He sat next to her and looked at her breasts. They were swollen. Her nipples were fire-engine red and twice their normal size.

"I didn't hurt you, did I, sweetheart?"

Sandi K. Whipple

She smiled as she shook her head no.

"I never knew a woman's breasts and nipples could be as sensitive as yours," he said, and took one into his hand and massaged it. She gasped when his thumb flicked her nipple.

Grinning at her with an evil look, he said, "I'll bet I could make you climax just by sucking, licking, and biting them. Should I kiss them and make them feel better?" He bent to take her breast into his mouth.

She giggled and hit him with a pillow. Pushing him away, she jumped out of bed. "You're insatiable," she said. She headed to the bathroom and he heard her lock the door amidst the sound of her giggling.

He was dressed and on the phone when she walked into the living room.

"Sorry, Mom, I can't, but if you'll promise me a steak, we could do it one night this week. Yes, I know the weather is changing and it's almost time to put the grill away. I will, I promise. I love you too, bye."

He turned to Angie and smiled. "You look nice. I was going to make you breakfast, but, as usual, there's no food in this house. Why don't we both play hooky today? You call Patti and beg her to work and I'll call my office to tell them I won't be in today. Then we'll go out to breakfast and while we're eating, we'll plan the rest of the day. What do you say?"

With a mischievous grin, Angie said, "its Tuesday so Patti's opening today anyway." She picked up the phone, spoke to Patti who agreed to work the entire day, then told him, "I'm all yours."

Sandi K. Whipple

She knitted her brow and asked, "By the way, why'd you bring champagne? Were you hoping to get me drunk and take advantage of me?"

Gary roared with laughter. "That was the plan. But it was halted in its tracks when you ripped my clothes off and took advantage of me instead. Not that I'm complaining." Still laughing, he added, "Put it in the fridge. Maybe later we can revert to the original plan, huh?"

"You're terrible, but I do so love that part of you. Let's go. I need sustenance." She stopped in her tracks, and made a thorough scan of the kitchen. "Hey, wait a minute. Where's my flowers?"

Stopping in his footsteps at the door, Gary turned around. "They were dead so while you were in the shower I put them in the garbage under the sink. Sorry, babe."

"They shouldn't be dead already, even without water from just last night. Wherever you bought them, they got good money out of you for old flowers."

Laughing, she pushed him toward the door with only two words, "Feed me."

In an attempt to make up for lost time, they saw each other two or three times a week. They found ways to be together every weekend.

They'd gone fishing and she found it wasn't a favorite past time of hers, especially since the weather was getting cooler. She wasn't overly fond of the bait either. She knew after he made her clean her first fish that it wasn't a sport she'd care to get into.

When she caught him cheating at miniature golf, she chased him with her club as he screamed for help.

Sandi K. Whipple

    They jokingly argued in the video store when she picked out a movie he said was a chick flick, but he finally succumbed. They watched the film together and at a sad point in the story, she saw tears fall from the eyes of her macho *Adonis*. When she later teased him about his reactions, he adamantly denied the tears and threatened her with bodily harm if she ever told anyone.

Sandi K. Whipple

CHAPTER TWELVE

Springfield issued final approval on the license for Gary's new partnership corporation. The attorney had already begun the process of the buy-out of Pederson's Plumbing and Heating, and anticipated a smooth closing within a week.

Gary's announcement to his employees was going to be a surprise. With the help of Tom's wife, Heather, the plans were in place for a celebration at La Virage. Employees would be told to bring a guest, spouse, or significant other to make the occasion not only business, but festive. Gary's attorney, Ralph, felt honored when he was invited to be a part of the event.

Gary told Angie he'd be taking her to a special dinner on Saturday. He hoped when he revealed to her that he was, in fact, the owner of Walgren's, she'd understand and not be angry. After all, so much time had passed since their first meeting, how could it possibly make a difference now?

Gary was amused when he thought of Tom, who was stumped by the whole thing and still wondering what surprise there could possibly be that Gary hadn't shared with him.

The night of the announcement festivities arrived and Gary's excitement was elevated when he envisioned showing Angie off and introducing her to his mother and sister.

When he arrived to pick up Angie, she answered the door wearing flannel pajamas. She looked like death warmed over. She was pale as a ghost, and she was sniffling. She could barely stand.

Sandi K. Whipple

Grabbing hold of her to keep her from falling, Gary kicked the door shut and guided her to the sofa.

"Sweetheart, what's wrong? You look awful."

"I feel awful, and my head hurts. I can't quit blowing my nose and I hurt in places I didn't know I had places."

Reaching out and taking her face in his hands, he knew she had a fever, and a high one at that. "Honey, you're burning up. Maybe I should take you to the hospital or a doctor or something."

"No, I'm sure it's just the flu. I woke up this morning feeling this way. Patti covered the shop for me and I've been in bed all day hoping I'd feel better for our special dinner. Now I've ruined everything and I even bought a new dress."

She began to cry as he picked her up and carried her to bed. He gently covered her with her down quilt. "Honey, I'll have to explain the surprise later. It's actually a business thing, so I can't get out of it now. I hate to leave you like this. Should I call Ruth to see if she can stay with you?"

"No. I'll be fine. I just want to sleep. You go and have a good time. Just promise you'll miss me."

"I already do sweetheart." He leaned over her, brushed her hair out of her face, and ran his fingertips down her face. When he kissed her forehead he said, "I'll come by tomorrow. Want me to bring you anything? Juice or something?"

"Maybe some apple or cranberry juice."

"Done. Goodnight, honey." It killed him to leave her.

****

Sandi K. Whipple

When he entered La Virage, his festive mood had been completely altered by Angie's illness and his inability to stay with her through her ordeal. When the day started, he'd been keyed up about the night's celebration and getting to share everything with Angie. Now, all he wanted was to be back in her apartment, holding and comforting her.

Ralph approached him when he entered the banquet room and shook his hand, congratulating him on the finality of the buy-out.

"I must say," Ralph said, "these festivities look to be very entertaining."

Gary looked around the room. Heather had done an incredible job of decorating and arranging everything. The tables were set in a U shape to include a microphone that had been set up in the center. There were embossed name cards at each plate. The head table included Ralph, his mother, his sister and brother-in-law, and an empty chair next to his own without a name card. The flower arrangements were beautiful. He wondered if they'd come from Angie's shop.

The menu included Gary's favorite, filet mignon, which he asked Heather for. There were over fifty people mingling throughout the area. They were all curious about the surprise.

Seeing Gary enter the room, Heather began to organize the crowd. There'd be business first, then dinner and music. She put the wait staff on notice and began shuffling everyone to their seats.

Once everyone was seated, Ralph stood up and announced, "Most of you out there haven't the slightest idea who I am, though many of you have spoken to me on the phone a time or two over the years. I'm Ralph Cragen. I'm Mr. Walgren's attorney and friend. He's been working on a business venture for some time, and I've had the pleasure of handling his legal affairs. As it has now come to be, I guess I'll let him explain the rest. Gary?"

Gary rose and took his turn at the microphone. "Thanks, Ralph, and," turning to the expectant faces, Gary continued, "relax everyone. We're still in business, I didn't sell out, and you all still have a job."

Though everyone laughed, there was no missing the many sighs of relief.

"Actually," Gary went on, "the situation is just the opposite. I've taken on a partner and we've just bought out Pederson's Plumbing and Heating. They have three locations spread over three cities. These locations are now the new offices of Walgren's Heating and Cooling Systems. The name change will be effective shortly."

Everyone applauded.

With both hands in the air Gary said, "Hold it, everyone, there's more. Rather than hire a new crew, we're going to keep Pederson's staff. They've already been notified of the buy-out and have been assured their jobs are secure."

Turning toward the first seats on the right, Gary addressed the occupants, "Katie, you and Lucy will be in charge of coordinating with the Pederson's office staff. I trust your judgment, so I'll leave it up to you how you want to change things around. Just keep me and my new partner up to date. The plumbing part will be new to all of us. I'm sure everyone will welcome all of Pederson's crew and make them feel like part of our family. You've all worked hard over the years and this expansion will be a lot of work for all of us at first. But, further down the road, we'll all be happy and fatter. I think you all know what I mean by that."

Everyone laughed and continued to keep their eyes on Gary.

"Now, before I introduce everyone to Walgren's new partner," holding onto a piece of paper with his hand in the air he continued, "and I have the legal document right here in my hand as proof, I'd like to thank Heather for setting up tonight's festivities. From the confused look on her husband's face, I'd say she really kept this a secret. Heather, everything looks wonderful and if you weren't already married to Tom, I'd marry you myself just for making sure there was steak on tonight's menu." Gary's sister rolled her eyes and his brother-in-law laughed.

"Now, getting to my new business partner, I'm sure everyone knows him. His name is Tom."

Heather began to cry in relief of having to keep the secret for so long from her husband. Tom stared at her. When she nodded her head and he saw her tears, he reached over to kiss her.

"You knew he was doing this and never said a word?" She nodded her head while dabbing at her eyes with her napkin.

Seeing that Tom was a little taken aback by his wife's tears and shocked by the news, Gary attempted to inject some comic relief by saying, "Tom, give her a Kleenex, and come on up here! I'm getting hungry."

Sandi K. Whipple

When he reached the podium, Tom shook Gary's hand and told him how shocked and grateful he was. Loud enough so all would hear, Gary said, "You've earned it, my friend."

Tom made a small speech that included words of praise for his working environment, his wonderful co-workers and, most of all, his gratitude to Gary for such a vote of confidence.

So as not to drag out the speeches, Gary again shook Tom's hand, turned to the diners, and said, "Okay, let's eat. Where's my steak?"

While Gary was finishing his dessert of chocolate mousse, a photographer approached him, explaining he was from the local newspaper. He'd been assigned to cover the event and added that Heather asked him to take a few photos for tomorrow's Sunday edition. Gary accommodated his request and quickly stood next to Heather with Tom on the other side of her. The photographer snapped a couple of shots.

The photographer and Heather then engaged in a conversation about the photos and the article for the paper. Gary gave a cursory thanks to them and returned his attention to his mother who'd been sitting quietly as she watched everyone.

Gary gave her a hug and a kiss on the cheek. "Hi, Mom. Thanks for your support. It would've all been for nothing if you hadn't been here."

She touched his face and told him, "Your father would be so proud of you, Gary. As for me, I need to sew the buttons back on my blouse because they all burst off with pride about an hour ago. By the way," she continued, "may I ask what happened to the surprise introduction?"

Gary's smile suddenly disappeared. "She's sick with a burning fever. I helped her to bed and I think she was dead to the world before I was out the door. I feel like a heel for leaving her like that."

"You did the right thing. But you'll go to her first thing in the morning, yes?"

"If I can wait that long."

His mother understood. "Now, I think you should mingle with this large family of yours. Ralph agreed to give me a ride home, so I'll be leaving soon." Grabbing his arm, she continued, "Gary, I love you."

At the sound of a fake cough, Gary turned and saw his sister and brother-in-law standing in front of his table.

"You snake you," his sister scolded. "You didn't even tell me anything about this deal. I should refuse to ever speak to you again. And I wouldn't, if I weren't so damned proud of you."

His brother-in-law wormed his way between the two of them and shook his hand, saying congratulations.

"So where's the mystery guest?" his sister said with a flippant attitude. "Mom told me you were going to make a surprise introduction. Is it okay to ask the why's and the where's and maybe the who's? And how come the empty seat?"

"No, it is not okay to ask," her husband told her. "Don't be so nosy. Come on, let's go mingle." Grabbing his wife's arm and moving away, he looked back and said, "See you later, Gary."

Sandi K. Whipple

With only a moment to finish his cup of coffee, Gary was approached one more time. Tom and Heather moved to his table and thanked him for a perfect evening.

Gary gave them a pleased smile. "You might not be so grateful for the next few months while we're trying to get everything situated."

With a few more polite conversations and many "Good nights," the festivities were finally over. Being a good host, Gary was the last to leave the restaurant.

As he drove homeward, the excitement of the announcement and the genuine pleasure evidenced by Tom's words and manner seemed to float out the open car window. Gary felt a sense of melancholy and loneliness. He'd been so excited about bringing Angie as the *coup de gras* of the evening. He wanted everyone to see this beautiful creature and understand that she was with him. Not with Carl or Alan, but with him.

He chastised himself for focusing on his inability to show her off instead of worrying about her at home, suffering alone in bed. He told himself he really was a selfish ass.

****

The following morning, Angie was grateful to see Aunt Ruth when she and Frank came by. They brought some breakfast treats, juice, and a newspaper, telling Angie to get lots of rest. Making it a short visit, they left for their Sunday outing.

Angie poured herself a glass of juice, retrieved the tissue box from her bedroom, and sat at the table to read the newspaper. When she turned the page to the local news section, she was suddenly accosted with the large photo of Gary and, *That Woman*. She barely noticed the other man. The caption read: "Above are Henderson and Walgren, the new owners of Walgren's Heating and Cooling. After a major buy-out of Pederson's Plumbing Company, Walgren's is now the largest Heating Cooling and Plumbing business in three states."

The rest of the words appeared to be a blur. So Gary, according to the caption, bought into the business he worked for. Angie assumed the other man must be the owner of Walgrens. Giving him a hasty glance, her eyes were stuck on the woman, the one she'd seen kissing Gary at La Virage. Angie's thoughts became a whirlwind of angry clouds. How could he do that to her? This was the special dinner he had planned? He bought into the business he worked for? Something that wonderful should have been shared with her. Because she'd fallen ill, did he feel he couldn't go alone and had to take that woman?

Angie's heart nearly lurched out of her chest. She now knew where she stood in Gary's life. Carl's words of a few months ago resounded in her head: *Once you know where you stand, you can then decide what to do and get on with your life.*

Angie hated him! Carl was right. He was slime. The tears came in buckets and she bent over from stomach knots.

When a knock sounded at her door, she almost didn't hear through her sobbing. With the paper still crumpled in her hand, she opened the door to see the slime, and screamed, "You bastard. I hate you!"

Throwing the crumpled paper in his face, she bellowed, "Don't you ever come near me again. You're slime, Gary. Do you hear me? You're slime. Don't call me, stay away from my shop, and stay the hell away from me. I don't ever want to set eyes on you again!" With that, she slammed the door in his face.

Banging on the door, Gary hollered, "Angie, let me in. What the hell's the matter with you? What's this all about? Come on, honey, I brought you some juice. Will you please talk to me?" He stood there dumbfounded. What just happened here? He knocked again, hollering through the door.

Still sobbing, Angie yelled, "Go away. I have nothing to say to you, not ever again. You can drop dead for all I care."

She heard him knocking and banging on the door for almost an hour before he finally gave up.

Completely exhausted and emotionally drained, she climbed into bed and sobbed for hours. He had no right to stomp all over her feelings, and he definitely had no right to manipulate her and make her fall in love with him. She'd done nothing to deserve this emotional pain.

Reaching to the bed stand for another tissue, Angie blew her nose, wiped her tears, and vowed: "Starting tomorrow, there'll be no more pain or heartache. I'll forget this ever happened and I'll wipe out all memories of him."

****

Sandi K. Whipple

Nearly two weeks had gone by before she could finally go to bed without crying herself to sleep. During that time, everything she did seemed to be robotic. Patti and Aunt Ruth tried to pry out of her whatever it was that brought on the obvious depression. She told them they were imagining things. Carl also tried by extending several invitations to lunch and dinner, but Angie declined.

Before realizing it, two weeks stretched to four and she still didn't feel good. She felt no excitement or happiness. In addition, when Patti walked into the shop and jabbered a mile a minute, flashing her new engagement ring, Angie's depression was magnified. Though she smiled and feigned happiness for the bride-to-be. She forced herself to be pleasant while assuring Patti that she would have the most beautiful flowers and bridal bouquet ever seen.

The workload in the shop kept them busy with little time for chitchat. Angie was grateful she didn't have to be polite and congenial as she struggled to get through each day.

Early one Sunday morning, as Angie sat finishing the paper and her third cup of coffee, Carl, whom she'd been treating like a stranger, turned up at her door.

"Hi, Carl. Come in," Angie said as she quickly cleared the table.

Carl kicked off her shoes, took off her coat, poured herself a cup of coffee, and sat across from Angie without saying a word.

Angie wondered why her friend was so quiet, because it sure wasn't the norm. "Is something wrong, Carl?" Angie asked.

Sandi K. Whipple

Carl looked Angie straight in the face and said, "You could say that. Want to know what it is? No? Well, I'll tell you anyway. I've had it with you, Angie. Before I leave here, we're going to have it out. I'm tired of you moping around. You cut me short at every turn and refuse to go to lunch or dinner or even come by my house. You've always got an excuse to hang up when I call. You don't want to do anything anymore. Patti says she's been working with a robot. Damn you, Angie, I'm your friend." Carl began to cry. "Don't you dare shut me out. Talk to me."

The stinging words and the emotional energy had the two women crying together.

"Carl, I'm just so miserable," Angie confessed.

"That's sure as hell obvious. It's that guy you're seeing isn't it?'

Angie nodded yes.

Carl slapped her knee and said, "I knew it! Want to tell me what's going on?"

Angie took a deep breath and recounted the scenario of her flu episode and how she had to break the date with him.

"And?" Carl was waiting for more.

"Well, the next morning I found out he left here, picked up another woman, and took her in my place."

"Get out of here! How do you know that?"

"I saw pictures of them together in the newspaper. Before that, when I was having lunch with Aunt Ruth at La Virage, I saw him with the same blonde and they were hugging and kissing. He was with that same woman in the paper, Carl."

Sandi K. Whipple

Carl interrupted Angie by saying, "What paper?" You mean our local rag? I never read it. I let my Jim keep me updated on the spinning of the world."

Angie continued with the story as though Carl had said nothing. "That morning I saw him in the paper, he came by and I told him to go away and never come back. There it is, all of it," she said, lowering her head. "I hate him for doing this to me. You told me once I knew where I stood, I could decide how to handle it and get on with my life. But God, Carl, I can't even function, so how the hell can I get on with my life?"

Carl was slowly shaking her head. "Oh, Angie, I'm so sorry. Boy, this guy is true slime. I don't know what to say to you." With a pause, she added, "I wish I could do something for you. Anything. I feel so helpless. You're my best friend and here I sit unable to do a damned thing to help you."

With a slight grin and hoping to lift Angie's spirits, she continued, "We could just get drunk and bash on slimy men the rest of the day."

With that, Angie did laugh for the first time in weeks. Thank God for Carl. They made small talk for the next several hours and Angie became somewhat animated as she explained her idea of expanding the shop and maybe buying a little house somewhere.

Angie's enthusiasm affected Carl and she began to chatter nonstop. "Angie, that's wonderful. Will you let me help you house hunt?"

With promises to keep Carl in the loop, and to work on her own attitude, Angie felt much better by the time her friend left.

Sandi K. Whipple

CHAPTER THIRTEEN

Tom, the new partner, rattled on in an excited tone. "I'd say we're fairly organized now and things are running smoothly. All five offices have estimates coming up, three weeks of jobs lined up and scheduled, and the Pederson crew has adjusted well. I'm even learning a few plumbing tricks. Katie's working her tail off to keep up. She makes sure the office staff is comfortable and coordinates with each office every day. Heck, she almost threw me out of my own office when I threatened to hire extra help for her, and . . . Gary, have you heard a word I've said?"

Looking up with a start, Gary said, "Honestly, Tom, no, I haven't. Sorry."

"You've been doing nothing but the grunt work for a while, and sometimes for fourteen and sixteen hours a day. Maybe you should take a vacation or something, Gary. If you don't figure out and fix whatever it is that's pulling you apart, you're going to kill yourself. You've even lost weight. We're all worried about you. Want to talk about it?"

With a heavy sigh, Gary placed his elbows on the desk. "To be blunt, Tom, I really miss her. I miss her so much my insides hurt. I really thought we were doing great. I planned to bring her to the company dinner and show her off so everyone would know she was with me. Sort of like 'she's mine' - know what I mean? I even considered proposing to her that night. She got real sick and couldn't make it. The next day I went to her place. She threw a newspaper at me, called me a bastard, and said she never wanted to see me again. For the life of me, Tom, I've no idea what happened or what I did. I tried for almost an hour to get her to open the door but she wouldn't."

Sitting across from Gary's desk, Tom leaned forward and placed a hand on the desktop. "Gee, Gary. I'm really sorry. Is there anything I can do?"

"No, but thanks anyway. I need to work this out on my own, if there's a way to do it."

While Gary struggled to formulate a plan to ease his pain or, he hoped, reconcile with Angie, if at all possible, there was a level of excitement brewing in the flower shop on the other side of town.

****

"Angie, it's for you," Patti said, holding the phone out to her. "It's Alan," she added with a questioning look.

"Hi, Alan. Yes. Really? Oh that's terrific. I know. I understand. No, I won't get too excited. Okay, but please call me as soon as you know. Yes, I will. Goodbye."

She turned to Patti and with an excited voice said, "That was the private investigator. He thinks he might have narrowed things down a little more as to where my brother might be. I would tell you more but I have an appointment and I'm running late. Anyway, I'll be out for a little while, so I'll see you later this afternoon."

"I've got it covered."

Angie headed out to meet Carl for the appointed quick drink and a preview of a property of interest.

Angie was elated when she met Carl at the house and she spoke quite rapidly. "What do you think? It's kind of neat, huh? I think I could make it really cute."

Carl chuckled. "Make it cute? It already is. It's like a European cottage. I just love it. It's the best we've seen yet."

"Well then, I guess it's time to make an offer and go to lunch. How about Di Nido Bistro? Or should we get burgers and go to your house so I can finally meet your kids?"

Carl chose Di Nido Bistro so she could have her luncheon toddy.

At lunch, Angie could think of only her shop expansion. "If they accept my offer, I'll need to start pricing the renovations. You know, racks, shelves, a larger counter, a sizable office, and I'll need to call Chicago to see if I can get some prices on six new flower coolers."

"Why would you get them from Chicago when the biggest cooling and heating business in three states has an office right here in Nasons Grove?"

"I had a bad experience with them so I'd rather deal with someone else."

"Really? What's the jackass's name? Describe him to me and I'll get him fired." Laughing, Carl added, "Where's my cell phone?"

Angie's chatter and her small giggles made Carl smile. She felt proud knowing she'd found a way to bring Angie back to her sunny disposition.

****

Sandi K. Whipple

Angie's offer on the new house was accepted and a flurry of activities filled her days. Before she knew it, she'd become engrossed with numerous tasks and details for moving into her new home.

Amidst unopened boxes and furniture, Angie gently chastised Aunt Ruth. "Will you please slow down? You haven't stopped since the moving truck left. There's no big rush to get it all done today. If you don't sit down for a while, I'm going to call Frank."

Laughing, Aunt Ruth told her, "You can't call him, or anyone else, dear. The phone isn't hooked up yet. But you win. Let's both sit down for a while." When she found an empty space on the sofa, she continued, "Angie, this place is absolutely adorable. Do you have any idea how proud of you I am? If God had seen fit to give me a daughter, it would have been you, I'm certain of it."

Angie reflexively crossed her arms and felt an emotional rush. With a tightening in her throat, she said, "Oh, Aunt Ruth, what a beautiful thing to say."

Aunt Ruth's endearing words made Angie's mind wander to her mother. She placed an arm around Aunt Ruth's shoulders and said, "I know we've never really talked much about my mother, but could you tell me something about her? Something that might help me understand why she did what she did?"

The two women settled into the soft cushions and Aunt Ruth began a little story. "Darling, no one could ever come close to explaining or understanding what Sylvia did. I do know that when she married your father, she thought she would live happily ever after, like a fairy tale. She expected to have a white picket fence, a family, and basically, a storybook life. That was unrealistic, of course, but then, she always did live in her own little fantasy world."

As she spoke, her eyes seemed to shine brighter. Aunt Ruth continued, "When your brother was born, she was so happy and elated that a team of firemen couldn't have brought her back down to the ground."

She continued, "Your father wasn't a rich man, but he made a decent living as a carpenter. They weren't poor, but there weren't a whole lot of extras either. When you came along, your mother talked about nothing but pink dresses, a pink bedroom, dolls, and little girl stuff. Your mother bought every girlie thing she saw. That's when the fighting started."

Aunt Ruth continued her now sad story with a heavy sigh. "It wasn't long before the ugly words turned to hitting. At first, it was just a few slaps, but every fight and argument grew worse than the one before. Your dad went ballistic every time your mother went on her spending sprees. I begged her to leave him before he really hurt her, but she wouldn't. She said she loved him, no matter what he did to her. He took the checkbook and had her removed from the account, giving him complete control over her. She couldn't even buy groceries because he didn't want her to have change in her pocket. He started drinking and before long, it was an every Friday occurrence."

Seeing the effect her words were having, Aunt Ruth felt Angie needed to know the entire truth so she went on with her story. "Your father drank every weekend, all weekend long, and the hitting got worse. The first few times he hit your brother in a drunken rage, your mother was devastated and threatened to kill him. He beat her even more and her depression worsened. When the abuse escalated, your father drank more and, of course, as he drank more, well, you see the cycle?"

Angie could only nod as she waited for the unhappy and disturbing revelations to continue.

Aunt Ruth squirmed on the sofa while she tried to find a more comfortable position. Placing her hands in her lap, she continued with a somber tone in her voice. "One day, in a drunken rage, your father slapped you. When Sylvia told me, she had the strangest look on her face. She said very determinedly, that if he ever hit you again, she would kill him. I never dreamed it would come to that. So many times I begged her to leave him. When she didn't, I just gave up asking. When I heard she'd shot and killed him, then turned the gun on herself, I thought, maybe if I hadn't given up, my sister would be alive today."

Aunt Ruth's quiet tears almost ripped Angie apart.

"Please don't cry, Aunt Ruth. I'm sorry I asked you to tell me all this ugly stuff and made you revisit the horror."

"There's no reason to apologize, dear. Sometimes it's good to finally get things out in the open."

In an attempt to change the subject, Aunt Ruth brightened and said, "Goodness, look at the time. Are you getting hungry? When Frank gets here, we can send him to the deli for sandwiches. And, we'll have another set of hands. I find it hard to believe there are so many boxes. Was all this stuff in that tiny apartment?"

Sandi K. Whipple

"It was. Can you believe it?" Angie said, trying to sound hearty.

****

The construction crew worked steadily in Angie's shop. Amidst noise and dust, as they knocked down walls and tore out floors, everything in the shop had thick plastic walls around it.

The foreman recommended a treated and painted concrete floor for the working area, telling her it would be cost-effective and low maintenance. He told her she could pick any color and even have a design. She decided against the design. When he suggested she close off the center back wall and move the door to the corner, she vetoed that idea. Gary put that door in and it was staying. Why? She didn't know.

A week later, the electrical work was completed along with the walls. Thank goodness they were no longer tripping over extension cords.

With the powder blue concrete floor finished and her spacious office set up in the far corner, she was thrilled to be ahead of schedule.

Frank and Aunt Ruth showed up to inspect the completed work. "Angie, now that I've sold my store and I'm retired, I get restless. Why don't you let me help you? I'd be happy to assemble your shelves and racks. Just let me know when and show me where you want them."

With an enthusiastic pitch in her voice, Aunt Ruth injected, "Frank, darling, what a wonderful idea. Aren't you a love? Great idea, Angie, don't you think?"

"I'd be more than grateful. I built up some pretty bad blisters last time I tried," Angie said as she rubbed her hands.

Frank went on, "You need to use an electric drill and driver attachment. It makes the job real fast and easy. I'll get you one and show you how to use it. It'll be an early birthday present."

Hearing his offer, Aunt Ruth gave him a scornful look. "You don't buy tools for women as birthday gifts," she told him with a chuckle.

Later that day, Frank finished assembling the shelves while Ruth set up three folding chairs and a card table for their pizza lunch.

As the lunched on Pizza Frank asked Angie, "So how are you managing to keep up with business with all this construction is going on?"

Between bites, Angie told him, "Patti and Carrie, the new girl I hired, adore each other." In fact, Angie was elated when she saw how well they worked together. "They take turns working out of my house and the little bit of room we're still using here. The walk in traffic has pretty much ceased because of the way the place looks of course. But between the three of us and Chuck and the van, we're keeping up with all the outside and telephone orders. Without walk in traffic, I'm not selling any nick-knacks or antiques. The girls never complain, but I know they're as exhausted as I am.

Angie closed her eyes, took a deep breath, and said, "I'm a little nervous. I hope I haven't bitten off more than I can chew."

"You'll be fine, dear." Aunt Ruth told her. "This expansion is not only a great business move, but it seems to have been good for you mentally. You've perked up quite a bit between working the shop and setting up your new house. For several weeks there, Frank and I were really worried about you, weren't we, Frank?" she asked.

Not waiting for a response, she continued to speak for the two of them. "You seemed so hollow and distant. But, my dear, you have nothing to worry about. You have your smarts, your drive, and you have us, doesn't she, Frank?" This time she paused, allowing him to add his comments.

"Yes, she does," he said with a smile.

The day had finally come to an end, and Angie felt a little more energized. She was happy to see Carl who came by to see the new changes. "Your shop is blue, your entire house is blue, I guess you're just a blue kind of girl, huh?" Carl told her.

Angie laughed.

"I can't believe how well you've mixed the different shades, even at the shop. The concrete floor is beautiful. With two kids, I wouldn't mind having that in my kitchen." Laughing at her own humor, Carl added, "But I'm sure glad you're not still blue. I can't tell you how happy I am to have my friend back."

Angie hugged her. "Let's go eat. I'm getting hungry. How about the deli?"

"Can't we go some place where we can have a drink?"

Angie laughed as she headed for the door. "Carl, you're incorrigible"

Over dinner, switching the conversation from the shop, Carl told Angie how beautifully she'd decorated her new house. "I can't believe you made the place look so great with all that used stuff you bought. Don't you dare ever let my Jim know you did that. He'll never let me buy anything new again."

    Angie smiled at the compliment. "Frank was a big help. He had the buyer of his store tell him any time someone brought in something nicer than normal. He even repaired and cleaned up a few things himself, thinking I might like them. I think he went so far as to bamboozle the owner into selling them to me for less. I think a little coaching from Aunt Ruth may have entered the equation somewhere," she laughed. "It saved me a lot of money since I hadn't counted on spending so much for the new coolers."

    "As smart as you are about business and money, I still don't understand why you wouldn't get them locally. I know they'd have been cheaper."

    "Please don't go there again, Carl."

    She didn't want to see or deal with Gary again or admit to anyone that she still hurt and dreamed about him. She wouldn't tell anyone she was wondering if he was missing her half as much as she was missing him.

    "Earth to Angie. Come back, girl," Carl said as she waved her hand in front of Angie's face. "Where were you? So, is it yes or no?"

    "I'm sorry, I was thinking about Patti and the new girl I hired and how well they get along." She hoped Carl wouldn't see through that fib. "Yes or no what?"

    "Will you let Ruth and I organize a grand opening for you?"

    Angie sensed a bit of uneasiness at the idea. "I'd rather not. I've been in business for close to a year and

Sandi K. Whipple

I'm already known and established. I think a grand opening at this point would be tacky."

"Okay then, I'll cover my mouth with duct tape and quit asking."

Laughing, Angie said, "God, Carl, I love you."

****

The next afternoon, Patti and Carrie were both working out of her house, and Chuck was in the van making deliveries.

When the extra coolers arrived, the men had to struggle through the front door because the back door was too small. Most of the floor was concrete and the customer service area was covered with carpeting. Angie was sick with worry that they'd rip it, or for that matter, scratch the newly painted concrete floor.

She stood by the huge windows in the front of the shop and watched the men come in and out. She happened to look across the street and was shocked to see Gary leaning against a building with his arms crossed, watching the delivery. Why in the world was he doing that? In an instant, all the past hurt feelings hit her like a steamroller. Should she walk across the street to ask him what was so interesting? No, definitely not. Best to let sleeping dogs lie.

She felt the need for distraction so, turning away, she strolled into her office. She sat at her desk shuffling papers, trying to keep herself busy so she wouldn't think about him. But it wasn't working. She put her face in her hands and began taking deep breaths so she could stay calm.

"Hello, Angie."

Her head jerked up. The shock of his presence made her hesitate but she finally responded. "Hello, Gary, how are you?"

"I'm doing okay, how about you? Congratulations on your expansion. The place looks great. I see your cute little apartment is gone. You staying with Ruth now?" Gary was rattling.

"No. I bought a house. I think I'm a little too old to be living at home. By the way, congratulations to you too, on your new partnership I mean. I read about it in the paper a few months ago."

"Thanks." Gary tried to remain calm. "So, you've been keeping busy?"

"Yes. I've been going out with my friends, setting up this new shop, and settling into my new house."

"How come you didn't use Walgren's for your new coolers, Angie?"

Angie couldn't believe he really asked her that. "Don't do this, Gary. You already know the answer to that."

Not wanting to continue a cold and evasive conversation, Gary put his hands in his pockets. "Can we go someplace and talk?"

"I don't think we have anything to talk about. Besides, I'm very busy. I have a lot of things to do. I hardly have time for idle chitchat." Angie began to shuffle papers on her desk in an effort to calm her nerves and prevent him from seeing her hands shake.

Leaning on her desk, Gary asked, "Is that what you think it would be? Idle chitchat?"

She refused to answer him and shuffled more papers.

Not wanting to plead but yet get his point across, Gary gambled and said, "I've missed you, Angie."

Angie raised herself from her chair and looked directly into his eyes. "I'm sorry to hear that, Gary. If you'll excuse me now, I have things to do. Good to see you though. Goodbye."

He knew from her tone of voice he couldn't engage her in conversation. He'd been dismissed rather curtly so he turned and walked away.

As he walked out the door, Angie wanted to cry, but she sure couldn't break down in front of the work crew and she couldn't leave the shop yet.

Her thoughts tormented her. She hadn't seen him in weeks. Actually almost two months. Why did he have to show up? Why did he say he was missing her when he had the blonde to keep him company? Hadn't she told him she hated him and to never come back? Didn't she mean it when she'd said she never wanted to set eyes on him again? Right now, she hated herself for letting him get to her this way. She returned to work and tried to forget him. There weren't enough papers to shuffle, or work to make it easy.

****

The next morning her new delivery van was painted and delivered. Angie didn't get much of a trade-in on the old one and was sorry she hadn't just donated it for a write-off. Chuck used the van to bring back everything for the shop that was still at her house.

Sandi K. Whipple

Patti and Carrie reorganized the shelves and put things away while they took turns with walk-in customers and the phone. Angie spent hours filling the new coolers with the huge flower delivery.

At 5 O'clock when Angie finally locked the door, she just stood in the middle of the shop and looked around. It was amazing how big it was without the apartment. She decided that as hard as it was to keep running the business during construction, it had all been worth it.

A week later one of her larger hotel accounts had chosen to put fresh flowers in every room, each day. When she suggested it to her other hotel accounts, they jumped at the idea. She even picked up a new account – for stocking the floral and gift shop at the hospital in town.

With the business load, Angie had the phone company install three roll-over lines. She was amazed to see a big increase in her paper work. What she thought to be a huge office was soon becoming cramped with file cabinets. All in all, she really had no complaints. She loved the activity of the newer shop, and adored her new house, even if she had to tolerate the many lonely nights.

Someone calling her name caught her attention. "Angie, line three is for you. It's your aunt."

"Thank you, Carrie." Grabbing the phone she said, "Hi, Aunt Ruth. What's up?"

"Dear, if you could spare an evening next week, Frank and I would like to take you to dinner. Frank wants to try the La Virage, since he's never been there. He wants to talk to you about something, though I can't imagine what, and he refuses to share it with me. I told him he was being impossible, but he laughed at me. I tried to act angry with him but I think he saw right through me. So, can you join us one night next week?"

Angie was tickled by the antics of her aunt. "Aunt Ruth, you're so funny. I'd love to. You pick the night and let me know."

"All right, dear, I'll check with Mr. Impossible himself and get back to you." She was giggling when she hung up.

Angie wasn't thrilled about meeting them at the La Virage and wished she'd suggested some place different. La Virage brought back memories she didn't want to entertain. Her aunt and Frank were important to her, though, so she had to go.

She left her office and walked back into the shop where she found Patti, who for the moment wasn't busy. "Okay, Ms. Right Arm of Mine, the time has come. You need to make a decision on the flowers for your wedding, and preferably today. I need to start designing and preparing and, as you know, there isn't much time left."

"Angie, I've got so many things going on, my brain is starting to feel like mush. Could I just talk you into doing it for me? Your work is great, and I've never seen anything leave here that wasn't beautiful. Even my mom says so. I'm willing to beg if I have to, please?"

Flattered by Patti's appraisal, Angie said, "I suppose I could, if you trust my judgment."

Patti gave Angie a big hug. "Oh, thank you. By the way, I want to ask you one more thing. I know I told you once I graduated and got married I'd be leaving, but can I retract that? I'd like to stay here until I decide what it is I really want to do." Giggling, she added, "Besides, I don't think you'd make it without me."

"Patti, you're one of a kind. Of course you can stay. I was sad at the thought of you leaving me." Angie adored her. "Now get back to work."

Angie walked into her office and closed the door. She didn't want Patti to see her cry. That phrase, *sad at the thought of you leaving me*, hit her like a slap in the face. Hadn't her mother left her? Hadn't her brother left her? And hadn't her *Adonis* left her?

Catching herself, Angie realized she hadn't thought of the word *Adonis* for a long time. For months, whenever she thought of him, and after she stopped pining away her days, the only word she associated with his name was Carl's favorite word, '*slime*'. God, would she ever stop missing him? It took her almost half an hour to stop crying.

CHAPTER FOURTEEN

Following a few days of flurried activities, Angie discovered she was looking forward to a quiet dinner with Aunt Ruth and Frank even though she still wished it wasn't at the La Virage.

Entering the restaurant and looking through the crowd, her eyes immediately located the table where Gary and Blondie had been together. Why was she tormenting herself? Did she expect to see them sitting there again? Chastising herself, she forced her thoughts to the only reason she was here, and that was her aunt and Frank. She needed to get a grip and stay in the moment.

Mr. Solis greeted her. "Ah, Miss Gibbons, how very nice to see you."

"Thank you, Mr. Solis. I'm meeting someone."

"Yes, indeed you are and I've been instructed to watch for your arrival. Follow me, please."

After hugging Aunt Ruth and Frank, Angie was seated. Before she could say anything to them, Angie felt her aunt's hand on her arm. Aunt Ruth turned to Frank and said, "All right, Frank, let's have it. I've been waiting for almost a week now to find out what's so hush-hush about this dinner."

Angie and Frank laughed at her antics, knowing she was trying hard to act perturbed, but they saw right through her.

Frank started laughing. "Ruth, couldn't we have a nice dinner and a nice visit first?"

Sandi K. Whipple

"Yes, Frank, you're right. Sorry for my outburst," Aunt Ruth said as she lowered her chin and pouted.

Frank laughed and took her hand in his. "No, you're not, Ruth, but it was a nice thing to say anyway."

Later, Frank commented on the restaurant's décor and ambiance. He went on to say their meal had certainly validated the restaurant's great reputation.

Her impatience rising, Aunt Ruth chimed in. "Okay, Frank, we've talked, drank, and eaten, so let's have it."

Frank laughed heartily. "God, Ruth, I love you." While Ruth blushed at his words, he reached across the table, and took her hand in his as he spoke: "That's one of the reasons I've asked Angie to this dinner.

Speaking to Angie, Frank said, "I guess it's no big secret that I'm in love with your aunt." He then began to explain a little about his life. He told Angie, "My late wife and I never had children so when she passed away, I was completely alone. I dealt with it, accepting that life just dealt me a lousy hand, and that's the way it was. Well, I was wrong. Life shouldn't be lived with such negative resignation." Putting an arm around Aunt Ruth's shoulders, he continued, "It took Ruth to make me realize that."

Offering a little more insight, Frank leaned forward and looked directly at Angie. "I know I'm pretty quiet sometimes and don't always say what's on my mind, but tonight is different. I asked you here, Angie, to ask you if you'd be upset if I asked your aunt to marry me."

Sandi K. Whipple

With a gasp and a hand flying to her mouth, Aunt Ruth became an instant waterfall of tears. She was only able to whisper, "Oh, Frank."

Angie's eyes filled with tears. She looked at him and smiled. "Gee, Frank, what took you so long?" She rushed around the table and hugged him and then her aunt.

Frank leaned toward Ruth. "Ruth, darling, I was actually asking you at the same time. You haven't responded, and I'm getting nervous here. Will you please quit blubbering and give me an answer?"

She just smiled at him and whispered, "I love you, Frank."

"Is that a yes, Ruth? Because if it isn't, you're paying for dinner."

When the emotions over dinner subsided, the bill was paid and Angie drove home.

****

After a long and soothing bath, her mind drifted back to the dinner with Frank and Ruth. How obvious it was they were in love. She was happy for them and what a sweet way Frank had proposed. She felt secure knowing her aunt would be safe and happy with him.

Frank hit the nail on the head with that phrase about life dealing one a lousy hand. How often had she felt that way about her own life? She suddenly felt cold and alone.

She tried to block the sadness and thought about her need for a cat, a goldfish, or maybe a dog. Or maybe she needed Gary, her very own precious *Adonis*. He wasn't hers though, was he? God, how she missed him.

If she could just erase the past, she would run to him with her arms wide open. But his moods, his damned "see ya," all the time, and his ability to just leave her and run straight to the arms of another woman, told her she couldn't forget the past. Was there more than one woman? Did Blondie have to share him too? Well, all Angie knew for sure was, she couldn't share him. Not with any woman, ever. Considering Blondie and the past circumstances, that meant just one thing. She would never have him.

****

The next afternoon, with their feet tucked comfortably under them, Angie and Carl were cuddled in each corner of Angie's sofa. They'd finally found some girl time.

With great enthusiasm, Angie brought Carl up to date on the shop's events and Patti's wedding.

"You should have seen Patti. Her dress was the most beautiful I've ever seen. Her mother outdid herself on the reception. I can't possibly imagine what it cost. They even served prime rib. And can you imagine honeymooning in Paris?"

With a heavy sigh, Angie continued, "I miss her already. It's going to be a long three weeks without her, but thank God she's not leaving me too. She's coming back."

Patting Angie's hand, Carl tried to comfort Angie. "I know how close you and Patti are, Angie, and

Sandi K. Whipple

I'm happy for her too, but you're rambling and we both know what that means. You need to talk to me, girlfriend. I can tell something's bothering you lately. And what did you mean by *leaving me too*?"

With a slight pout on her face, Angie confessed, "I guess watching Patti so happily married, and with Aunt Ruth marrying Frank soon, I'm just feeling lonely. My parents left me, my brother left me, and the Slime left me for Blondie. I just feel so alone sometimes, Carl"

Carl placed her hand on Angie's knee. "You're still miserable without him, aren't you? You've been hiding it all along, and I didn't even see it. Great friend I am."

"Don't say that, Carl, you are my friend. My best friend."

"You still want this guy, don't you? Even though he treated you like crap and he's a cheating slime, you still miss him?"

"I guess I do. When he showed up at the shop, I thought I'd faint. Then when he left, I felt like I'd been punched in the stomach."

"What?" Carl said as she sat straight up. "You never told me that. Why didn't you tell me that? More smut about the grubby slime and you said nothing? Let me get us a beer and you can tell me all."

By the time Angie finished relating the events of that day, she was crying. "So I sent him away again. I look back now and wish to God I hadn't."

Knowing Angie needed some cheerful conversation, Carl tried to be light-hearted. "Why don't you just go over to his house after dark in a black negligee, tell him he holds the secret to make you quit hating him, and just get it on? I'm kidding, of course. But if he told you he misses you and you still miss him, maybe you should talk it out and forgive and forget. Just go over to his place and do it."

"I can't, Carl."

"Why not?"

With a schoolgirl look on her face, Angie told her, "Because I don't know where he lives. We always ended up back at my place. Then he usually spent the night. I never thought to even ask him where he lived." After a moment of silence, Angie added, "Let's have one more beer and go eat somewhere."

Carl couldn't help laughing at her friend. "Angie, tell me, how can someone always be hungry, and never have food in the house?"

Sandi K. Whipple

CHAPTER FIFTEEN

When Patti entered the shop after her return from her honeymoon, Angie gave her a big hug with her words bubbling over. "Hi! Welcome home. I want to hear all about the honeymoon. Don't look at me like that, you goof. You know I just mean Paris, not the personal stuff."

Their laughter and giggling filled the shop for hours and in between phone orders and floral preparations, Angie heard about the Eiffel Tower and all of Paris. She even thumbed through dozens of photographs.

"Okay, Patti, I need to leave, but first, I have to share business details. I've made a schedule out for the next two weeks, and you and Carrie will both be working a lot of hours. I have a convention to attend this week in Chicago. When I get back, I'll be busy getting things together for my aunt's wedding. It's going to be a small affair, but I'd like to make it extra nice."

Shuffling through papers and arranging them in a neat stack on her desk, Angie continued, "While I'm gone, you'll be in charge of all the delivery orders since you've been doing them longer than Carrie. Why don't you have Carrie take care of the drop-ins and phone orders, and I'd like you to take care of the banking."

Seeing the expression on Patti's face, Angie stopped shuffling papers, placed her hands on the desk, and looked at Patti. "I realize I just gave you a ton of information. Are all these okay with you?"

Grinning at the serious note in Angie's voice, Patti reassured her. "I've got it covered, Angie. You know I can handle it."

"Okay, so you have the work book, the daily delivery schedules, the name and number of the hotel I'll be staying at, the ..."

Patti told her louder than was probably necessary, "Chill out. I've been doing this stuff for a year. I paid attention, you know. Just go and don't worry."

"I know you can, Patti, I'm sorry. I guess I'm just a worrier by nature."

"You're going to find a little time to party hearty in Chicago, aren't you?"

"I think not. See you when I get back." With that, Angie left the shop and she wistfully hoped she'd also left her worries behind as well.

****

Following an uneventful two hour drive, Angie arrived in Chicago and was delighted that the convention hotel had been easy to locate. The check-in process was less time-consuming than she'd anticipated and the cheerful bellman not only assisted her with the luggage but led her to a well-appointed room. He held the door open for her and when she walked to the far wall and looked out the picture windows, she was dazzled at the incredible view of the city. Angie thought for sure she'd enjoy her stay, gain some feedback, and learn some new things to warrant the $170-per-night price tag.

She unpacked her suitcase, put her toiletries in the bathroom, and sat down at the desk that faced the panoramic view outside her window. She called Aunt Ruth, as promised, and told her she'd arrived, safe and sound.

After chatting for a few minutes, Angie said goodbye and rummaged through her convention packet. Eager to familiarize herself with the list of activities, she examined the convention brochure. As she scanned the offerings of the first day's events, she began to relax and enjoy the peace and quiet. Maybe this change of pace would be good for her, maybe even fun, she thought.

At the end of the second day, Angie went back to her room, sat at the desk, and pondered the activities of the convention. She was disappointed to realize the first day had been a bit boring. The second day wasn't much better. When she thought about the costs for the convention and the hotel, she decided to stick it out and at least try to get her money's worth.

At the end of the fourth and final day, she visualized the long drive home. After a busy day, she knew she'd be tired and she hated driving in the dark. With that in mind, she chose to have dinner in the hotel dining room, take a hot bath, leave an early wake-up call, and drive home in the morning. When she entered the dining room, she requested a table in the far back corner. The waiter had just delivered a glass of Merlot when she heard, "How's the wine?"

Without any thought, Angie knew instantly whose voice just jolted her. With a racing pulse, she turned her head slowly and looked up to see that incredible face and those flashing black eyes that she'd been sorely missing. Not wanting to appear too eager and, in order to maintain her composure, she took a few moments to respond. Holding her glass of wine, she said as nonchalantly as possible, "I thought you lived in Nasons Grove. What brings you to Chicago?"

Gary struggled to keep his voice steady. "My mother had an appointment with a specialist and it's too far for her to drive by herself, so I brought her. We're staying here." Without asking, he pulled the chair from the table. "May I?"

Without waiting for an answer, Gary sat in the chair across from Angie. The waiter magically appeared, placed a second setting and menu, and asked for Gary's cocktail order.

Not taking his eyes off Angie, Gary told the waiter, "A draft beer, please." Looking directly into her eyes, he said, "You look great, Angie. I saw in the lobby there was a florists' convention here. Is that why you're in Chicago?"

Holding her glass with both hands in front of her face, she replied, "It is. I must say, though, I'm pretty disappointed. I've never been to a convention before, and I had high expectations. I thought I'd learn all kinds of new stuff, but I think I know more than most of these yoyo's." She put her glass down on the table with a coy expression on her face. "Oh, quit laughing, Gary, I'm serious. I'm thinking it was a big waste of time and money. Between the fee for the convention and the cost of the hotel, I'll be eating hamburger with macaroni and cheese for six months."

Sensing she was beginning to relax, Gary asked, "Is it okay if I stay and have dinner here, with you?" With a slight laugh he added, "Don't worry. I won't add to your hamburger and macaroni demise. I'll pay for my own dinner. Yours too, if you'll let me."

She knew it wasn't a good idea to sit here with him, but she couldn't bring herself to say no.

"Sure, why not? Especially if you're buying. But what about your mother?"

"She's resting in her room. So, where were we? Oh yeah. You don't have to convince me you're smarter than most of these —what did you call them?—*yoyos*? I watched you take a mediocre flower shop and turn it into a thriving business. Most first-time business owners struggle and never expand let alone as quickly as you did. I give you a lot of credit, Angie."

She felt a sense of pride with his compliment. "Thank you. That was a nice thing to say. So tell me about your new partnership. Things working out okay for you?"

With a more serious tone in his voice, Gary responded, "The first few months were rough, trying to reorganize and reschedule, but everything seems to be running pretty smoothly now. We're busy as hell and sometimes I work until nine or ten and just go home and crash." Hoping to get the subject matter to a more personal level, Gary stalled the conversation by signaling the waiter. When he arrived, Gary asked, "Would you please bring the lady another glass of wine and another beer for me?"

When the waiter left to retrieve the drink order, Angie said, "I really wasn't going to have any more wine, but I guess one more won't hurt."

Sandi K. Whipple

With a mischievous grin, Gary lowered his voice, "You know, as long as I'm paying, you could let me get you drunk so I can try to take advantage of you."

When he saw Angie's eyebrows go up and her face turn pale, he quickly added, "That was supposed to be a joke, Angie. Maybe it was in poor taste. I'm sorry. Maybe you're right, maybe I am slime."

With that, she spat wine all over the table and they broke into raucous laughter.

The unintentional comic relief provided a relaxing mood and made for a comfortable dinner. They drifted into pleasant conversation and, for all appearances it seemed nothing had ever gone wrong between them.

When dinner was finished, Gary paid the check as promised and casually walked Angie to her room. Knowing it was a daring move, she explained that her room was huge, and even held a small refrigerator. She gingerly invited him in for a drink.

Without hesitation, Gary accepted. "Sure, thanks."

Angie placed her purse on the desk and turned toward the small refrigerator. Gary ambled toward the large windows and stood gazing out at the panorama of the Chicago city lights. Gently, so as not to break his apparent nostalgia, Angie placed a cold bottle of beer in his hand and stood by his side.

Without turning, Gary said, "Nice view from here. My mother can't handle heights so our rooms are on the ground floor."

Angie too was gazing at the night lights. "Well, as pleased as I am with the view, I didn't ask for this room. I agreed to the cheapest room available at the time I booked it – and even then I had to take a Valium and lie down."

He was laughing at her when she smiled and asked, "Why are you laughing? You've been it doing it since you sat at the table in the dining room."

"I'm laughing because you say funny things and generally, when I do, you laugh too. I love to see you laugh, Angie, and I miss hearing it."

Sensing his own vulnerability, Gary drained the last sip of beer. "Thanks for the beer. Housekeeping counts them, you know, and you'll be charged for it. Want me to leave the money for it, or maybe a Valium?"

Laughing, they walked to the door. Before turning the doorknob, Gary turned to look at her. "I'd like to kiss you goodnight, Angie."

She looked up at him but remained silent. Gary told himself she hadn't said no so he gently put his arms around her with the intent of kissing her on the lips, nothing more. When she reached up and put her arms around his neck, everything changed and Gary's heart began to pound.

The anger over the transgressions Angie thought him guilty of began to melt away. Although she was skittish about returning to the familiar territory that had inflicted such emotional turmoil upon her, she threw her concerns to the wind and her tongue began to seek his. Her entire body ached for him.

After kissing for what seemed an eternity, Gary pulled his head up to lay gentle kisses on her eyes and in her hair. He was almost breathless. "God, Angie, I've missed you. I can't get you out of my mind no matter how hard I try. I think about you all day, every day. Then I dream about you at night. Why can't we work out whatever it is that's keeping us apart? Are you as miserable as I am?"

"Probably more, and I've missed you more than I can say. Stay with me tonight, Gary. Please?"

With a small stab of fear in his heart, Gary quietly asked, "Are you sure it's what you want Angie?"

Her kiss told him she was beyond sure. He moved her toward the bed. Gently and slowly he began to remove her clothing. Nothing could make him rush this night. He intended to savor every precious moment because his craving for their lovemaking was not going to be quickly satisfied.

His small, light and gentle kisses over her face and neck were giving Angie goose bumps. Her blouse and slacks slowly settled on the floor.

Gary kept her standing while he continued to cover her with his soft kisses. His arms reached behind her as he kissed her neck. He unhooked her bra, pulled it away, and tossed it toward her other clothes on the floor. He held her lacy panties on both sides, and, as he slowly went to his knees, gently pulled them down with him, lifting one foot and then the other. Gazing at her complete nakedness, Gary inhaled her beauty with his eyes and for a moment, he could only stare at her. His heart began to beat faster and the air in the room became oppressive as he inhaled deeply. He felt his temperature rise and his skin was hot and sultry. Her magnificent body and his deep feelings for her nearly brought tears to his eyes.

Sandi K. Whipple

He gently backed her to the bed, sat her down, and began removing his own clothes. All the while Angie watched him in a mesmerized state. She could sense a fire awakening in her and igniting unbearable heat throughout her entire body.

He added his clothing to the array on the floor and lowered himself to his knees in front of her. He took her face in his hands. Their kiss was long, slow, and passionate. He moved to her neck and shoulders, kissed one side and then the other. Gary lifted her hand, kissed the top and played his tongue over the palm. One at a time, he took her fingers into his mouth and sucked them. Reaching up and taking a breast firmly in each hand, he kissed one, then the other, moving back and forth, kissing them with only his lips.

With her head flung back and her eyes closed by the sensations of his touch, Angie lifted her arms and wove her fingers through his hair. He covered a breast with his warm mouth. She gasped, inhaling as much air as her lungs would allow.

That sound, that glorious gasp of hers, sent waves of thunder through his body and settled in his groin. He moved from one breast to the other, teasing each nipple with his tongue. He gently sucked one for a brief moment and then, switching to the other, increased the pressure. As he teased and nibbled her flesh with his teeth, her throaty murmurings became more intense. Tasting her and hearing her moans of pleasure mirrored his many dreams of their lovemaking. When the sucking and nibbling subsided, her eyes were still closed. He gently laid her on her back with her feet still touching the floor.

Sandi K. Whipple

Kissing the tops of her soft white thighs, then the sides, he slowly moved to the warmth of her inner legs. Shivers of heat shot up her spine, and her desires began to spin almost out of control. She tried to sit upright but he gently held her shoulders on the bed and said, "Relax, Angie, and let me make love to you."

Her woman's innermost point of desire began to swell under the sensuous movements of his warm mouth and tongue. As his tongue caressed her, she became lost in her own world.

Knowing she was close, Gary moved his mouth to her thighs, kissing and fondling her as he waited for her breathing and panting to slow. When he sensed her calmness, his mouth and tongue reignited her desire and she was once again transported to that other world. Twice more he pushed her cravings to the edge, then stopped.

Grasping his hair with nails digging into his scalp, Angie pleaded, "Gary, please, I can't take this."

"Yes, you can, my love."

Lifting her, he placed her in the center of the bed and covered her body with his, propping his weight on his elbows. He showered her face and hair with wet kisses. He started stroking as if he were in her, but still refused to mold their bodies. She began to match him stroke for stroke. She moved from side to side as if begging him to enter her.

Using his knee to separate her legs, he still refused the release of her wet-hot desire. Her moaning and squirming became louder and stronger. He rose to his knees and pulled one of her legs toward his mouth, licking her foot and calf. Placing that leg over his shoulder, he raised the other toward his mouth. With both of her legs now over his shoulders, he barely entered her, stroking in and out with only an inch or so of himself. A little at a time, the strokes entered deeper, then deeper.

She tried reaching behind him to pull him into her, but her reach was too short. When he felt she could stand no more of the teasing torture, he entered her as deeply as possible, and then he slowly pulled out of her. Repeating the same sensual move over and over, his pace began to quicken. When she screamed his name, he was plunging deep inside her over and over again. Their release was simultaneous, loud, emotional, and seemed everlasting.

Gasping for air with a pounding heart, Gary fell to Angie's side and inhaled deeply. As his mind began to clear, Angie brushed her hair from her eyes, turned on her side and snuggled into his arm. Their hot bodies, glued together by wet skin, formed a physical bond and their hearts perceived a new cohesion.

Emotions welled up in Angie's heart and with no forethought, she asked, "Am I, Gary?"

"Are you what, sweetheart?"

"Your love?"

"You are," Gary whispered. He tightened his arms around Angie and sleep came to them quickly.

The morning light was flooding her room when the ringing phone awakened them. Gary lay half asleep as Angie spoke on the phone.

"What is it, Carrie? Is everything okay at the shop? It's too early to be open yet. No, it's okay. Just tell me what he said. Thank you for letting me know, but you didn't need to set your alarm and get up early for this. Calm down, Carrie, it's okay that you forgot to call last night. I'll take care of it. Yes, I have his number." Not sure what today would bring, she added, "I'll try to be home today before the shop closes. Otherwise, I'll see you tomorrow, bye."

When he heard *just tell me what he said*, Gary sat up. After last night, he knew he had to keep his jealous temper in check. After all, "he" might be a client.

Angie placed the phone back in the cradle, turned back to Gary, and wrapped her arms around him. "I'm hungry. You need to feed me."

Gary shook his head and laughed in her face. "When aren't you hungry? If you want me to feed you, then you need to let me get up, unless the sustenance you have in mind doesn't come from room service."

She pretended to hit him on the arm. When she stood up, he casually asked, "Everything okay at the shop?"

"Yes. Carrie just wanted to give me a message since she spaced out last night and forgot to call; she thought it might be important."

Carefully choosing his words, Gary asked, "So it wasn't pressing or important and all is A-okay?"

"Sure. It was just Alan. He wants me to call him. Carrie said he sounded a little upset that he couldn't reach me."

Gary sat straight up and started throwing on his clothes. He thought to himself, one of her damned boyfriends again and she couldn't even be subtle about which one.

Sandi K. Whipple

Gary's body language told of an urgency that alarmed Angie. She tried to keep her voice calm as she asked, "Are you okay? Is something the matter?"

Gary continued to dress and with a gruff tone, said, "No, not a damned thing is the matter, but I got to tell you, babe, after last night, I sure as hell didn't expect this."

With shock in her voice, Angie said, "Expect what? What's the matter with you?"

With a rising voice, he angrily told her, "Nothing's the matter with me. Nothing at all. Too bad I can't say the same for you."

As Gary headed for the door, Angie screamed out, "Don't you dare leave me again, Gary. If you do, it will be the last..." and she heard the door close.

She couldn't move! She stood staring at the closed door, unable to focus or discern a thought. Minutes passed and she continued to stare. She felt her breathing slow and her mind started to clear. She wasn't only baffled, angry, and confused, but the emotional pain had returned like a speeding train. She once again felt rejected and abused but before the clouds of depression descended upon her, she needed to take a shower and pack her clothes.

After showering, she started packing and her thoughts began to collide with one another. He hadn't changed one iota! The moody bastard! He makes love to me as if I'm the only woman on the whole planet, then up and walks out on me - again. This time, there wasn't even the good old "see ya." She knew there wasn't a chance in hell it was due to anything she'd said. She'd done absolutely nothing to deserve this inexcusable treatment again. Maybe "Blondie" let him get away with this crap, but she wasn't going to. Her anger told her there wouldn't be another round like this, and he could drop dead for all she cared. One thing was certain: she was mad as hell — fighting mad.

While checking out at the registration desk, Angie glanced toward the restaurant. Humph! She thought. There he was, having breakfast as though he didn't have a care in the world! She guessed the woman with him was his mother. At least it wasn't the blonde, thank God.

She signed her bill and asked the desk clerk to break a hundred-dollar bill. She walked into the restaurant and strolled directly to his table. As she looked at Gary's mother, Angie smiled. "Please pardon the intrusion."

Turning to Gary, she threw some crumpled bills in his face and said angrily, "Here, this should cover my share of last night's dinner." She quickly turned on her heel and stomped out of the restaurant. Take that, you smug bastard, she thought.

Harriet Walgren looked at her son who was wearing a mask of embarrassment. In a sweet quiet voice and with a grin, she said, "Dare I ask what that was all about? And how nice of her to be willing to pay her share of last night's dinner. Kind of renews one's faith in the fellow man." With her last words, she laughed heartily.

"Knock it off will you, Mom?"

"Anything you care to share or talk about, Gary?"

"No," he snapped.

Sandi K. Whipple

His mother was still laughing.

As she sat and sipped her coffee, Harriet Walgren observed her son and realized the *reason* behind this little scene that just took place wasn't a laughing matter. He looked so lonely she wanted to cry for him. "You know, Gary, I'm not blind. I can see you've been depressed and unhappy. I'm concerned. Is there anything I can do to help you?"

Gary was uncomfortable in confiding his thoughts and emotions to his mother, but the grave concern on her face was more than he could handle. "There's not much to tell, Mom. I made several attempts at something and I failed. You know I don't take failure very well."

"Are we talking *failure*, son, or are we talking *rejection*?"

With a bit of surprise in his voice he said, "You're perceptive, Mom. How'd you guess?"

Keeping her voice steady, his mother responded, "Probably when that beautiful woman with fire in her eyes threw that money in your face. No man or woman can look at the other with as much anger as that unless there's real feeling involved."

Lowering his head and his eyes, he admitted, "I thought she was the one, Mom. I've never been as happy as when I was with her. We had some wonderful times together. I thought I made her happy, but I guess I was wrong."

"Why do you think you were wrong?"

"Because I'm not the only man in her life. She's also seeing a guy named Alan and another guy named Carl." Following an intake of air, he continued, "I love her so much, Mom. There's no way I could ever share her. I thought I could deal with it if I could have her in my life at least part-time. I tried, but I just couldn't do it. I figured not having her in my life at all was better than knowing she was with another man."

"It isn't working though, is it? This not having her in your life at all."

Gary now sat up straight. "How can you tell? What gave it away? Was it the fact that I can't even function like a human being anymore?"

With a shrug of her shoulders, she said, "That was a clue, yes. Does this woman know how you feel about her? Did you ever tell her you were in love with her?"

"No. Not in words anyway. Every time I was set to tell her, she'd somehow bring up either Alan or Carl. Then when she did, my jealousy jumped right in front of me and forced me to walk out. Weeks later, sometimes months later, we'd try again, but it was the same thing all over again."

"So this has happened several times."

There was no mistaking Gary's sarcasm. "Ha! More than I care to count."

His mother gently wiped her mouth with her napkin. "I'm sorry, Gary. It breaks my heart to know I can't help you. I don't think anyone can. You'll need to reach inside yourself and work this out on your own. But I'm here for you. You know that, don't you?"

"Yea, Mom. And thanks."

Gary then sat back in his chair and rubbed his chin as if in deep thought. "You know, before she stomped out of here, I should've asked her if she returned poor concerned Alan's call. I wonder if Carl knows about Alan and vice versa." Gary appeared to be deep in thought before continuing. "Well, she can have Alan – and Carl too, for that matter. I'm through playing her juvenile 'pit 'em against each other game.' No more."

Gary stood up and retrieved the check. Looking at his mother he said, "It'll probably be a quiet trip home."

CHAPTER SIXTEEN

The drive home from Chicago was a blur for Angie. The inner struggle to hold on to her self-esteem and self-respect was almost unbearable. For a number of miles, her anger and rage drove the car and she was shocked to realize she was passing most vehicles that were doing the speed limit. The honking of horns brought her back to reality and she shuddered at the thought of a potential collision.

It had been a nightmarish drive and when she pulled into the parking lot of her shop, she sighed deeply and thanked God for getting her home safely.

When she turned off the engine and alighted from the car, she stood for a minute and inhaled deeply telling herself she needed to get a grip, throw her shoulders back, and get on with her life in as normal and healthy a manner as possible. No man was going to get her detoured from having a successful business and she sure wouldn't sacrifice her years of struggling solely for the purpose of having a wonderful bed partner. She'd carry on and she'd soon find the memories of Gary slowly fading. At least that was the plan.

Feeling as though she'd just experienced an epiphany, Angie tilted her head upward, sucked in her abdomen, straightened her shoulders, and entered the shop. "Hi, Carrie. I thought I'd drop by before heading home. I have one hell of a headache. If there's nothing pressing, I think I'll go home and put my head on a pillow." Realizing she was rambling, Angie took a considerable pause while Carrie stood staring at her. To break the silence, Angie added, "Where's Patti?"

Sandi K. Whipple

Carrie wasn't sure how effusive her response should be so she chose a little humor. "She's talking to that scary guy from Gardner's Funeral Home. You know, the one who gives me the creeps."

The description made Angie laugh. "I have a confession to make Carrie. The guy gives me the creeps too, but he spends a lot of money with us, so I guess it's okay for him to act a little creepy, don't you think?"

With hesitancy Carrie replied, "I guess so. And, ummm, do you want Patti to call you at home?"

"No. I can't remember the schedule. Who's opening in the morning, you or her?"

"It's Patti's turn. Oh, did you call Alan?"

Angie was turning toward the door when she said, "Not yet, but I will."

Carrie sensed something was not quite right with Angie. She asked, "Angie, you sound funny. You okay?"

Too quickly, Angie replied, "Of course I am." Seeing the concern on Carrie's face, Angie suddenly felt a need to put her at ease. She simply stated, "It was just a long and boring drive home and I hate being in a car that long." Going out the door she gave Carrie a slight wave. "I'll see you tomorrow."

As she drove home, Angie's mind wandered back to Chicago and she mulled over the events of the convention. She felt she'd learned absolutely nothing. Every time she thought about the cost of those three and a half days, she cringed.

When she thought about the mental cost of the night with Gary, she felt ill. She knew she had to accept that it was finally over between them. Not that there'd ever really been any *them* in the first place. Oh sure, the sex was the best ever, but it seemed that's all he ever wanted from her. It was sex with her and love and romance with Blondie, whoever the hell she was. But that was then, and this is now, and she swore she was going to pull herself up by the bootstraps and move on down the road.

****

The next morning, Angie was engrossed in the newspaper when the sound of the doorbell startled her. She opened the door and was baffled upon seeing Aunt Ruth holding a notebook and a stack of papers. "Aunt Ruth, what are you doing here so early in the morning?"

With her usual calming smile, Aunt Ruth replied, "It isn't early, dear. It's ten o'clock." She entered the room hesitantly. "I thought you took the day off to help me go over the arrangements for my soon-to-be small reception. If you're busy, or would rather do it another time..."

"No, I'm not busy. I just spaced it. Let's sit at the kitchen table. Want a cup of coffee?"

"No thank you, dear. I'm only allowed one cup a day and I had to sneak a second when Frank left this morning to go to the travel agency."

Angie had a dismayed look on her face. "Travel agency? Are you going somewhere?"

"He's booking a cruise today for our honeymoon. Angela, you knew all this. What's going on with you?"

"It's nothing. I've just been a bit of a space cadet lately."

Sandi K. Whipple

"Lately, you say? Let's see now, what does that mean? A few days or a few weeks? No, I believe it's more like several months — on again, off again —for almost a year." Placing the notebook and papers on the table, Aunt Ruth turned and faced Angie. "You know, I would never pry into your personal life, but I think it's time you tell me what in the world it is that has you living on an emotional roller coaster – and don't you dare start with that *I'm fine* stuff."

Angie felt a lump in her throat and stinging of her eyes. "I can't talk about it, Aunt Ruth. If I do, I'll just start crying."

Aunt Ruth feigned the sternness of a schoolmaster. "Well, I suggest you get upset - then together we might be able to work out a solution to your emotional crisis. I think I noticed the beginnings of depression and mood swings when we had lunch at the La Virage. I also suspect it might have something to do with your Gary Adonis. I can still see the look on your face when you saw him kiss and hug that blonde woman."

Angie grinned and tried to lighten the mood. "Why, Aunt Ruth. You think you're pretty sly, huh, and don't refer to him as *my* Gary Adonis."

"I'm serious, Angela. Stop joking around and trying to avoid the issue."

With a sigh of resignation, Angie crossed her arms and began to explain, "It's not a very long story. Gary and I have been seeing each other on and off, more off so it seems, since that first time you met him in my old apartment. Anyway, each time we saw one other, things were wonderful between us but it only lasted for what I consider a short time."

Feeling the rising pain of memories, Angie sat down in a nearby chair and continued, "Then, out of the blue, for no reason at all, or any reason I understand, he'd get mad and storm out, hollering, 'see ya.'

Angie needed to take a short break and sipped her coffee. As she exhaled a deep breath, she began again. "Do you remember when I was so sick and you brought juice and a newspaper to me? The night before, Gary and I had a dinner date. He told me it was a very special occasion. When he came to pick me up and saw how sick I was, he acted real concerned. He said he didn't want to leave me alone, but said the dinner had something to do with business and he couldn't get out of it. He stayed a while and even tucked me into bed saying he'd be back in the morning with juice."

Wanting to get the story finished, Angie became somewhat agitated as she went on telling her tale of woe. "After you came by, I sat at the table waiting for him and when I opened the paper, there he was! On the front of the local page was a picture of him at his special dinner and he was with that same woman from La Virage. It hit me between the eyes! He left me sick at home in bed and went straight to her."

With her voice rising a bit, Angie once again felt the familiar sting in her eyes and she fought back her emotions. "I was devastated. When he showed up, I threw him out. I ran into him a few days ago at the Chicago convention. We had dinner together and did a lot of talking. We even spent the night together. I was stupid enough to think we'd finally put all the ugliness behind us. Carrie called my room the next morning to give me a message and when I hung up, he put on his clothes and stormed out.

Angie was exhausted from the retelling of the event and wrestling with the memories. With utter confusion on her face, she looked up, "For the life of me, Aunt Ruth, I can't find two things to put together that make any sense and I've sure as hell tried."

Before saying a word in response, Aunt Ruth walked to the bathroom and returned with a box of Kleenex. "Here, sweetheart. Tell me something. When things were good between you, did you try to ask him why he kept walking out?"

"Of course I did," Angie said, as she dabbed at her eyes. "His explanation was always the same. He said he allows things to fester and build up then he goes into one of those moods. That's all he would say. He never said or hinted at *what* festered or built up."

Seeing her anguish and tears, Aunt Ruth felt helpless. All she could say was, "You're in love with this man, this Gary Adonis, aren't you?"

Holding a tissue to her face, Angie replied, "Hell, right now, at this very moment, I hate his guts and I hope he drops dead."

Sitting across the table from Angie, Aunt Ruth tried to be consoling. "I may not have a lot of experience in matters like this, dear, but I think when people profess such hate they generally mean just the opposite. Are you emotionally up to another attempt? You could always try to get with him and see if things can be worked out."

Sandi K. Whipple

With eyes almost ablaze, Angie quickly retorted, "No, I'm done. I just can't bring myself to try any more. Besides, he's got the blonde, so he sure isn't home alone suffering without me."

Feeling at a loss of words, Aunt Ruth could only add, "All right, dear, but you know if there's anything I can do, you need only ask."

"Of course I know that," Angie replied. "But now, I'd like to think happy thoughts and your wedding is even better than happy thoughts."

Wiping away the last of her tears, Angie smiled and said, "What do you say we start working on your wedding reception? You can't possibly know how thrilled I am for you and Frank. Seeing you together is the highlight of my life."

Silently agreeing to change the tone of the conversation, Aunt Ruth said, "Thank you, Angela. And yes, let's get to work. Though the wedding itself will be a small ceremony with just a few people, I'm afraid the reception has grown a bit larger than we originally planned. Do you think we'll need to change the location? I'm worried because the invitations are already printed."

Angie picked up her coffee cup and was putting it in the sink when she turned around. "Don't worry about it. The La Virage has three different banquet rooms, and I'm sure one of them will be large enough. Now let's roll up our sleeves."

The table was soon littered with paperwork, lists of names, and seating arrangements.

****

Sandi K. Whipple

Three days later as the work day was drawing to a close, Patti looked over the plans for Aunt Ruth's flower arrangements for the wedding chapel and the La Virage restaurant. She looked up at Angie and said, "They're going to be absolutely beautiful." With a childish pout, she added, "I hate you because I think they're going to be even prettier than mine were."

"You think so?" Angie asked with a smirk.

Softly and in a very serious tone, Patti said, "It's nice to hear you laugh again, Angie."

Angie was struck with the thought that she hadn't laughed so freely since, hell, when was it? So long ago she couldn't remember? She admitted to herself she'd been poor company for Patti and many others. She felt badly that she'd created an atmosphere of sadness. In a conciliatory tone, Angie attempted a slight confession. "You know, Patti, I suppose you're right. I've had a lot of things on my mind lately and my preoccupation made me pretty unfriendly. I promise to try and straighten up and fly right from here on in, okay?"

She shooed Patti out the door telling her to go home and tend to her husband's needs.

With a quick hug and a wave of her hand, Patti hollered, "Bye."

At a nearby table in the shop, Aunt Ruth had been quietly attending to her lists for her wedding, all the while observing the activities of Angie and Patti. She'd even eavesdropped on their shoptalk. Following Patti's departure, she finally had Angie's undivided attention and began to chatter excitedly as she listed all her concerns. "I guess that's it. We're ready to go. The invitations are out, the meal arrangements are made, Mr. Solis is taking care of the music and decorations, I have my dress, and you're doing the flowers. Though I wish you'd change your mind and let me pay you for them. By the way, Frank's recovered from the shock of the guest list for the reception. You know, I could have choked him when he said I left the president off the list. I'm not even nervous, not yet, anyway. Do you think I'll get that way the closer we get?"

Grinning at her Aunt's nonstop babbling, Angie attempted to reassure her. "Aunt Ruth, I think you'll be the calmest, most beautiful bride anyone has ever seen."

With widened eye, Aunt Ruth said, "Oh dear, don't say that in front of Patti. It might hurt her feelings. You and I both told her the very same thing at her wedding."

Angie grinned broadly. "Aunt Ruth, you're just way too wonderful!

****

A few weeks later, the wedding ceremony was a beautiful event and one to remember. Aunt Ruth and Frank had tears in their eyes when they looked at each other as they spoke their vows.

When the newlywed couple stepped out of the chapel into the sunlight, they gasped upon seeing the surprise limousine that Angie had secretly hired. Aunt Ruth giggled like a schoolgirl when she climbed in. "I've never ridden in a limousine before. I feel so important." Angie was touched when she heard Frank tell Aunt Ruth that she was far above and beyond important.

Following a short drive, the newlyweds exited their personal chariot and were escorted into the La Virage banquet room. Frank immediately scanned the room full of people. He took hold of his bride's elbow and asked just how many people had been invited to the shindig.

Hearing Aunt Ruth reply, "It's okay Frank, I brought along a Valium for you," Angie nearly choked with laughter.

The dinner entre chosen by Angie was Veal Picatta. Everyone commented about the exquisite meal, the wonderful service, and beautiful table settings. Angie was pleased to have added a little of her own personal touch to her aunt's wedding memories. The festivities were highlighted with a toast to the new bride and groom. When the new couple cut and shared the three-tiered wedding cake, another surprise was presented.

Startled by the sound of music, Frank turned to his bride, placed a finger under her chin, and raised it so he could look directly into her eyes. He asked with a little sternness in his voice, "Who arranged for the music and how much is this going to cost?"

Feigning distress, Ruth said, "Frank, will you stop? We could buy Microsoft if we wanted to, so quit acting like we're paupers." Turning to her niece, she said, "Angie, dear, could you please reach in my purse and give Frank a Valium?" The diners at the head table overheard the bantering and all laughed in unison, including Frank.

Sandi K. Whipple

The band announced the Bride and Groom Set. Frank escorted his bride to the dance floor as all eyes followed. As they glided in unison to the rhythm of the music, their timing and movements created a sense of oneness. The amazed onlookers stared in silent admiration. Angie was equally in awe of their complete focus on one another and as she watched their loving eyes, her thoughts began to wander.

She began to feel the rise of emotions and melancholy as she drifted away with thoughts of Gary. She hadn't realized the music had changed and that other guests were now twirling and gliding on the floor. Thankfully, her thoughts were chased away when Frank approached and touched her arm. With an outstretched hand he asked, "May I dance with the wedding planner?"

Angie was deeply moved and, while dancing, confessed to Frank that Mr. Solis had insisted on furnishing the music. With an intake of breath and a gentle squeeze of her hand, Frank told her, "You know, don't you, that I couldn't care less how much she spends or what she spends it on. Between us, we're more than okay. I just enjoy giving her a hard time so I can watch her feisty side get ruffled."

Angie smiled up at him. "Not only do I know that, Frank, but I get the feeling Aunt Ruth does too. I think it's a game you both enjoy playing and I find it touching. I love you, Frank, for the happiness you've given my aunt, and because you're part of our very small, but loving family."

When the flurry of activities and the dancing finally ended, Angie waved goodnight to the newlyweds and thanked everyone who attended. When she was

Sandi K. Whipple

finally able to drive herself home and collapse into bed, she slept a dreamless sleep.

The next day was Sunday. It was a beautiful day of sunshine and balmy weather. Deciding to pamper herself, Angie grabbed a blanket and a book and drove to the park down by the river. She sat on the blanket, donned her sunglasses, propped herself on her elbows, and indulged in her favorite pastime of reading.

Sandi K. Whipple

CHAPTER SEVENTEEN

For the past few weeks, after Chicago, what seemed to be an eternity of fighting mood swings, struggling with depression and anxiety, Gary was exhausted. He dragged himself into the office to face yet another day of thinking about Angie. The only thing on his short list of "good things" was the easier commute to his main office in Nasons Grove rather than driving to Green Bend. He was thankful for the smartest move he'd made by putting Tom in charge of that location.

Walking into his office, he was greeted with a big smile from Katie. "Good morning, Mr. Walgren. Your timing is perfect because your sister's on line one."

"Thanks, Katie." Entering his office, he picked up the phone and hoping he could hide his gray mood from his sister, he forced a cheery tone. "Hey, Sis, what's up?"

"Gary, I'm desperate and need a big favor. If you'll help me out on this one, knowing how you love, I mean, well, I promise to, uh, promise to ..."

With a chuckle, Gary said, "What's the matter with your voice? I know, you can't even say the word, you tightwad. Go ahead, try again, I can wait."

"Okay, smartass. I promise to cook your favorite steak the next time you're here. There, I said it. Happy now?"

Teasingly he said, "Would that be a New York steak?"

With a gasp, she replied, "Gary, that stuff is over ten dollars a pound. Could the steak be small?"

Not letting her off the hook, he responded, "Minimum two pounds or you can forget whatever favor you're calling about."

"Sometimes I hate you, Gary, you know that?"

Gary's roar of laughter was heard throughout the entire office. "Deal or no deal then?"

Conceding to his demands, she told him, "All right, it's a deal."

She altered her tone of voice and said with sweetness, "I need someone to watch the brats this weekend, from late tomorrow morning until Sunday about dinner time. Can you pick them up or should I have them sent to your condo in the morning by special delivery?"

Smiling, he decided to keep his sister on edge. "You seem pretty eager to get rid of them. Is this something I can threaten to tell your husband about so you'll be forever indebted to me?"

"Did I mention the fact that I hate you?" she said.

Her words stung a little and he immediately had a mental image of Angie. Trying to stay focused, he responded, "You did, and trust me when I say, you're not alone."

There was a slight pause in the conversation so, without allowing his sister to ask any questions, he quickly added, "Why don't I just come by today and take the little monsters off your hands. You can pick them up any time Sunday."

Keeping her off guard so she couldn't ask any questions, he told her, "Besides, I need to have a conference with them about their language. Mom told me they recently referred to me as *Mr. Poo Poo Head* and that language just cannot be tolerated."

He added a last jab: "And I do so love it when you're indebted to me."

They were both laughing when she told him, "I really hate you," and hung up.

Gary hung up his phone and sat thinking about his sister. It was fun sparring with her. He realized it'd been a long time since they'd had any real fun together. Thinking of past jovial times with her, he walked to the outer office and asked Katie if there was anything that couldn't wait. She grinned and informed him there was nothing that couldn't wait or be assigned to someone else.

"That's good. I need to do some grocery shopping. I have my sister's kids coming for the weekend."

With a wave of good-bye, he told her, "Have a nice weekend, Katie."

****

Now Sunday, and the weekend half gone, after feeding breakfast to his niece and nephew, Gary decided to take them out for some fresh air. They walked down to the waterfront so his nephew could look at the boats. His niece informed her brother and uncle that the boats were boring and she wanted to go play on the swings.

As they entered the park, his nephew found a Frisbee lying under a tree. There wasn't anyone else around either. "Uncle Gary, can we play with this for a while?"

Sandi K. Whipple

Gary told him, "As long as you put it back under the tree when you're done. It's not yours, so you can't keep it."

The children and Gary began tossing the Frisbee to one another. After a few minutes, it was thrown too hard and went flying further than expected.

Angie was engrossed in her book when suddenly a Frisbee came from out of nowhere and hit her in the face. Her book went flying across the blanket and her sunglasses were pushed into her face before sailing away. She felt a trickle by her right eye and before she could attend to it, she heard a scream. Sitting upright on her blanket, Angie shielded her eyes, and a short distance away, she saw a little girl running toward her.

As she neared Angie, the child was frantically crying out, "Oh, lady, I'm sorry. Are you hurt? My Mom's gonna really spank me."

Angie was trying to clear her muddled thoughts and regain her bearings in order to answer the little girl. Without any forewarning, she heard: "Did you apologize to the lady?"

Oh my god! Angie thought. *I know that voice.*

Slowly looking up with a bit of hesitancy, her heart skipped a beat. It was him! Timidly, see looked up at Gary. "She certainly did, but I'm not hurt, see?"

Angie had retrieved her sunglasses and was putting them back on when the little girl saw a tiny trickle of blood near one eye. Looking up at Gary, the child said with panic in her voice, "She is too hurt, she's even bleeding. Look! It was an accident, honest." Yanking at his sleeve, the child asked, "Am I in trouble?"

Before Gary could respond, a little boy joined the group. He stood next to Angie and looked at her eye. With a wave of his hand, he straightened up and said, "Aw, she's not hurt bad. It's hardly bleeding, and anyway, she's not even crying. Can we go play on the swings now?"

Gary leaned down to the little girl and tried to reassure her she wasn't in trouble. He patted her on the head and told her to go play on the swings with her brother. As the two children ran off, he yelled for them to stay where he could see them.

He turned back to Angie. "Looks like the Frisbee pushed your sunglasses into your face and cut you just below your eye. I'm sorry, Angie. It was my fault. We were playing and I guess I wasn't paying attention."

Gently rubbing her face, Angie responded with an air of indifference. "I'm fine, really, and it's no one's fault. Accidents do happen often with children."

Not sure if she was convincing in her attempted indifference, she continued, "How are you, Gary?" Looking toward the children, she said, "Busy, I can see."

"I'm just baby-sitting and they got restless so we headed over here."

"Oh. You must live close by."

Gary pointed in the opposite direction and said, "I do. I've got a condo overlooking the river in that building over there."

Angie tried hard to appear nonchalant. "It must be nice, living by the water, I mean."

"It's better than sleeping here in the park, I guess."

Sandi K. Whipple

Gary had been more than surprised when he realized who the lady was when his niece cried out about the Frisbee. He was cautious as he spoke with her. He didn't want to say anything that might turn her away. Tentatively, he said, "You look great, Angie. How've you been?"

Holding her emotions in check and still trying to be indifferent, she answered, "Fine, thanks, I've been busy for sure. I've had a number of weddings and just received a new hotel account. I'd say things are pretty good."

Gary scrambled for additional conversation as he didn't want to end this encounter. "I'm going to take the kids for ice cream. Want to join us?"

Angie responded a little too quickly saying, "Thanks, but I don't think so. I have plans in a little while." Pointing to the children on the swings, she added, "They're adorable, Gary."

Looking at them, he smiled. "They are, aren't they? I pretty much love them as if they were mine. I guess I'd better get over there before they start losing interest again. Take care, Angie."

Gary ambled away and she watched the threesome leave the park hand in hand. They certainly seemed to adore him. They must be Blondies' kids. His relationship with her must be pretty serious if he's come to love her kids as his own. Angie's mind reeled and she felt numb.

She packed her blanket and book and headed home for a quick look at her eye. When she pulled into her driveway, she was shaken when she realized she didn't remember the drive home. She'd been too focused on her thoughts of Gary. All she could think of was the fact he really was lost to her now. There'd be no more forgiving or future attempts to get him back. She'd always held on to a small ray of hope that they'd settle their differences and finally be together.

Any hope of that happening faded today when she saw him laughing and playing with another woman's children. On the other hand, he wasn't wearing a wedding ring, so maybe they weren't married yet.

Angie's thoughts began to swirl and then became muddled. Was there a chance she could get between them? But did she want to go back to sharing him? If nothing else, she could play his game as well as he did and give him a taste of his own medicine. Maybe better.

Although it would take time and some careful planning, she could give Blondie a run for her money. She could even pull the same see ya vanishing act as his, and it would serve him right! All she had to do was come up with a plan. She needed to be completely prepared the next time she ran into him. Angie struggled with her jumbled thoughts and erratic emotions.

That same evening, Gary's sister arrived at his condominium to pick up her children. "Thanks for taking the monsters. Have they eaten?" she said.

Gary walked toward his sister's car with a devilish grin on his face. "Yep. They each had a candy bar, six cookies, and two Mountain Dews. I'll be unplugging my phone so don't even think about calling me later to help scrape them off the ceiling."

"Thanks a million, Gary. That's just great. You *are* kidding, aren't you?"

Sandi K. Whipple

She turned to leave but a thought halted her departure. She turned back to Gary and asked, "What's this about hurting a nice lady in the park and making her bleed?"

"Oh that! We were playing Frisbee and it hit a woman in the face. No big deal though. She turned out to be just fine. The Frisbee pushed her sunglasses into her face and left a tiny cut near her eye. She thought it was funny. Anyway, I knew her."

Almost knowing the answer before she asked, she said, "Knew her? From where?"

Sensing his sister knew more than she was letting on, Gary's defenses crumbled. "It was *her*. I turned to mush the minute I realized it. I even invited her to go with us for ice cream. She refused, of course, saying she had plans. I almost asked her with which guy, but decided against it."

With a sad expression and a lowered tone of voice, he continued, "Life sure sucks sometimes, huh? Get your brats and go home. Say hi to the other *sometimes ass* for me. I need to go drown my sorrows or maybe just drown, period."

"Okay, Big Brother. Whatever you say, but I feel terrible because you ran into *her*. You wouldn't have been in the park if it weren't for my kids. Hence, you wouldn't have run into your past. I sure wish I knew who this woman was. I'd like to kick her teeth in for hurting you like this."

Gary didn't want to hear any more. He changed the subject by saying, "I'll be calling you to set up a time to make your payment for this weekend. In case you forgot, I like my New York steak medium rare."

Sandi K. Whipple

Steering the children to the car, she smiled at Gary and said, "God, I hate you."
"I love you, too," he told her.

Sandi K. Whipple

CHAPTER EIGHTEEN

Angie agreed to drive Aunt Ruth and Frank to the airport when they left for their honeymoon. Glad to have a diversion, she clutched the steering wheel to steady herself from the constant laughter inside the car, thankful that their bantering kept her in stitches throughout the ride.

Aunt Ruth's voice interrupted any potential negative thoughts in Angie's mind. "Frank, are you sure we have everything? You never know what will happen with the weather. I think I packed jackets, but looking back, I think they might be too lightweight. Did you grab the bag of medicines from the shelf in the bathroom like I asked? And did you pack the hand mirror?"

"Yes, the jackets are fine, yes, and yes! I'm beginning to think I shouldn't have grabbed anything. Maybe you're too nervous for this trip, Ruth. Maybe we should just stay home."

"But it's our honeymoon Frank, and I've never been on a boat before."

Frank was rolling his eyes and shaking his head when he said, "Honey, when it's big enough to hold over two thousand people, it's called a ship, not a boat."

Angie knew this honeymoon was going to be extra special. They'd both been too young and too broke during their first marriages.

Aunt Ruth's squeaky voice broke Angie's thought. "Oh Frank, I'm so nervous. Can we afford this, I mean, really?"

Frank held her hand and gazed out the car window, attempting to hide his amusement. "No, dear, we can't, so when we get home I'll help you look for a job."

Angie nearly ran off the road with more laughter.

The flight from O'Hare would take them to New York where they'd board the *Grand Princess* for their twenty-one-day Mediterranean cruise. What could be nicer or more romantic for two people in love? Angie couldn't have been happier for them.

Angie sat in the airport while they checked in. Before long it was time and they arrived at the security area. "Okay you guys, your chariot awaits. Have a great time, bring something back for me, anything, just so I know you missed me."

Once the hugs and goodbyes were complete, Aunt Ruth started to cry. Frank gently took her by the arm and led her through security. Angie heard him say, "Don't cry, sweetheart. This is supposed to be a happy occasion for us."

Angie's drive back to Nasons Grove was depressing and long. She thought of her aunt and Frank and knew she'd miss them, but her heart was heavy. She had no special person in her life to enjoy a cruise with, but more importantly, she had no one in her life to indulge her as Frank did Aunt Ruth. Angie's self-pity pointed to the fact that everyone she knew, except herself, had a special someone in their life. *Damn it!* She thought. *It was Gary's fault she was all alone. His and Blondies'.*

Angie knew she'd done nothing wrong, but he sure as hell had. She'd never walked out on him. She'd never taken up with another man or cheated on Gary. She'd even tried to ignore and get past his mood swings, his 'see ya's, and that Blondie. She'd forgiven him more times than she cared to count. Her bruised ego and battered pride altered her thoughts. Pretty soon she'd set her plan in motion. Then he'd see how it felt.

****

The intercom buzzed and startled Gary as he sat at his desk staring at the scenery from his office window.

"Mr. Walgren, Miss Gibbons just called."

Before Katie could say any more, he quickly rose from his chair, opened his office door, and asked, "What did she want, Katie?"

"To tell you the truth, she was rude."

"Really? Tell me what she said."

"She said this was the last time she'd call our *inefficient* office. She demanded we send the bill she'd been requesting for over a year. She said the workman's name was Gary, and she described you perfectly, Mr. Walgren. She expects to hear from someone by five o'clock today. Then she hung up." With a pout on her face, Katie continued, "She was really rude, Mr. Walgren, she had no right..."

Gary interrupted her. "I'm sorry you had to deal with that, Katie. It's my fault and I'll take care of it. I promise."

"Thanks, Mr. Walgren."

In the meantime, back at the floral shop, Angie felt terrible about the manner in which she'd spoken to that poor girl. But, hey, she rationalized, wasn't all fair in love and war? Well, this was both.

Sandi K. Whipple

It was five o'clock, time to close up. She began to think her plan had failed. She thought for sure her nasty message would've made him call by now.
Stepping out of the shop, she turned to close and lock the door when a shadow reflected in the glass. She jumped and leaned back.

"Hey, it's me, Angie. I didn't mean to startle you. I'm sorry," Gary said.

"Well, you did," Angie said with an edge in her voice. "What are you doing here anyway?"

"You know damned well what I'm doing here. You knew as soon as I got wind of your nasty message, I'd show up."

"I haven't the slightest idea what you're talking about, Gary. If you'll excuse me, I'm on my way home."

"I'm not finished with you yet, Angie, and if you leave, I'll just follow you."

"Suit yourself."

She climbed into her car and pulled away. She checked the rear-view mirror to see if he really intended to follow her. He did, and was. When she pulled into her driveway, he was right behind her. In fact, he was so close to her car he nearly hit the rear fender.

She refused to look up and acknowledge him, so he hollered, "I want to talk to you, Angie. Right now, and I mean it. This isn't over."

She took her time unlocking her front door. He had ample time to catch up to her and was standing alongside her when she pushed the door inward. She was as angry as he was. He followed her into the house. *So far, so good,* she thought. She set her purse and jacket on the sofa, kicked off her shoes, and turned to face him. Boy, did he look furious.

With hands on her hips, she said, "All right, Gary, what?"

"Explain the message you left at my office today."

With sarcasm dripping from each word, she explained, "Gee, Gary, I was just trying to do the right thing. I pay my bills, and I owe no one. I've never paid for the door or wall in the shop, so I thought, now that you're a partner, you could make sure I get the bill so I can make it right. I've been asking for the bill for a year now. If you think it was nasty to try to do the right thing, then I apologize. I also suggest you relax and calm down a little. The veins are sticking out in your temples and forehead."

She walked slowly to the refrigerator, opened it, and bent way over as if she were looking for something. Holding that position, she turned her head to him. "I'm gonna have a beer. Want one while you try to calm down?"

His eyes never left her backside.

The distraction garbled his hearing and when he realized she'd spoken, he said, "What?"

She held up two beers, tilted her head again and asked if he wanted one.

"Sure, if it's okay with you."

She sat at the kitchen table and pointed to a chair, so he sat.

Gary was baffled and nearly stumbled over his words. "You knew I did that work at the shop on my own, Angie. You knew it had nothing to do with the company."

"Well, I didn't before, but as I do now, I'm sure you expected compensation for your work. I'll get my purse and write you a check."

When she stood, he let her take two steps before he grabbed her and turned her to face him.

"What are you up to?"

"I just want to make sure you're compensated for all your hard work, Gary."

"I don't want your money, Angie."

She looked directly into his eyes when she spoke. "I see. Well, if you had a different form of compensation in mind, I'm not sure if ..."

His mouth stifled her words. Pretending to struggle at first, she finally wrapped her arms around his neck, and without hesitation, matched his hungry, aggressive kiss. Their actions bordered on violence. Backing her up to the sofa, he threw her jacket and purse across the room. He tried to remove her blouse but the buttons were too small, so he mumbled, "To hell with it," and ripped it wide open. Buttons flew everywhere.

He pulled the torn blouse down her arms, reached behind her, unsnapped her bra and threw it toward the jacket and purse somewhere on the floor. Not once did his mouth leave hers. When her skirt fell to the floor, he nearly threw her down on the sofa. He ripped off her panty hose and panties. Hanging on to her, he removed his own clothing.

Wasting no time, he tore his shirt open, sending his buttons to join hers.

Sandi K. Whipple

As he kicked off his shoes, he removed his jeans and underwear. Quickly covering her body with his, he thundered into her without hesitation. Her warm and wet feminine parts instantly enveloped him. She'd been ready. With his blood hot enough to make his body explode, he pounded her with the fire of a wild animal.

Within minutes, they lay spent and gasping, unable to speak. Sometime later, Gary rose and picked her up, asking where the bedroom was. She only pointed. Lying her on the bed, he rested his warm body over hers. Neither of them spoke. Kissing every inch of her face and soft smooth lips, he entered her again. This time he was slow and gentle. Hearing her catch her breath with each erotic movement, he slowed his pace. As his slow stroking quickly brought his probing manhood back to life, she lifted herself into him, wanting him to push deeper into her. She reached for his buttocks and pulled him into her. She wanted control of the stroking. Her up- and-down movements increased and he met her stroke for stroke. Her moaning told him her release was near. When she cried out, her convulsion and inside contractions forced him to join her in rapturous climax.

They clung together in each other's arms for over an hour, again without speaking, yet both were wide awake. Angie was the first to break the silence.

"I'm hungry."

"You're always hungry," he said, tightening his hold on her to let her know he wanted her there, next to him. "And I'll bet you a pound to a dozen donuts there's no food in the house either. Speaking of which, this looks like a really nice place, Angie."

Angie responded sarcastically. "All you've seen is the sofa and the bed.

"Is that a complaint?"

"I never said it was or wasn't." She jumped up to pull a nightshirt from the drawer and headed to the kitchen.

Gary walked to the living room in search of his jeans. He thought teasing her a bit would lighten the mood. "Gee, Angie, you used to be a better housekeeper than this. There're clothes all over the place. I guess I owe you a new blouse too, huh?"

Walking to the kitchen, he heard her chuckling at his last remark. He took a sip from the beer on the table and, finding it warm, asked, "You got another cold one?" She reached into the refrigerator and handed one to him.

Swallowing the cold liquid, Gary cleared his throat. "You don't have much to say. Am I supposed to say anything here? Maybe I should ask you how this happened when we weren't even speaking. If you expect me to say I'm sorry this happened, you'll be disappointed, 'cause I'm not the least bit sorry."

She turned to face him. "I hate it when you're right. There's nothing to eat in this house."

"I could take you somewhere for dinner if you like."

Hoping he would agree, Angie asked, "If I order in, will you stay and have some?"

"Sure, I'd like that."

She ordered a pizza with everything but anchovies. He pulled a twenty-dollar bill from his wallet and paid the delivery boy. They made idle conversation while eating and he wondered how she could eat so much and still have a body like Venus. He sat and stared as they ate.

While she cleaned up the table, she noticed him watching at her.

She'd tilted her head to the side and, in the sexiest, raspiest voice he'd ever heard come out of a female's mouth, he heard, "What are you looking at?"

"You. Every single inch of you. I'm making a mental note of all the body parts you have that my tongue hasn't caressed." He wanted to map out that entire body with his tongue.

"It's nine o'clock, Gary, and that's real close to my bedtime."

Remaining silent, he watched as she moved toward him. Towering over him, she stood and looked down at him in the chair. Even in his bare feet with just a pair of jeans on, he was an absolutely perfect Adonis. She wondered if he knew how handsome he truly was. Did he know he was capable of frightening her and delighting her at the same time with that incredibly masculine physique of his?

Enough of that, she told herself. Didn't she need to get on with her plan to get him to spend the night? Then, when he didn't go home, wouldn't Blondie go berserk? After seeing him in the park with her kids, she figured they must be living together. Yet, here he was, with her. The guy was truly *slime*. She could enjoy herself in the process of her plan, though, couldn't she?

She straddled his legs, scooted herself into him as close as she could and placed her arms around his neck. He sucked in a quick breath when she began to rock her body against his. His instant arousal told her he was ready for her again.

In a way that no one else was capable of doing, he'd sensitized her breasts earlier. Now they began to ache for his warm mouth and tongue. At this moment, she wanted more than anything to lose herself in him. His body had become a weapon when it was near her, especially with the hot throbbing inside his jeans.

Reaching beneath her nightshirt, he massaged and thumbed both breasts, never taking his eyes off hers. He stopped only long enough to disrobe her. She tried to put her arms around his neck but he placed them gently behind her where he took her hands firmly in one of his. Placing his other hand in the center of her back for support, he set her torso back so far she was now lying on his knees. Leaning over, he sucked hard as he pulled a breast into his mouth. His tongue made circles around and over her nipple and it swelled instantly. He teased her with his teeth and tongue, knowing how sensitive she was. He knew how to satisfy her, and at this moment, he wanted nothing more. Her breathing was a loud rasping pant. Without hesitation, he swiftly moved to her other breast, sucking it with his hot mouth.

She tried to move, but her balance was off. Her feet didn't quite reach the floor and he held her firmly in place.

"When you straddled me, Angie, were you telling me you wanted me again?"

Between his words, he lightly bit and sucked on her nipples. Her moaning grew louder and her head moved back and forth.

Sandi K. Whipple

"I'm going to show you that you belong with me."

He lifted her just enough to lower his jeans and kick them off. Sitting back, he swiftly slid into her. Keeping a firm grip on her hands behind her back, he used his other to grab her buttocks. When he pulled her firmly against his throbbing erection, he rose and carried her to the bedroom – all the while remaining inside her.

He was gasping when he sat down and slid backward onto the bed. She tried to move from him but his firm hold on her hands behind her wouldn't allow her to budge.

"God, I love filling you, being completely inside you," he whispered. He released her hands and pulled her toward him. Again he massaged and caressed her breasts, which drove her wild like a wanton tigress.

Angie soon gained control and sat straight up, taking every bit of him inside her. She rode him as though it was the last time she'd ever make love. As she was reaching her peak, he flipped her over, never pulling out. He pulled her legs over his shoulders and leaned far enough forward to lift her buttocks. Once again, he filled every inch of her. He moved slowly all the way in, then all the way out, over and over, as he watched her facial expressions of pleasure and release. Every nerve and muscle in his body screamed to give her more.

Hearing her loud moaning, gasping, and crying out, he wanted the world to hear and know of their erotic union. His and hers. Gary and Angie.

"Gary, please."

Did Alan or Carl make her beg?

Again he heard "Please."

Sandi K. Whipple

Suddenly, the whole world exploded for them. Neither of them knew who cried out, they only knew they heard the sounds of screaming out. Eventually, as they clung tightly to one another, they slept.

He awoke alone. His clothes were folded neatly at the foot of the bed. Looking at the clock on her nightstand, it read 7:30. After a quick shower and rinse of his mouth with toothpaste, he dressed and headed to the kitchen. He found her there, showered, dressed, and placing a coffee cup in the sink.

She turned, walked past him, and opened the front door. Looking straight at him, she said, "I wrote you a check for the wall and door, but I tore it up. I believe after last night, you've been compensated enough. After all, it was just a little drywall and a steel door. That's why you did the work in the first place, right, Gary? So you could get me in the sack? Well, my compliments to you on your success. Now get out."

More than shocked by this twist of her personality, Gary was mortally stung by her hateful words. He was unable to move or utter a single word.

"I said, get out," Angie repeated.

With a shaky voice and complete bewilderment, Gary said, "Angie, you have to know the things you just said aren't true. Why are you doing this? I know it isn't over a door and a few pieces of drywall. Please don't do this." In a pleading voice nearing hysteria, he nearly yelled at her. "Talk to me, Angie! Tell me what it is. If you make me leave like this, Angie, I won't be back."

"That's what I'm counting on, Gary. Now go."

Sandi K. Whipple

Without looking at her or even glancing back at her doorway, he walked to his car. She hollered after him, "See ya!"

Leaning against the inside of her closed door, she knew this finale was an academy award performance. If her plan to piss off Blondie by keeping him out all night worked, well, it sure wasn't worth it. There was no way Blondie could feel the pain Angie was dealing with at the moment. She'd merely wanted to screw up Gary's relationship with her and give him a taste of his own medicine.

She hadn't counted on the effect her behavior would have on him or herself. She'd just witnessed the most devastating hurt look on a man's face. But, wasn't that what she'd wanted? Wasn't that what she'd planned — to hurt him? To get even for Blondie and all those 'see ya's?'

The mental picture of his face tore at her conscience. Maybe it wasn't what she wanted after all. But, it was too late for second thoughts. The damage was done and she felt a growing sense of regret. She felt a foreboding that she would suffer a new agony born from her behavior.

CHAPTER NINETEEN

For weeks after she'd maneuvered and placed her great plan into action, Angie threw most of her time and energy into her shop. Her self-respect was on the line and she tried to ignore her feelings of regret. Her only consolation was that her business was successful.

More often than not, Angie considered selling the building and buying a larger facility. She'd recently hired two more young girls, which had grown her staff to include five, and, along with a delivery driver, they all seemed to be tripping over each other. It was obvious the shop was too small to function properly. She decided to spend some time with Carl and share her thoughts about an expansion.

Angie just walked into the house when she heard the doorbell, then the sound of the opening door. Smiling, Angie turned and saw Carl with her arms full. "Knock, knock, who's there? It's the nosy bank lady carrying beer."

They laughed and went into the kitchen, opened a beer, and sat down.

Angie began the conversation. "Carl, I need your advice on something. Just hear me out, and then give me your opinion, okay?"

Carl sat straight up. "Oh God, no. Has the 'slime' done something to you?"

"I haven't seen or heard from him in months. Not since the episode here at my house."

"Episode? What episode? You never told me about an episode. Especially not here at your house. How did he know where you lived? You've been a very bad girl, Angie. There's smut about the 'slime' and you didn't share it with your best friend? You will enlighten me, right?"

Angie was tickled by her friend's child-like demeanor. "Yes, but another time."

"All right, shoot."

Angie began with excitement in her voice, "Here's my situation. I'm cramped at the shop again and it's getting harder to function. My list of clients now consists of every hotel and one motel in town, seven restaurants, the hospital, three funeral parlors and a catering service. Add to that the weddings, bar mitzvahs, telephone orders and walk-ins." She continued to itemize and verbalize her thoughts, "And on holidays, well... I can't keep my shelves stocked because I have no space for inventory. I thought I might start looking for a larger place. Should I keep the building and rent it out while I go rent space somewhere else? Should I buy another building and rent or sell this one?"

Carl's hands were pumping the air. "Wow! Slow down Angie. But, way to go, Girlfriend! I had no idea you were that busy. Are you asking me what I'd do if I were in your shoes?"

Angie nodded yes.

"I'd buy another building on contingency. That way you could move into the new spot right away. In case your old building doesn't sell right away, you only pay rent on the new one until the old one sells, so both escrows will close pretty much at the same time. Just don't rent if you can avoid it. My bet is that, once you find a new building, you'll sell the old one as soon as it goes on the market."

Angie's face now wore a frown. "I'm worried about the remodeling costs of a new building and a larger mortgage. I don't want to be in hock till I'm ninety years old."

Carl became more serious. "The real estate market is hot right now, Angie. You'll make one hell of a profit on the old building, and even have a nice chunk of capital to work with after you make the down payment on the new one. You already have all the expensive coolers, so you won't have to buy more equipment. You can increase your stock a little at a time. You might even consider buying a large building and renting out what you don't use. The rent might even make your mortgage payments. Once you decide where you're going to park yourself, just let my bank take care of the rest. We'll have all the financing, title and escrow paperwork done for you. I promise you, the transaction will leave you stress-free so you can concentrate on getting the new shop set up."

Angie grinned and said, "I knew there was a reason I loved you."

"Damn. I thought it was for my charming personality and excellent advice on 'slime.'" Carl then added, "Do you need to think more about this or can I get excited about real estate shopping? I have one condition though. After we agree on my new assignment, I want the hot details on the 'slime'."

CHAPTER TWENTY

With a stack of paperwork in front of him, Gary sat back in his chair. "Well, Tom, that should just about wrap up this job. Tomorrow I'll head over to the Pearson Clinic. That job should be a doozie. It's a big building. The duct work alone will take four guys a couple of weeks."

Tom looked at Gary with concerned expression. "Gary, I need to talk to you about something."

"You sound upset. What's going on?"

Sitting back in his chair and eyeing Gary, Tom said, "Ever since you made me a partner, you've been hitting the field more and more, doing a lot of the grunt work. I think I should be out there and you should be in the office. It should've been you who interviewed the last five guys. You're getting the short end of the stick here and it bothers me."

Gary asked, "Can you handle the bids okay?"

"Sure," Tom answered with a question in his tone.

"Can you handle the office stuff?"

"Well, yes." Tom responded, wondering where Gary was going with his questions.

"Do you like those five new guys you hired? I mean does it look like they'll work out okay?"

"I guess so. What's that got to do with what I just said?" Tom was getting exasperated with the questions.

"Everything. I'm doing what I like to do. Bastard that I am, I dumped all the other crap on you. I think you got screwed in the deal. I know the company keeps growing and your end can get pretty hectic. If you need help, just hire another guy to help you. You own half the company and don't need my permission."

"See, that's what I mean, Gary. We used to talk all the time. You wanted to know everything that was going on and I wanted to tell you. For months now, you've worked in the field ten and twelve hours a day, and then you've gone straight home."

Tom went on, "Most of the time, you work two or three hours after you've sent the rest of the crew home for the day. The people from the new plumbing shops don't even know who you are, and Lucy and Katie can't remember what you look like. I'm watching you grind yourself into the ground and it's bothering me."

Placing his hands on the desk, Tom tried to control his frustration. "I almost don't recognize you these days. You've lost interest in everything you worked your ass off to build up."

For several minutes, neither said a word. Finally, Gary asked, "What time is it?"

"Three thirty. Why?"

"Call Katie and tell her we'll be out of touch the rest of the day and to reschedule any other appointments you have. Tell her to notify all offices of the same thing. Let's go have a beer. I'll meet you at Lindy's in half an hour?"

"Done."

****

Although Gary didn't frequent the place the way he used to, Lindy's was a great bar. Dark and not crowded except on weekend nights. And everyone adored Bridgette, the owner. When Gary walked up to the bar, he spotted Frank sitting on a nearby stool.

"Hey, Frank. Good to see you. Can I buy you a beer?"

"Good to see you too, Gary. Yeah, I've got time for one. I haven't seen you in a long time. When did I see you last anyway?"

"I was on a job downtown and I helped you move some boxes and furniture into a small apartment."

"Oh yeah, that's right. My wife's niece had her old flower shop there that used to have a little apartment in the back."

Without a blink of an eye, Gary said, "By the way, congratulations. I saw your wedding announcement in the paper. I met Ruth once. She's a nice lady. You got lucky, you old goat."

They chuckled.

"So, the flower shop is no more, huh? Too bad," Gary said. "Rumor has it she was doing real well."

"Better than well. She's actually still there, but she just sold the building and bought a bigger one down by the waterfront. She's one smart cookie, you know. Ruth and I wish there were something we could do for her."

"Do for her? Does she need money? I'm sure she could get a loan."

"No, nothing like that. The girl labors like a worker bee. She sends the girls home when she closes shop and does all the clean-up stuff herself. She's there till nine or ten most nights. She even takes paperwork home and that's how she spends her weekends. My wife takes it pretty hard sometimes when she won't come to visit or go out with us."

Gary was perplexed by this tidbit of information but remained neutral in his response. "Well, she's single and a very attractive woman, Frank. I'm sure she dates on occasion. She didn't strike me as the nun type."

"Ruth's never seen her date anyone since she opened the shop. And, if she's seeing someone, she sure keeps it to herself, but it's none of our business. Listen, I have to go. Thanks for the beer. It was good to see you."

Seconds after Frank left, Gary heard a voice from behind: "Hi, Bridgett, give me a beer, will you? Get another one for this sourpuss, too."

Looking at his friend Tom said, "We haven't done this in a long time, Gary. Especially the playing-hooky-from-work part."

"Yeah, I know. There's no reason we can't kick back once in a while. Hell, we're the bosses."

Tom grinned. "I'm all for it. I called Heather and told her I was meeting you for a drink. She said it was about time the two lug nuts got together for the male bonding thing, though I'm not sure what she meant by that."

With a frown on his brow, Tom asked, "So, are we going to sit here and talk shop or are we really going to talk?"

"Makes no difference to me, you pick," Gary replied as he shifted his weight in the chair.

Tom leaned forward. "Okay. I vote we really talk. I'll even let you start. Maybe you could start with whatever it is that's been driving you into the ground for months."

Gary rested his chin on a hand. "I'm trying to keep myself busy. You know, Tom, I figured if I just work and sleep, then I won't have time to think. I know you've got the guys and the office under control. Hell, you do a better job than I ever did. To keep busy, I work in the field. End of story."

Tom knew Gary was holding back. He wasn't going to let him off the hook that easily. "I don't think that's even the beginning. This is me, Gary, your friend. Come on."

When Gary didn't smile at that remark, Tom knew whatever it was that was driving him so hard had to be pretty bad.

Gary broke the momentary silence. "You've probably already figured out what's been bugging me."

Tom shrugged his shoulders. "I base everything on logic and fact. I've seen neither where you're concerned, so I've had no way to figure it out."

Gary began to open the doors of pain and slowly confessed, "It's her, Tom. It's always her. When I'm happy and upbeat, it's because of her. When I'm depressed and miserable, it's because of her. There's times I'd like to turn her over my knee and wallop the hell out of her, but, the minute I'd set eyes on that cute ass of hers, I'd forget what I was doing."

Gary told Tom about the last episode with Angie and offered scant details of the night's event. Then he added, "I haven't heard from her since. She's probably keeping herself pretty busy between Alan and Carl."

Sandi K. Whipple

Gary sat back in his chair and said, "That's the whole story in a nutshell. Sucks, doesn't it?"

With amazement and disbelief, Tom sat back in his chair. "Holy shit. She really said that about compensating you? This is ugly."

With a somber expression on his face, Gary said, "Tell me. I'm trying real hard to forget her, Tom. I thought busting my ass would work. I just can't get her out of my head. I met some broad one night and got her number and I really had every intention of calling to ask her out. I didn't. I just couldn't bring myself to go out with another woman and wish or pretend it was Angie."

Tom jumped in saying, "I've got to tell you, I'm one hundred per cent lost here. I love Heather with all my heart and soul, and I can't imagine what I'd do if she pushed me out of her life—especially in an on-and-off manner. You know," Tom mused, "maybe a woman could understand or make sense of this. Have you thought about talking to your sister?"

Gary spoke with a tinge of anger in his voice. "Hell no. I haven't thought about talking to anyone. Not until today, with you. I didn't see much point in it. I might try to talk to Sis. She might have an idea why a woman would act like this with her on-again-off-again act." Gary had talked enough and needed some air. "Mind if we finish these and go?"

"No problem."

They drained their beer bottles, hollered a good-bye to Bridgette, and left.

****

Sandi K. Whipple

On his drive home, Gary purposely drove downtown past Angie's shop to see if she'd moved out yet. The lights were on. He pulled to the curb across the street, turned off the headlights and engine. There she was. All by herself, packing up boxes. Nothing had changed. She was still so strikingly beautiful. He sat there picturing her sensuous lips and that inviting smile of hers. He was remembering every curve and contour of her delectable body. He thought of her fair silky skin covering her shoulders and neck and those sensitive delicious breasts. He could see every freckle in the small of her back.

Did she ever sit alone in the dark thinking about him? Why was he even here? He knew he couldn't persuade her to come to him, wanting him as he wanted her. Turning the key to start the car, he realized that for the first time since he was a child, he was crying.

The next day he called Tom into his office. "I really need to get the hell out of Dodge for a while. Think you can do without me for a week or so if we plan it a little in advance?"

With a grin, Tom told him, "It kills me to hurt your feelings pal, but we can get along just fine without you now. For a while anyway. Ain't it a bitch not to be needed?"

Gary was dead serious when he responded, "I'm used to it by now."

"Hey, I'm sorry, Gary. I didn't mean it like that. Feel free to deny me beer for at least sixty days. So, where are you going? Is it okay to ask?"

"I thought I'd go deep-sea fishing. I haven't been in years.

Sandi K. Whipple

"It's fine with me," Tom told him. "The fact that you're going somewhere to kick back is great. You can go tomorrow if you want. Katie and Lucy are the best at shuffling things around to meet any situation."

"Don't try shoving me out the door yet," Gary told him with a laugh. "Hell, I'm not even packed. I thought I'd go in a few weeks. That's pretty much the peak of the fishing season, and it gives me plenty of time to plan ahead, you know, set up the charters and stuff."

"Want me to drive you to O'Hare when you go?"

"Yeah, sure. I'd appreciate it."

"Not a problem. And Gary, I'm glad you're doing this. It's been a long time coming."

"Do me a favor, will you, Tom? I'd rather no one knows where I'm going or when I'll be back. I'm not even going to let my mom or sister know. I want to be completely alone."

"No problem, my lips are sealed." Tom put a finger to his mouth and raised an eyebrow.

CHAPTER TWENTY-ONE

The move into her new building hadn't killed her, but Angie swore to never do it again. The packing was easy compared to unloading boxes and sorting the contents. And boy was it slick the way it worked out so that she only lost one day of business. The electricians and plumbers did all the work on the new building in advance while the old shop kept open for business. Thank God for professional movers. On one Sunday, paying them extra of course, they moved everything to the new shop and even hooked up the coolers and water.

She'd filled three storage rooms with plenty of inventory and felt comfortable that the shelves and racks would remain full.

One entire section of the new building was now filled with small sized antiques, the most difficult area to keep stocked.

Thinking back on the days that she and Carl searched and viewed properties, Angie knew what a find this building turned out to be: two floors with nearly three thousand square feet. Her shop and the antique store occupied the ground floor. A good-sized brokerage firm rented the entire second floor. They were tenants of the previous owner and, when Angie assured them she wouldn't raise the rent, had chosen to stay and sign a new lease. Angie made a killing on the old building and realized a terrific profit. To top it all off, the second-floor tenants were paying ninety percent of her new mortgage each month.

She'd been working nonstop for so many weeks that she lost track of time. Before she knew it, her mind wandered and she found herself thinking of the last time she'd seen Gary. How long had it been since she'd been a fool and played her vicious game of revenge?

Her revenge had backfired badly and she was now alone and emotionally numb with no one to blame but herself. She began to understand why the physical and mental exhaustion was enveloping her.

On the bright side, she thought, her business was wonderful. She had a terrific staff and Patti could now run the shop as well as Angie, allowing her some time for a much-needed vacation or just a little time away. But where would she go? Glancing at the clock, Angie realized it was late and decided to call it a day. She headed home hoping to get a good night's sleep.

Angie awoke the following day feeling as though she hadn't slept a wink. She seemed to be in a daze as she fixed some coffee and moved about the kitchen. Sitting at the table with a fresh cup, the silence of the house was broken by the ringing of her phone. It was Aunt Ruth.

"Hello, Angela, I just want you to listen and don't utter a word until I'm finished, okay?"

Oh boy, now it's Angela, she thought. What on earth could she have done wrong?

"You got it, Aunt Ruth. I'm all ears."

"Good. Frank and I decided last week that you need to get away for a while. You've nearly killed yourself with the moving. Angie, we're worried about you. Your business used to make you happy but lately you act as if it's a job or chore. We've made arrangements for you to take a week's vacation. And, you can't say no. Frank says it's a done deal. So, come over, pick up the tickets and dossier, and have dinner with us."

Angie was so touched by their love and concern for her she gratefully accepted the dinner invitation — and the trip. How strange that she'd just been thinking of a break the night before. She was so bone-tired she didn't even argue with herself as to whether or not she should take a vacation. A different environment is what she needed. She kept her promise and had dinner with Aunt Ruth and Frank and graciously accepted the ticket.

****

On the day of her departure, Angie looked at her packed suitcases and felt a tugging reluctance. She struggled with self-talk and had to convince herself she was going to enjoy this trip, no matter what. She'd lie on the beach, get a tan, and maybe check out a few nightspots. Carl came by to bolster Angie's enthusiasm and help pack.

"Angie, you really are going, aren't you? New clothes, new shoes, and even a new haircut, which, by the way, I like. So, your room is kind of like an apartment, you say, with a stove, refrigerator, and fully stocked kitchen?" Teasing her, she went on, "Hell, Angie, you could change your mind and stay home. You have all those things right here, except food in the kitchen of course."

Angie laughed at the inside joke. "But this is right on the beach. I can open the sliding door, step on to the sand, and it's only 35 yards to the water. I can lie in the sun right outside the door and it's only a few steps further if I want to take a swim."

In an attempt to be cute, Carl said, "This is one of those all-inclusive packages, huh? With booze included? Damn, Angie, I should go with you, and between us we could put one hell of a dent in their liquor stock, huh?"

Changing the subject, Carl said with a more serious tone, "I wish you'd let me take you to the airport. Those shuttles are expensive. Besides, there's always six or eight people crammed into those things. Don't they take hours with all the stops to pick up other people?"

"The van is stress-free, Carl. Just the most perfect kind of driving there is, so will you drop it?"

"Okay, I tried. Your chariot should be here soon. Give me a hug good-bye so I can go home and start missing my best friend."

Angie gave her friend a bear hug. "I'll see you in eight days and I'll bring you back a sombrero."

The van arrived and soon Angie was at the airport, on the plane, and headed for rest and relaxation.

****

Arriving at the Camino Real Hotel in Mazatlàn, she was thrilled to see the property was really right on the beach. The private bungalow was much nicer than she'd imagined.

As she unpacked, Angie mused about the things she'd do here for a whole week by herself. After two or three days of sunbathing, a little shopping and playing tourist, what else was there to do, especially since she'd be on her own? She felt more alone than she had in her whole life and the loneliness hit her hard. She lay across the bed and started to cry.

With no more tears to shed, Angie chided herself for such a lengthy pity party. She told herself it'd be smart to make the best of things so she grabbed the tourist brochures on the table. She was happy to see there was a coffee shop for light dining, and a fine dining restaurant too. The in-room menus and her travels had made her hungry. Determined to get herself together and enjoy this week, she quickly dressed, brushed her hair, and headed for the restaurant.

The following three days of sunbathing, reading, sleeping, and fine dining hadn't helped rid Angie of her loneliness. If anything, the solitary vacation added more discontent and anxiety. At least the shop at home kept her busy with little time to think. The romance novel she'd read in which the guy and girl got together and lived happily ever after depressed her more. And boy, was happily ever after fiction! That sure as hell didn't happen in real life, not to her anyway. And here she was, living proof.

Feeling guilty about her situation, she wondered if things would've been different if she hadn't tried to get even with Gary, or if she hadn't been dead-set on giving him a taste of his own medicine. Better yet, what if he'd needed to 'fess up" that night at her house and she'd blown the whole thing?

I've got to think about something else, she told herself. She grabbed her beach towel, suntan lotion, and book and headed to her bungalow. She took a shower and caught a cab to downtown where she could ogle the souvenirs.

Lunch at the Shrimp Bucket offered a reasonable measure of fun and enjoyment. With a lighter mood, Angie joined a game of kick ball in the street with some local children. Her afternoon had been surprisingly pleasant. By the time she arrived back at the hotel, it was dinnertime. She asked the concierge to have her packages taken to her bungalow and headed to the dining room.

****

After a full day of fishing under the hot Mazatlàn sun, Gary was famished and felt grimy. He headed to his hotel room for a shower and change of clothes.

He was pleased with the accommodations and the spaciousness of his room. It held a king-size bed, a wet bar with a small well-stocked refrigerator, and a small seating area with a writing table and chairs. There were ornately decorated sliding doors that led to a large balcony overlooking the ocean. He wondered what more he could ask for. He instinctively knew the answer to that: someone to share it with. He could ask for Angie but asking wasn't necessarily getting. He popped a beer, slugged it back, and stepped into the shower.

Feeling a little more refreshed, he headed to the dining room instead of the coffee shop where he'd eaten most of his meals. Everyone on the fishing boat recommended the Camino Real restaurant, saying it was one of the best in Mazatlàn.

Sandi K. Whipple

He thought it must be pretty good when he saw a large number of diners. He found the maître d' and requested a table for one. There would be a twenty-minute wait so he headed to the lounge for a beer. He chose the last seat at the bar farthest from the entrance.

As he tipped his beer, his eyes scanned the crowd. Settling upon a strikingly attractive woman sitting alone at a table, he thought, Boy! Did she look like Angie! It couldn't be her though, because Angie had shoulder-length hair. This beauty had a short and very stylish cut. Besides, what would Angie be doing in Mazatlàn? Wow, he thought, all these miles from home and he couldn't stop thinking about her.

"Gibbons, party of one, your table is ready."

His head jerked to the direction of the table. He watched her as she reached for her handbag and rose from the chair. She turned in the direction of the doorway so he couldn't see her face. He had to know. Was it really Angie and what could she possibly be doing here? Maybe she wasn't alone. What fool would let her dine by herself? His eyes followed her from a distance. He knew that walk!

Seated, Angie began to read the menu.

Gary couldn't stop himself. He walked across the dining room and before she could look up, he quietly said, "Hello, Angie."

He could see she found it difficult to speak.

She forced herself, smiled and said, "Hello yourself. This is a coincidence, isn't it? What brings you all the way to Mazatlàn?"

"I'm on a fishing trip, how about you?"

Sandi K. Whipple

"A trip Frank and my aunt gave me as a gift. I didn't want to accept but when Frank said the ticket wasn't refundable, I had no choice."

"May I sit for a few minutes while I wait for my table?"

"Sure," she said and pointed to the chair across from her. Angie didn't want to show too much enthusiasm so she kept the conversation light. "Is this fishing trip a gambling group wagering on who'll land the biggest catch?"

"No, nothing like that. I love to fish and haven't been down here for a long time. We decided the business could get along without me for a week, so here I am. I've been here for four days."

Still somewhat shocked at seeing Angie so unexpectedly, Gary guarded his words to hide his pleasure. "I like your haircut, Angie. I saw you from the bar and at first I didn't think it was you; the hair was too short. I heard your name announced, and when you got up to head for the dining room, I recognized that walk."

Angie chuckled. "You recognized my walk? I didn't know people could be identified by their walk. That's a new one on me."

He wondered why she was alone and gingerly approached the subject of any possible relationship. "So how's Alan doing?"

With a slight smile, she responded, "Working hard and promising to surprise me soon.

He felt an invisible punch to his stomach. Was he hearing the end of any potential reconciliation between them? Was this the end of their story?

Sandi K. Whipple

The maître d' announced, "Gary, party of one, your table is ready."

With a heavy heart, Gary rose from the table. He'd been shaken by Angie's presence, the news that Alan had a surprise for her, and now, he couldn't find a reason to linger. Unable to think of a way to depart graciously, he simply said, "It was good to see you, Angie. You look terrific. I hope everything works out for you with Alan."

Angie was struggling to retain her composure while hiding her desire to prolong their conversation. Even though they'd only engaged in mere chit-chat, she wanted more time to fill her eyes with the sight of him. She refused to let him know her true feelings because of the distrust she held in her heart. She heard herself say, "I'm sure hoping it will and it was good to see you, too."

Gary's throat felt constricted as he said, "Good-bye, Angie."

Turning to leave, his mind reeled with the knowledge that Alan and his forthcoming surprise were obviously very important to Angie. His appetite suddenly faded. He apologized to the maître d' saying he no longer needed a table. As a heavy cloud of depression began to engulf him, Gary wouldn't allow himself a last look at the woman who'd invaded his daily thoughts and dreams. He left the restaurant and walked dejectedly to his room, where he paced and struggled to calm his mind. From the in-room refrigerator, he took a beer and walked out on the balcony. Maybe some fresh air would help, he thought. He stood at the railing. Staring out over the evening shadows and the cerulean waters of the ocean, he couldn't stop his racing thoughts.

Sandi K. Whipple

    Angie had intimated she was in Mazatlàn by herself, but if things between her and Alan were so tight, why would he let her come here alone? Didn't he want to be here with her, day and night, the way he did? Evidently Alan didn't love her as much as he did. Hell, he thought, she wasn't even wearing an engagement ring.
    His trip was now a complete bust. The thrill of the ultimate catch no longer held any excitement nor was he interested in wandering alone on the sunny beaches or manufacturing conversation with the teeming tourists. He couldn't stay in Mazatlàn with Angie so close by and suffer the torment of not being with her.
    With a hasty decision, he called the front desk to say he'd be checking out in the morning. He then contacted and instructed the concierge to cancel the rest of his fishing charters. When he finally got through to the airline, he eagerly charged the additional fare and booked the early morning flight home.

****

Angie boarded her return flight to the states, boasting a golden tan accentuated by her stark white sleeveless top. As she walked to her seat, she was in a mental fog, unaware of the number of admiring eyes that followed her movements.
    She was thankful she'd chosen a window seat. She fluffed her own carry-on pillow and placed it against the windowpane. Silently she prayed that sleep would relieve her of the mental exhaustion she felt from wrestling with thoughts of Gary. She kept her

sunglasses on to hide her swollen eyes and, minutes before the plane lifted from the runway, she was in a dreamless sleep.

After retrieving her luggage, she stood at the designated location waiting for the shuttle that would take her back to Nasons Grove. Angie whirled in surprise at the tap on her shoulder. "Carl. What in the world are you doing here?"

"You left a copy of your itinerary and I decided there was no way I was going to let you ride a cramped shuttle. So now you get your own private chauffeur and I get to hear all about this wonderful trip of yours. Good plan, huh?"

Hugging her friend, Angie said, "It was a great plan." Angie hoped her sunglasses were dark enough to hide her eyes. "Thanks for being so thoughtful. You're a true friend and I love you."

"I love you, too. Now, let's get your luggage to the car and get out of this madhouse."

The drive home was filled with gossip and laughter, all the while Angie struggled to keep the conversation light and airy. She just couldn't deal with any more heartache and she was more determined than ever to alter her attitude. She told herself she needed to focus more on her floral shop and the wonderful people in her life.

****

Angie dove into her daily routine without a skip, and before she knew it, she'd been home for more than a month. She'd found a few minutes of respite and was sitting in her office. Her thoughts wandered to her embellished descriptions of her fantasy Mazatlàn vacation, maybe even out-right lies, to Frank and Aunt Ruth. She'd wanted them to know how grateful she was and how much she'd enjoyed their thoughtful gift. She purposely chose not to divulge her happenstance meeting with Gary for many reasons, the main one being she dared not entertain any thoughts of him.

Everyone appeared to be tickled with the souvenirs she brought home and she embellished the story of each purchase. Again, she didn't mention to anyone that Gary had been in Mazatlàn.

Her thoughts again wandered as she asked herself, *What, pray tell, are the chances of experiencing a coincidence like that?* Her attempt to see him before her scheduled flight home failed. The desk clerk informed her that a Gary Henderson was not registered, nor had there recently been a guest of that name. If she'd been able to see him, what would she have said to him anyway? That she loved him? That she was better for him than Blondie? Of course, if that were true, he'd be here with her now, wouldn't he? Frank was right when he said life sometimes deals a lousy hand.

Still mulling over the events of that meeting, she recalled the surprised look on the waiter's face when she'd asked for the check just moments after Gary left her table. She explained she wasn't as hungry as she'd thought and quickly paid for the glass of wine. Without a second thought, Angie had hurriedly returned to her bungalow where she grappled for her key. When she unlocked her door, she'd frantically run into the room and threw herself across her bed. She'd hoped to find solace and escape from the emotional turmoil of the encounter.

Gary had looked so good. Nothing about him had changed and he was still the most handsome man she'd ever seen in her life. He was truly Gary Adonis - just not *her* Gary Adonis. He'd said *we* decided on this trip. *We* who? Had he meant Blondie, and where had she been? He hadn't ask if he could join her for dinner, and, furthermore, the maître d' had announced his table for one, not two. Maybe Blondie wasn't a fan of fishing.

Still dissecting her trip in her mind, Angie realized there hadn't been one damned thing about it that had been relaxing for her. She'd wanted to pack her souvenirs and go home immediately, but her departure wasn't until the next day. She felt it had been the longest and most unnerving twenty-four hours she'd ever lived through.

CHAPTER TWENTY-TWO

After a week back at work, Angie found herself still depressed. She sighed with an air of despair and attempted to refocus her thoughts. She desperately wanted a more positive attitude. She considered the shop's activities and knew that business was better than she could have ever imagined. Her investment in this building was a great move and the bonus was, her staff of fabulous people whom she'd come to love. They were like family and, having seen their loyalty, her heart filled with pride.

Patti was deliriously happy in her new marriage, and Carrie had an adorable boyfriend who cherished the ground she walked on. Even Chuck had met a nice woman and was becoming serious about her. Aunt Ruth's happiness and contentment were an answer to Angie's prayers. Her best friend adored her husband and they had two wonderful children. Then there was Gary, who had Blondie and her two kids.

With an elbow on the edge of her desk, Angie rested her chin in her hand. Here she sat, she mused, the only one she knew who had no special person in her life. Her depression grew and she fought the hot and salty tears forming in the corners of her eyes.

She knew she had to chase away the black clouds threatening to darken the rest of her day. With little thought, she grabbed the phone and called her best friend.

With a forced cheerfulness in her voice, Angie responded to Carl's hello, "Hey, girlfriend. I need to get out of the shop before I go crazy. I've covered everything here for the rest of the day, so can you get away for a long lunch?"

With the usual giggle in her voice, Carl told her, "I already have keys in hand, silly girl. Tell me where to meet you and I'm out the door."

"How about Di Nido Bistro?"

"I'm halfway there. See you in a few."

****

The restaurant was in the middle of the lunch rush but there was always a table available for Angie. She'd been seated for only a few minutes when Carl walked into the room.

Angie waved and said, "Over here, Carl."

As she approached the table, Carl asked, "How did you beat me? I drove like a fool looking forward to an afternoon of smut and gossip."

"First of all, I had very little traffic and, as for smut and gossip, sit, dear friend, and we shall begin. But, first things first. Want to order a drink?"

Angie described the seemingly deserted roads and the uncommon light traffic when the waiter arrived to take their drink order.

When he disappeared, Carl said, "Traffic schmaffic, Angie. I'm going to skip the chitchat and dive right in. I knew when I picked you up at the airport that Mazatlàn hadn't renewed or energized you." Carl was trying to make a slight joke of the serious questions, thinking it might lighten Angie's mood. "Either Mexico was not all it's cracked up to be in those gorgeous brochures, or you went fishing and the big one got away.

Were the ocean waters too cold and the beaches too rocky?"

Although she was rambling, Carl sensed her friend had definitely been out of kilter since her return and she was determined to find out why. "Want to tell me what happened there or just tell me it's none of my damned business? You know I'm dying to hear it all."

Grinning at her friend who obviously cared about her, Angie decided to unload her burden and began her story by saying, "Actually, I was pretty hyped when I left here. I thought a change of scenery would help clear my mind and set me on a new course. For a couple of days, I stretched out on the beach and caught up on some reading. I even had a fun shopping spree and found a great restaurant near the beach. One night, I was waiting for a table in the hotel restaurant and, by a strange coincidence, guess who was also there, on a fishing trip?"

With a loud gasp, Carl put her hand to her mouth. "No way. I don't believe it. What are the odds of that happening? Did he see you? Did you talk? What the hell happened?"

Angie explained, "The place was busy so he sat with me and we talked while he waited for a table."

Carl couldn't contain her impatience to hear the details and with an excited voice she said, "Talked about what, Angie?"

Recalling the scene in her mind, Angie's obvious sadness altered her mood and Carl noticed her immediate change of tone when she answered. "As I look back now, it was just a brief encounter and I realize we didn't talk about anything important. He told me he was there on a fishing trip and I explained I was there, compliments of my Aunt Ruth and Frank. He did say he liked my haircut. Then his name was called for a table and that was pretty much it."

Carl felt disappointed in the lack of details so she inquired more. "Was he alone? I mean, like, you know, really alone? And I don't mean with a group of fanatical gill lovers."

Angie sighed. She knew Carl was trying to inject some humor for her benefit but Angie couldn't shake her sadness. She went on with her story. "I don't know. The next morning I checked with the front desk for his room number thinking if we could just sit and talk, I mean really talk, we might have been able to work things out. I was stupid enough to think that maybe, if I looked him in the face and told him I loved him, that . . . well, it might matter to him."

Carl nearly yelled, "Then why in the name of God didn't you do it?"

"The girl at the desk said no one by that name was listed as a guest, nor had the name ever been registered. I guess he was staying elsewhere and was just there for dinner."

As though a light bulb had gone off in her head, Carl reflexively leaned forward and clasped her hands together. With her eyebrows arched and an expression of amazement, she said, "Angie, be serious for a minute. Do you realize you've never told me the 'slime's' name? For that matter, I don't think I've ever asked."

"It's . . ."

"Your drinks, ladies," the waiter interrupted.

Sandi K. Whipple

Sensing the impact of her words, Carl paid no attention to the waiter and immediately interrupted her friend's response. "Anyway, if you don't want to talk about this, just say so and I'll quietly remove my tennis shoe and stick my sock in my mouth," Carl said with a grin.

Grateful for a respite, Angie sighed with relief. She needed relief from the conversation and she didn't want the feelings of depression to dampen the afternoon.

They'd been chattering away when yet another waiter appeared with a bottle of champagne nestled in a silver ice bucket. Just as they began to question the waiter, Mrs. Di Nido approached the table.

"Hello, Angie. I apologize for intruding. I'd like to personally thank you for the special services you have been providing to Di Nido Bistro. I know my husband did, but I don't believe I ever thanked you for the special delivery on the night of my anniversary." She continued, "I'm sure you went out of your way that evening, as did that handsome young man with you who bowed at our table ... well, you made my husband and I proud to know you." Not wanting to intrude any longer or monopolize the conversation, Mrs. Di Nido quickly added, "I do hope you enjoy the champagne."

"Thank you," Angie told her, and before she could introduce Carl, Mrs. Di Nido departed as quietly as she approached.

Carl looked at her misty-eyed friend. "Oh, Angie, don't you dare start crying. I hate it when you do that. And did she say 'the handsome young man with you'? You never told me about this or any handsome young man."

Sandi K. Whipple

Carl scrambled for words in an attempt to stem the flow of Angie's tears. Once again she tried humor and said with a raised glass, "Let us drink and be merry while you tell me all . . . I'll call my Jim later and tell him he's our designated driver so he'll come get us."

Seeing the sparkling glass of champagne in front of her, Angie looked up and said, "I don't know, Carl. I don't react very well to this bubbly stuff. Once upon a time I got very drunk on it and was pretty sick the next day."

Not losing a beat, Carl said, "It appears to me you survived it. Look, follow my lead. You just drink a glass of milk first to coat your stomach. Be sure to eat something and take three aspirin with four glasses of water before you go to bed. Hence, no hangover or headache the next morning." Laughing, she added, "Believe me, I did it all when I was in college."

With that, Carl waved at the waiter. "Could you please bring us two large glasses of milk? After that, we'd like to order. Eating first is part of our program."

With a confused and comical expression on his face, the waiter asked, "I beg your pardon?" Angie and Carl looked at one another and broke out in laughter. As they roared at the inside joke, Carl gave Angie an unobtrusive glance and applauded her efforts to lighten Angie's state of mind.

The chatting, giggling friends drank their milk and fed their laughter with white moustaches. They devoured their lunch but took their time as they savored each bite of the incredibly delicious dessert. To their amazement, they also emptied Mrs. Di Nido's champagne. They agreed it was a perfect reason to graduate to champagne cocktails.

Following a few hours of bubbly consumption, they became quite drunk. "Okay, Angie, let's play a game of *to tell the truth*. You're first because I thought of it. Now, give it up. What's the 'slime's' name?"

Feeling giddy, Angie confessed her personal name for Gary. "Adonis," she said. "And, he really is one, too. He's picture-perfect and gorgeous." At that point, Angie's thoughts became a little confused and she posed the question: "Do you think men can be beautiful?"

Realizing that her friend was wandering off course, Carl said, "Whoa, let's go back just a teensy bit here. Did you say *Adonis*? That's not a name, Angie. That's a Greek god."

"Exactly, Carl. You got the point. I rest my case."

Carl turned and hollered, "Waiter, more of this bubbly stuff, if you please. We're drinking to a slime God." Turning her gaze back to Angie, she blinked her eyes a couple of times to adjust her focus. "Now I see why you're so upset about not having this guy. Hell, if an Adonis God walked into my life, then just walked out again, I'd start digging in, too."

Angie had a quizzical look on her face. "What's that mean, digging in?"

Carl looked up from her glass and said, "I lost you, girlfriend. What were you talking about?"

"I haven't the slightest idea," Angie responded with a giggle and a wave of her hand.

Sandi K. Whipple

They poured more champagne and tried to make sense of one another's words as they laughed and carried on like schoolgirls. A grumbling sensation in her stomach caused Angie to say, "Have we been here long enough to check out the dinner menu? We did eat lunch, didn't we?"

Carl was having difficulty with her focus as she tried to read her wristwatch. "Gee, have we been here all day? If it's time for dinner, I suppose I should go home. I'm not gonna cook so my Jim can order take-out. Want to join us and finally meet my brats?"

Angie was feeling a bit wobbly. "I think I'd just like to be dropped off at my house. Maybe I'll join you another time."

"Okay then, girlfriend," Carl muttered. "I'll call my Jim and he can come get us."

Rummaging through her purse, Carl found her cell phone. She fumbled with the keypad for a minute and finally managed to call her husband. "Jim, honey, my friend and I had a wonderful afternoon, but we've had a little more liquid for lunch than we planned. Could you be a love and come play chauffeur?" Listening to his response, she said, "Well, don't open it, honey, come get your wifey first and then we'll open one together and play house. Okay, see you in a few."

As she folded the cell phone, she looked at Angie. "He was just getting ready to sit down and have a beer with my brother. He said he'd abstain until he had us safely home." With a sheepish grin on her face, she continued, "You know, whenever I offer to play house, there isn't anything he wouldn't do for me."

Sandi K. Whipple

When Jim and Carl's brother arrived at the restaurant, they were greeted by a sight to behold. With elbows propped on the table, the two women were in the midst of a giggling attack and the tabletop was in disarray. Realizing the two delinquents were going to be a handful, Jim silently thanked his lucky stars he'd brought his brother-in-law along for help.

As the men walked toward the table, Angie glanced up and looked through blurry eyes at the approaching men. Not trusting her sight or believing what she saw, she sat upright and rubbed her eyes. In between blinks, she felt she was falling into a swirling dark cloud. She knew she was awake but then again, she was frightened at the thought of having slipped into the middle of a nightmare. "No way," she said out loud. "I'm hallucinating!"

Angie tried to focus on the faces of the two men who now stood at the table. For what seemed like an eternity, Angie fought to gain some self-control and find a way to clear the hallucination or awake from the nightmare. Feeling squeamish, she leaned over the tabletop, raised herself from the seat, cupped her mouth, and whispered with urgency in Carl's ear, "Psst. Psst. It's him!"

Carl turned her head to focus on Angie's face. With slurred words, she asked, "Him who?"

Shaking a hand in Carl's face, Angie repeated, "Psst. I'm telling you, it's him!"

Trying to point a finger directly at Gary, Carl said, "You mean him? Aw, c'mon Angie, that's just my brother."

Sandi K. Whipple

Carl was also having difficulty focusing but, when she finally got a clear look at Angie, she was alarmed. Her friend was now ashen with all color having drained from her face. Angie didn't look well and furthermore, she'd suddenly become more than agitated. It must be the champagne, Carl surmised. "Angie . . . what is this *him* thing all about?"

Carl had no more completed her words when a lightning bolt struck her. She nearly jumped from her seat and her elbow knocked her glass, spilling the remaining champagne on the tabletop. Not realizing her words were audible, she squealed loudly, "Oh my God! No! You mean he's the *slime*?"

Shielding her face from Gary, and with slurred words, Angie said, "That's the one all right, in the flesh. If you're really my friend, Carl, you'll tell him to go away."

Concern for her friend had erased all awareness of her surroundings and, as Carl turned to face her brother, she yelled, "You heard her, Gary. I mean you, slime. Go away and the hell with you. Go away now, this minute. My friend doesn't want you here."

Unable to make sense of his wife's antics, Jim grabbed Gary's shoulder and said, "Want to flip to see which one you get to carry out of here?"

Gary pointed to Angie. "Nope. I'll take this one." He continued, "But you keep them busy and in their seats while I go pay the check and tip their poor waiter."

Trying to keep his laughter in check, Jim hollered, "Give him a nice tip. I have a feeling he's earned it."

Sandi K. Whipple

When Gary returned, Jim had both purses over his shoulder. He told Gary to get the girls' shoes from under the table. With shoes in tow, Gary stood and joined Jim in laughter. Approaching hysteria, Jim said, "Okay, on the count of three."

Gary pulled Angie up and out of her chair and she began to scream, "Get your hands off me, you slime." With her arms flailing, she yelled louder, "Help. Somebody, anybody, I'm being kidnapped. Stop this man. He has no right to remove me from the premises. Help."

Gary threw her over his shoulder and headed for the door.

When Jim pulled Carl up from her chair, she too started screaming. "How can you stand there while that slime is dragging my best friend away?" Carl was waving and yelling in Angie's direction. "I'm coming to help you, Angie, hold on. I won't let that slime hurt you."

Having witnessed how Gary handled his delinquent, Jim followed the lead in an instant. He put Carl over his shoulder and headed for the door. When they managed to get their inebriated and screaming loads to the car, Gary threw Angie in the back seat while Jim wrestled Carl into the front. Gary told Jim to drop him with Angie at her place, saying he would catch a cab later to retrieve his car.

Angie wouldn't stop screaming for help and she continued to holler about being kidnapped by the slime. From the front seat, Carl bellowed at Gary saying he was a beast and nothing but slime. Both men felt the pangs of constricting stomach muscles as they struggled to keep their laughter in check.

Jim steered the car with his left hand and held on to Carl with his right as he drove. The comedic situation was right out of a movie, but he was able to maneuver the car —although with difficulty – to Angie's house. He handed Angie's purse to Gary and asked if any help was needed with his flailing victim.

As he pulled Angie from the car and grabbed her shoes from the seat, Gary gave Jim a quizzical look. Laughing as he said, "I can handle her."

With the sound of the back door slamming shut, Jim pulled away from the street and headed home. Carl screamed through the front window, "You're slime, Gary. I hate you! You're pure slime, Gary."

As he struggled with Angie's purse and shoes, Gary tried to hold her upright as she walked. Thankfully, he was able to unlock and kick open her front door. In the time it took to maneuver her to the sofa, she'd calmed down a bit and he was able to set her down gently. Her hair was a mess from the wrestling match and Gary bent over to remove a few strands from her face. He was surprised at his own loving tone. "You sure can be hellcat when you're drunk, Angie."

Angie tried to sit up and focus her mind. "I'm not drunk. I just had a few drinks with a friend. That's all. You can go now."

With the scent of her cologne lingering in his nostrils, Gary's heart was beating rapidly with her apparent dismissal of him. He just couldn't say good-bye to her again. "Are you ever going to tell me what I did to piss you off so badly? You're killing me inside, Angie."

"Ha!" she said as she tried to straighten her clothes. "Isn't that just too bad? Let's play *to tell the truth*, Gary. I go first," she said with fire in her eyes. "The truth is, I hate you, and your truth is you like blondes. By the way, where is your Blondie?"

Before he could respond to her attack, she continued, "Is she good in the sack, Gary? Better than me? Well, my other truth is, I don't give a damn. Now get out."

Stunned at her accusations, Gary tried to remain calm. "No one, Angie, and I mean, no one, is better at making love than you. I resent you referring to our lovemaking as just *being in the sack*. Is that all it was to you?"

Now it was his turn to keep her at bay. He continued, "And, as far as a Blondie goes, I have no idea what you're talking about. There is not now, and has never been, a blonde or a Blondie."

By now, tears were streaming down her face. Angie could bear no more of his lies as she hollered, "Get out, Gary."

Panic-stricken, Gary reached out to her. "Angie, please talk to me."

Waving his hand away from her, she could only holler more loudly, "Please, get out. Please go, now."

As his confusion and pain grew, Gary felt there was no room for discussion or explanation. Angie was beside herself. He moved slowly toward the door.

"You sure enjoy throwing me out, Angie. Okay. You win! Have it your way!" Gary closed the door

Sandi K. Whipple

behind him and Angie sat with only the sounds of her sobbing.

CHAPTER TWENTY-THREE

Three days had gone by since Carl and Angie had succumbed to a liquid lunch and the day had ended in a wrestling match. Carl refused to take any of her brother's phone calls and she instructed Jim to tell Gary to stay away from her house. With anger in her voice, she also said if he called, she'd damn sure tell him off.

Gary phoned anyway, and when she answered unwittingly, he said, "Carolynn, will you please tell me what the hell is going on? I have no idea what I did to get you so mad at me."

With exasperation in her voice, Carl said, "Okay, Gary, I'll tell you. First of all, Angie is my best friend. Evidently you were having problems with some blonde so, in order to make her jealous, or to simply appease yourself, you two-timed with my friend. Then, after you got her to fall for you, you had the gall to flash the blonde woman in Angie's face. You weren't even discreet about it. I'm glad she hurt you, Gary. It serves you right. You tore her to shreds and now she hates you. You're slime, Gary, and I hate you too! Bye."

Gary was dumbfounded! He sat staring at the phone in his hand for almost five minutes before he set it down. What in the world was going on? What just happened here? Did everyone hate him? And what was this about another woman and not being discreet? He hadn't even looked at another woman since meeting Angie. What the hell was she talking about when she referred to a blonde? That was the same accusation Angie made.

Sandi K. Whipple

Pacing the room, he knew he hadn't been able to get in a word with his sister as she ranted on the phone. If he had, he'd have told her that the woman he'd been having problems with was Angie. Bottom line, Carolynn had no idea what she was talking about.

Trying to make sense of the chaos, Gary was totally baffled as he tried to dissect the past conversation. How could Angie be hurt by anything relating to him considering she had Alan or Carl to run to? Hell, he had no one to run to and, from the looks of things, he didn't even have his sister any more.

He wondered how and when Carolynn met Angie. He couldn't recall any recent conversations with her about a new friend. She'd never mentioned... All of a sudden, like a flash in his head, it hit him! He ran his hand through his hair, rubbed his face. Before he could unravel any of the mystery, his cell phone rang.

It was Tom. "Gary, I need a favor. I promised Lucy I'd take care of a couple of estimates in Green Bend by 6:30 tonight. I have an appointment with a Mr. Krenshaw at 5:00, so I don't think I can make Green Bend in time. If you can't do it, I'll have Ted leave a job early and drive over."

Gary could hear the urgency in Tom's voice. "Not to worry, and I'll let Lucy know. Who's Krenshaw anyway, do I know him?"

Tom sighed with relief. "I don't think so. I know I don't. He told Katie he's an independent journalist doing an article on heaters from the old days up to now. You know, the old-fashioned boilers and stuff? Katie thought it would be good publicity for us, so she set it up. I got stuck with it because some guy recommended me."

"Better you than me," Gary said with a chuckle. "I'll think of you while I kick back with my feet up on your desk. See ya."

****

Tom arrived at the appointed time and place for his appointment. While shaking hands, Mr. Krenshaw told Tom to call him by his preferred name, Alan. Alan steered the brief chat to his reason for the meeting and reaffirmed he was doing a story for an unnamed publication. He didn't think Tom was suspicious of his cover as a journalist.

With a notebook in hand, Alan posed his questions as a writer. "Well, Tom, let's start with you. I need some background information such as where you were born, where you grew up and where you attended school. I'd also like you to tell me how you got into this business – you know, things like that."

Having never been interviewed for a story, Tom found Alan's questions to be quite personal. Not wanting to insult him, he chose his words carefully. "I'm sorry, Alan, but my background won't make for very interesting reading. Simply stated, when I was real young I left Silo, Montana where I grew up, drifted through the northern states, moved to Illinois, met my wife, got married, moved here and learned the business from Mr. Walgren. That's my whole life story in a nutshell. Pretty boring, huh?"

Smiling, Alan responded, "I wouldn't exactly say that. If you're happy, then it's all pretty much academic, don't you think? And you do appear to be quite happy."

"Actually, Alan, I am. My life is pretty close to what I've always wanted."

For the next few minutes, Alan posed, and Tom answered questions about the company's history. As Alan closed his notebook,

Tom took that as a signal that the interview was over. He stood up, extended his hand and asked, "So when will this article run and in what magazine?"

Alan needed to continue playing the journalist. "As I told you, I'm independent, so, when I have the article ready for publication, I'll need your signature giving permission to run it. At that time, you'll know which magazine. I'll be including photos of old and new furnaces as well as some background information on the owners."

"You can get all that information from my secretary," Tom offered.

"Okay, great. I'll follow up with her."

As Alan rose from his chair, Tom said, "Then I guess we're finished here. Thank you for taking an interest in our company. I'll look forward to seeing and reading the article." Tom extended his hand.

"You're welcome," Alan responded.

As they shook good-bye, Alan thought to himself how fortunate he was to have found Tom and then to be shaking his hand, the hand of Angie's brother - and right here in Nasons Grove. Who would have believed it?

Sandi K. Whipple

His mind raced with so many thoughts of the long journey he'd been on to find Tom. If an auto mechanic from Chicago hadn't led him to Springfield, and a bartender from Springfield hadn't led him to Nason's Grove, well... Alan recalled the interview with Angie's Aunt Ruth. He had given his word that she would be the first to know of his findings, good or bad. Ruth didn't want Angie to be alone when she learned the outcome.

With excitement rising, Alan couldn't wait to tell Ruth he'd found Angie's brother and Ruth's nephew! He imagined the whoops of joy when they realized the huge bonus – a niece for Angie and a great-niece for Ruth! What a story! And it's all right here in town.

Alan shook off his daydreaming and searched for his car keys. He hurried to his car, nearly stumbled as he got in, fumbled with the ignition, and careened into the street. He doggedly steered the car straight toward Ruth's house.

****

The estimates on the two jobs took very little of his time and it was still daylight when Gary drove back from Green Bend. With thoughts of Angie and all the recent events running through his mind, he decided to stop off at Ruth's house. No one knew Angie better than her aunt. If anyone had any ideas or suggestions about this screwed-up situation, it would be Ruth.

He felt it was a risky attempt and possibly a waste of time, but he needed to make one last attempt at clearing up the confusion between him and Angie, once and for all. Gary needed some answers. He could hardly tolerate the constant anxiety that kept him from sleeping and operating on a healthy level.

He was hopeful that Ruth would be willing to talk to him and shed some light on the subject of Angie's life and perhaps tell him what was truly troubling her. For days he'd wrestled with her accusatory words and still, he had no idea what she was so disturbed about.

If he poured his heart out and professed his love for her niece, perhaps Ruth would be agreeable to sharing her perspectives. There was only one way to find out.

Gary parked his car on the street. Walking to the front door, he reached out to ring the doorbell. Before he could ring, the door suddenly opened. With her head turned away from him, Gary realized Ruth was obviously speaking to someone. He cleared his throat to make her aware of his presence. Turning at the sound, Ruth looked at him and immediately reacted in surprise.

Gary took the lead and said, "Hello, Ruth. I hope I didn't startle you. I came hoping to talk to you about something - if you're not busy." As he spoke, he saw the silhouette of someone in the entryway behind her. "I'm sorry," he said and began to back away. "I should have called first. I'll come back another time."

"No, Gary, it's fine. Please, come in. Alan was just leaving."

Gary felt a stab in his heart. He stood stunned and looked straight at his perceived rival. What was he doing in Angie's aunt's house?

Turning quickly from Gary, Ruth said to Alan, "Thank you again." She gave him a hug. "I'm so excited for Angie I'm ready to burst. I can't wait to see the look on her face. Good-bye."

Alan said, "Good-bye." He gave a nod to Gary as he walked past him and departed.

"Please, Gary, come in," Ruth said returning her attention to him. "What is it you wanted to talk to me about? Would you like a cup of coffee or maybe a beer?"

Ever more perplexed, Gary spoke softly. "I think I may have come at a wrong time, Ruth. Maybe even too late from the sound of your conversation with Alan."

"Too late for what, Gary? Come in, sit down, and tell me what brought you here."

Seated in the warm and cozy kitchen, Ruth gave him a beer and poured a small glass of Chambord for herself. As he waited for her to settle in a nearby chair, Gary wondered if this might be a wasted trip. Maybe he'd waited too long to make sense of everything. Evidently, Alan's timing had been perfect since he was about to do something to make Angie very happy.

Ruth interrupted his thoughts as she seated herself and said, "Now, talk to me."

She listened intently to Gary's beleaguered story while sipping her drink. As Gary droned on in great detail about the events of the past, his heartache, his sleepless nights, and endless anxiety, she fought the urge to interrupt. It was better to hold her tongue and allow Gary to vent his frustrations and purge his soul.

With a deep sigh, Gary sat back in his chair. "So, I guess that's all of it, Ruth. I love her very much, but I think I may have been operating on hope alone."

Ruth patted his hand and giggled. "Oh, Gary, I have so many things to tell you. I have a feeling you're going to be just as happy and excited as Angie will be with Alan's news. First, I think we'd better get you another beer. I have a feeling you're going to need it."

Gary sipped the cold beer as Ruth began to unravel the cobweb of events that had ensnared his heart and soul for so many months. She slowly explained everything she knew, including the particulars surrounding the fact that Alan was a private investigator.

Gary recalled that Angie had, in fact, briefly told him about her brother, but that was in the beginning of their relationship. She'd mentioned that her friend Carl had helped her hire a PI. Looking back he realized, the PI's name was never used! He was just referred to as the *PI*.

As Ruth continued to unravel more details, he started to see he'd also neglected to communicate fully. He cringed inwardly when he thought about his sister's children. He was guilty of not explaining to Angie whose children they were.

Ruth then confessed that for many months, she'd had a growing suspicion that her niece had been harboring considerable feelings for him.

Feeling more relaxed now that some of Gary's confusion had been clarified, Ruth said, "So you see, Gary, you've never had a reason to be in doubt."

For so long, Ruth had wanted nothing but happiness for Angela and she became animated with excitement at the thought of setting some wheels in motion to accomplish just that.

"Now, Gary," she said, "if you don't mind my meddling, I have a plan as to how we can handle this entire thing."

Ruth's willingness to share all that he'd just heard caused a weight lifted from his heart. He felt almost euphoric as he agreed to let her handle things. She was quite ecstatic herself as she filled him in on her plan.

Ruth concluded her plan by saying, "Once things are ready to go, I'll introduce myself to my nephew and his wife and I'll tell them of the plan. I'll make sure they're at Di Nido Bistro on Saturday night. I'll get in touch with Carl to set things up. Oh dear! Wait till I tell Frank."

They talked for a short time longer but their eagerness to put the plan in motion drove Gary out the door. He hugged Ruth and told her he couldn't find enough words to express his gratitude. She shooed him away with a grin.

In an attempt to shore up Ruth's terrific plan, Gary called Tom and told him not to make any plans for Saturday night. When Tom asked why, Gary said there would be a surprise coming.

"Damn, Gary. Last time you had a surprise for me I almost had a stroke. Is my wife in on this one, too?"

Laughing, Gary told him, "No, she isn't. So you'll leave Saturday open then?"

"Sure, I guess so," Tom replied with a questioning tone.

Gary excitedly told him, "Great, and by the way, a wonderful angel of a woman named Ruth will be calling you with more details. I think you'll be more surprised than you were the last time. See you Saturday night," Gary said and dashed off to his next mission.

As he headed for his sister's house, he silently thanked Aunt Ruth for opening his eyes and he chided himself for his stupidity. Carl was a nickname! His sister's nickname! He'd hated it her whole life thinking it made her unfeminine. Due to his insane jealousy he'd never put it together. When he reached the driveway of his sister's house, Gary jumped from his car and ran indoors without knocking. He found her in the kitchen and grabbed her in a huge bear hug. He spun her around in circles and yelled, "I love you, Sis. You're Carl. Did you hear me? You're Carl."

Carl was stymied and shocked by her brother's about face. Slamming her hands on his shoulder tops, she yelled, "Let me go, you slime. And hell, yeah, I'm Carl. Tell me something I don't know already. And why are you here? You know you're not welcome," she said, trying to look angry.

He let her go. "Now, listen for once and let me finish," he told her. As he broke the lengthy news to her, she stood open-mouthed. He rattled on and on and she became more shocked. Listening as intently as possible because Gary was talking so fast, Carl began to get a glimpse of the pain and suffering that her brother had endured.

She watched him pace while listening to him run on.

"All I had to do was ask her, but no, I had to let my damned jealousy and insecurities get in the way. But, isn't it great? Anyway, you'll need to get in touch with Ruth and Frank to work out the details. Got a beer?"

Carl stared at her jubilant brother and thought he was going to have a heart attack from an overdose of adrenalin. Feeling a warm rush of sisterly emotion, she finally found her voice and was able to speak. "You're still slime," she said affectionately.

****

Gary was inwardly bursting with pride when he reflected on the bridge he'd rebuilt between himself and his sister. He appeared to strut down the street over the next few days as he waited for updates on Ruth's great plan.

When his sister called, she told him Ruth had set everything in motion and then explained, "I called Mr. Di Nido and apologized for the drunken episode in his restaurant. He was amused and said none was needed. I also swore him to secrecy," she said to Gary. "I explained everything and he promised to help out. Angie is the only one who doesn't have a clue."

With great animation in her voice, Carl continued, "Ruth is really giddy, especially after meeting her new-found nephew and his family. Mom's excited and said she can't wait till Saturday and meet the feisty woman who's had you acting like a love-sick school boy."

"I'll bet," Gary said with a chuckle.

****

Sandi K. Whipple

Angie had been in a black mood for quite some time even though she'd survived the hangover. Carl had advised her incorrectly; the aspirin hadn't prevented a day-long headache. Nor did any of the remedies take away her embarrassment of the drunken scene with her and Carl, Jim, and Gary. How could she ever walk into the Di Nido Bistro again and hold her head up?

Furthermore, how could she escape beating herself up for saying all those ugly words to Gary? She knew she had way too much to drink but he hadn't deserved that kind of tongue-lashing. She was ashamed of her behavior and wanted to continue hiding in the shop.

Patti's loud voice made Angie jump in her chair. "Angie, line three is for you. It's Carl."

"Hi, Carl, what's up?" Angie inquired.

"Hey, girlfriend, you got plans for Saturday night?"

"Well, as a matter of fact, Tom Cruise and I had words yesterday and Robert Redford hasn't returned my call, so I guess I'm free, why?"

"Very funny!" Carl said. "Anyway, my mother-in-law has agreed to watch my brats and my Jim is going out with the guys for some of that macho bonding stuff. Want to have dinner with me at Di Nido Bistro? My treat."

Angie felt a lurch in her stomach. "Are we still allowed in there after our drunken episode? I'm embarrassed to even step foot in there, Carl."

Carl wanted to reassure her friend. "I called the next day and apologized for both of us. Mr. Di Nido said no apology was necessary. He actually thought we were very entertaining. Can you imagine that? Anyway, how about Saturday? I'm buying, as I mentioned."

Angie brightened as she felt somewhat exonerated. "How could I say no when I get to leave my wallet at home? Want me to drive over and get you?"

"No, I'll be out running errands, so I'll pick you up between 6:30 and 7:00, if that's okay."

"That's fine, and Carl?"

"What?"

"I really am leaving my wallet at home." They laughed and hung up in unison.

****

On Saturday, Angie rode to the restaurant with Carl. When they entered the lobby, Carl looked around and said, "I've always wanted to see the back banquet room. Mind if we snoop before getting a table?"

"A snoop won't hurt," Angie said, "but just a quick snoop!"

They walked through a set of double doors marked *banquet*. Carl said, "Oh, they have a ladies room over there. I left the house so fast, and I need to powder my nose."

Deliberately walking slowly, Carl made sure Angie entered the ladies room first, then, with a snicker, she tiptoed out.

When Angie realized Carl was nowhere near, she called out her name. Hearing no response, she stepped from the ladies room and into the banquet hall. Opening her mouth to call out for Carl, Angie's words were replaced with a loud gasp when her eyes were suddenly filled with the sight of Gary.

"What are you doing here?" she said with astonishment rising in her voice.

Turning to leave and escape any confrontation, she found the exit door was locked.

Angie immediately pivoted on her heel and found herself face to face with him. Angrily she barked, "Open this door, Gary, and I mean it!"

"No." he said and stood his ground.

With more fury in her voice, she said, "What did you say? I said open this door right now!"

He leaned against the wall, planted his feet, and crossed his arms. He had a mischievous smile on his face as he casually retorted, "I told you, no."

Completely bewildered, Angie almost pleaded, "What the hell is this, Gary?"

Standing still, he told her, "We need to talk, Angie, and being locked in the same room together seems to be the only way we can do that."

Pacing back and forth, Angie spoke with wrath in her voice, "I have nothing to say to you, Gary. If you're in a mood to talk, I suggest you go find your sweet little Blondie and talk to her."

Still standing motionless, Gary asked, "Would you be kind enough to tell me who this Blondie person might be? I mean, do you know her name?"

Angie's breathing increased. With fire in her voice, Angie's words erupted as she spewed her anger. "I don't give a damn what her name is. I saw you together, hugging and kissing. I tried to ignore that because I foolishly thought I was in love with you, but then, you left me in my sickbed and ran straight to her. I couldn't – and wouldn't - deal with it, no matter how much I loved you. Don't try to deny it either because I saw your pictures in the paper. Now let me out of here. I have nothing more to say to you!"

Frozen in his place, Gary didn't want to fuel the flames and have her run away. With a lowering of his voice, he calmly said, "You say you *loved* me, Angie. Is that past tense?"

"Yes, it is," she said. She practically stomped her feet as she continued to pace. "I was stupid enough to think I loved you, but I wised up. Now let me out of here. I have nothing to say to you so this conversation is finished." She tried to push him aside and grab the door handle.

Gary blocked her exit with his body planted in front of the door. Knowing she couldn't budge him, he took the opportunity and said, "If you have nothing more to say, that's fine. Tell you what, I'll talk and you can listen."

"What?" she said, unable to curtail her loud voice.

"Angie, if you'll just hear me out, everything will make sense."

Taking his lead, Angie leaned against the wall and gave Gary a condescending look.

Gary began to share his thoughts and feelings. "Every time we had words and I walked out on you, it was because I was full of jealousy. I couldn't stand it. I couldn't stand the thought of sharing you with other men. The thought made my blood boil. The first time you mentioned Carl, I wanted to find him and kill him."

Angie's eyes grew enormous and her hand flew to her mouth.

Gary continued, "Then I missed you so much, I came back in an attempt to get over it. Each time you said his name I went crazy. I just couldn't handle the thought of sharing you. When I thought I'd learned to control my jealousy and anger, you started talking about Alan and my blood started boiling all over again."

As if she'd been hit on the head, Angie ran her hand across her forehead. With astonishment rising in her voice, she tried to hide her own guilt and took the offensive by saying, "That's it? That's what this was all about? You really are an ass, Gary. Carl is my best friend and it was just the other night that I found out she's your sister. And Alan is the private investigator I hired to find my brother."

"I know that – now," he said. "I knew you'd hired a private detective but you never told me his name. When you talked about him it was always just 'the private investigator', or the PI."

Angie was in disbelief! How did all of this confusion get started? *My God,* she thought, *Carl is his sister and Alan is.?*

Gary was still talking. "Every time we made love, I thought we were back on track. Then Carl and Alan would come up again. I got jealous again and walked out."

Gary shifted his weight and dropped his crossed arms. "There you have it, all of it. But I do love you, Angie."

"And what about Blondie's two kids you had in the park that you've come to love as your own?"

Sandi K. Whipple

"They're Carl's kids, my niece and nephew."

With widened eyes and an audible gasp, she lowered her voice and said, "Oh my God! If you'd just once talked to me or asked me before walking out, we would've known all this and — what - what did you say?"

Catching her breath, she had a flashback of his words and said, "Did you say your niece and nephew?"

With an apologetic demeanor, Gary said, "You're right – I'm an ass. Looking back, I guess I also was pretty close to slime. And yes, I said those two kids that I've come to love as my own are my niece and nephew."

He paused and rubbed his chin. "By the way, if Carl is your best friend, how come you didn't know they were her kids?"

Before Angie could respond, he continued, "And, there is not now, nor has there ever been, a Blondie! That woman you saw me with at La Virage is my business partner's wife."

Gary wanted to lay all his cards on the table. "I also have a confession to make. The Walgren's Company is mine, and always has been. I didn't buy into it. What I've done is bring a friend into the business as a full partner. His wife helped to set everything up behind his back so we could surprise him. At La Virage, she was so excited for her husband that when she left, she thanked me with a hug and a kiss on the cheek. It was nothing, Angie. And yes, the picture in the paper was her, and she was standing next to her husband, Tom, my new partner.

In an attempt to remain calm, Gary uncrossed his legs and placed his hands in his pockets. "Don't you see, Angie, we've both been jealous fools here. We've been suffering and hurting each other through assumptions and misconceptions, and for absolutely no reason. Furthermore, I've never called my sister by her nickname. I hated it as kids and I still hate it. I was just so insanely jealous that I never put the two together. And never once did you refer to Carl as she, or her. I fell in love with you the day I delivered the flower coolers to your first shop and I haven't looked at another woman since. I love you so much it hurts sometimes. Does any of this make sense to you now?"

Angie felt like a deflated balloon. With a contrite voice, she whispered, "You mean there never was another woman?"

"Never."

"And you love me?"

"I love you."

"And you've *always* loved me?"

Smiling, Gary reached his arms out to her and said, "Always. Angie I love you and I want to marry you and spend the rest of my life with you."

Angie was now frozen in place, tears running down her face, trying to absorb what she just heard him say. She looked at him and in a whisper she asked, "What did you just say Gary?"

"I just asked you to marry me Angie."

Two steps toward him and she was in his arms sobbing with joy, sorrow, relief, and love.

"Oh Gary, yes and yes and yes!" She kissed him for a long time and they could both taste the salty tears of relief and happiness.

Sandi K. Whipple

Angie told him, "I've been in love with you from that very first day, too." Suddenly stepping back from his grasp, she asked, "How in the world did all this bubble to the surface?"

"That's the best part and I think you'll be surprised when you find out." Looking at his watch, he said, "She should be unlocking the door pretty soon."

"She who?"

"Carl, of course."

Before his words were completed, they heard a click. Carl stuck her head in the door and said, "Are you still alive in here or do I need to call 911?"

Seeing them in each other's arms, she smiled and added, "Come on, you two. Let's get this show on the road. I'm starving," she said as a way of keeping Angie in the dark.

Angie moved away from Gary momentarily and hugged her. "I love you, Carl.

Releasing Angie's grasp, Carl responded, "I love you, too, Angie, now come on, let's get to it."

"Get to what?" she asked Gary as he took her hand and followed Carl.

When they entered the dining room, Angie gasped in surprise and stopped in her tracks when she saw the group of familiar faces. Carl kept walking toward the back where a long table had been set up and her husband, Jim, was waiting for her. Among the crowd, Angie saw Aunt Ruth and Frank. She saw Gary's mother, whom she remembered from Chicago. She was standing next to a man and the blonde. Evidently that was Gary's partner with his wife. Bewildered, she wondered why they were all here. She stood frozen as though she'd stepped onto another planet.

Aunt Ruth walked slowly toward her. "Angie, darling, won't you and Gary come sit by me? I think you know most everyone here. Have you met Harriet, Gary's mother? Of course, you know Carl and her husband, Jim." Turning to the other couple, she continued. "I don't think you've ever met Gary's business partner and his wife. Come shake hands and meet Heather. I'm certain you'll rather enjoy meeting her husband, Tom Henderson."

Angie's head snapped to attention and she froze in her steps! She stared up at Tom and instantly felt a burning sensation in her throat. He was smiling down at her and she saw his eyes become glassy as if he were about to cry. Inhaling deeply, her voice failed her and only a whisper was heard. "It's you."

"Yes, Buttons, it's me," Tom replied in a barely audible murmur.

She threw her arms around him and held on to his strength and their joint past. Over and over, she repeated, "Where have you been all these years?"

"The last nine and a half, I've been right here in Nasons Grove. Until Alan Krenshaw told Aunt Ruth who I was, and she came to see me, well, I had no idea we'd both been in the same town for so long. I didn't even know I had an Aunt Ruth."

Holding on to her and trying to keep his tears from soiling her dress, he bent his head into the crook of her neck and said, "When I finally went back to Silo to get you, there was no one there. I asked the neighbors why the house was empty, and they said it had been that way for several years since the terrible tragedy. When I asked about you, they said some woman came and took you away and that's all they knew."

Clinging to one another and reliving past memories in a flash, Tom went on, "For a few years, I tried everything to find you, but I couldn't. I guess a lot of the reason was because you'd changed your name. After Alan found me, he was able to put a zillion pieces together and went straight to Aunt Ruth."

Lifting his head from Angie's shoulder, he sought out Ruth's smiling face. Looking into her eyes, he added, "And she took it from there, along with Carl. They jointly put together this surprise."

Turning ever so slightly so as not to release Angie from his grasp, Tom placed an arm over his wife's shoulders. "This is my wife, Heather. Heather, this is my sister, Buttons." He choked back his tears and said, "I mean, Angie."

Heather hugged Angie and, with sparkling eyes also filled with tears, said to her new sister-in-law, "I can't tell you how wonderful this is. For years, Tom talked about you and how he wanted to find you. It's great to finally meet you. I guess you didn't know you had a niece, did you?"

Angie nearly suffered whiplash when she quickly turned her head. "Tom! You have a daughter? Oh, that's so wonderful."

Tom filled his chest with a large gasp of air. "I've got to tell you, Angie, this has been the longest week of my life — waiting for tonight —you know, after hearing the story from Aunt Ruth," he paused and grinned and then continued, "including the part about her plan to throw you two hard heads together."

Suddenly the enormity of all the past events hit her. She turned to Gary who'd been silently standing by her side. "If my brother is Tom Henderson, then your last name is Walgren."

Tom started to laugh when he realized that right up to this moment, Gary had never confessed that part to her.

"Yes, sweetheart, my last name is Walgren."

The tears from many flowed freely as the Di Nidos scurried around and searched for tissue, then laughter ensued for the duration of the evening.

Gary introduced Angie to his mother, telling her that she was the woman he was going to marry. Harriet hugged her and gave her a wink of understanding.

Not to be outdone by the family reunion and the reconciliation of her son and Angie, Harriet silenced the crowd. They became mesmerized as she unfolded the story of the Chicago encounter. When Harriet described the scene in the restaurant where Angie threw money in Gary's face, the room erupted in an uproar.

When the evening came to a close, there wasn't a single person who didn't fully understand the impact of the reunion of a brother and sister. If that wasn't enough to comprehend, the somewhat public announcement of a proposal of marriage crowned the event and guaranteed memories for a very long time.

Later that night at home, Angie shed more tears as she spoke of the roller coaster of emotions she'd been riding. Drained and exhausted, she cuddled next to Gary on the sofa. She looked up at him through reddened eyes. "All this time I never knew your last name. I can't believe it. I changed my last name to Aunt Ruth's so many years ago, the name Henderson in that newspaper article never clicked. I just thought the other guy in the picture was Walgren, and you were Henderson."

Gary kissed her forehead and told her, "You knew my last name, sweetheart."

"No, I didn't, I swear."

He held her close to his chest and said, "Let's play *to tell the truth*." With the crooked grin she so loved, he continued, "To tell the truth, you've known my last name since the first time I visited your apartment back at the old shop. Your aunt was there and we all shared Chambord. You even told your aunt what it was. Don't you remember?"

"How could I, if I didn't know until tonight? What did I tell her?"

Laughing, he said, "You told her my last name was Adonis."

With a jolt, she sat upright, looked at him, and said, "Why, you snake. You were eavesdropping from the shop, weren't you?"

"I actually like that name – *Adonis*. It has a certain. . ."

She stifled his laugh with her kiss.

****

Sandi K. Whipple

EPILOGUE

Just over a year later, Angie was sitting next to her sister-in-law, Heather, and her new found niece, while they watched Aunt Ruth at play with the new edition to the family, Gary and Angie's son, Alex.

Heather reached over and took Angie's hand in hers and said, "Angie, I can't believe how much he looks like Gary. Of course, Tom has now decided he wants a boy. It looks like this family is going to grow by leaps and bounds."

Grinning, Aunt Ruth injected, "Isn't that what families are supposed to be all about? Growing? I know Frank and I would love to have a dozen more kids running around, wouldn't we, Frank?"

As Gary nudged Frank and told him not to answer, Heather screeched, "A dozen more kids? Was that each, or together, Ruth? Hey, Angie, feel free to jump in anytime. I could use a little support here."

Angie was laughing so hard her sides began to ache. What a wonderful way to spend a Sunday afternoon, she thought. The entire family, together. "Aunt Ruth, will you please put Alex down? You spoil him so much, I'm afraid he'll grow up to be a brat. You've already given him so many toys I'm thinking you own stock in Mattel."

Gary, Frank, and Tom shared a beer on the other side of the room. They stood listening to the banter and laughed among themselves.

Amidst all the joviality in the room, Alex had crawled, unnoticed, to the other side of the room toward his father. He sat on his padded bottom and, with his

Sandi K. Whipple

little outstretched arms, he reached upward. Gary bent down, picked up the pleading child and said, "Come here, Mama's little *Adonis Junior*."

Hearing his words echo through the room, Angie and Aunt Ruth nearly choked with laughter.

Heather and Tom looked questioningly at one another and said in unison, "What did he say?"

THE END

Sandi K. Whipple

**Intentionally
Left Blank**

Sandi K. Whipple

ABOUT THE AUTHOR

I moved from Illinois to San Francisco, California, as a young teenager, but I now live in a great small town in North Dakota, where one could almost expect to see Andy, Barney, or Aunt Be at the Post Office.

I'm a Veteran and was an Air Traffic Controller in the United States Army.

A few years ago, I was in a wheelchair for eleven weeks, and reading two and three romance novels a day. A friend suggested I give writing a try. The end product was *Loving Adonis*.

Now that I've discovered what fun and enjoyment writing can be, there's another in the works, to be out soon. Details can be found at: sandikwhipple.com.

Other books by this author: ***Twisted Engagement***
****

David started inching along the wall, pulling Lilly along with him, totally unaware he was sliding right towards the chief.

Reaching a small opening with his back exposed, the chief couldn't see the knife David was holding at Lilly's throat, just the gun in his hand up in the air. With that, the chief decided to take his shot.

The bullet hit David in the upper left side of his back. As if in slow motion, he slid to the ground. The knife he held slid clear across Lilly's throat.

When Glenn reached to location the shot had come from, he saw Lilly's body in a heap on the ground. He stepped over to David's lifeless looking body and raised his own pistol to shoot the bastard himself.

Gently pushing his arm away the chief said, "Don't waste the bullet. He's a goner. I got him right through the heart. Even though he's dead, if you do that, I'd have to arrest you." Slowly taking the gun from Glenn's hand he added, "Just check on the woman, I think she's hurt pretty bad. I see a lot of blood."

Sandi K. Whipple

**Intentionally
Left Blank**

Made in the USA
San Bernardino, CA
14 October 2014